THE GIRL AT
THE END
OF THE WORLD

OTHER BOOKS BY RICHARD LEVESQUE

TAKE BACK TOMORROW

STRICTLY ANALOG

DEAD MAN'S HAND

UNFINISHED BUSINESS

THE DEVIL YOU KNOW

FOUNDLINGS

THE GIRL AT THE END OF THE WORLD

RICHARD LEVESQUE

This is a work of fiction. Any resemblance to persons living or dead is
purely coincidental.

Cover illustration & design (c)2015 Duncan Eagleson. LA photo
(c)f11photo, motorcyclist photo (c)Andrey Armyagov

ISBN: 1491276932
ISBN-13: 978-1491276938

DEDICATION

For Kari and Olive
Survivors

ACKNOWLEDGMENTS

I am grateful for the input, advice, and encouragement I've received from friends and family as I have worked on this project. Several people read early drafts of this book and offered me valuable insight and support. My thanks to Chris Pellitteri, Tamara Trujillo, Heidi Guss, Janna Anderson, Elli England, and my wife, Karianne Levesque.

CHAPTER ONE

The world ended the day I turned 15.

I don't know who you are or when you're reading this, but if you're anything like me and remember how things used to be, I suppose that first sentence might remind you of the kinds of things teenagers used to read—things filled with angst and drama, lots of hand-wringing and butterflies in the stomach. Or maybe you're from a long ways into the future and stories have gone back to being about that sort of thing; maybe people in your time have the luxury of being able to worry about heartbreak and loneliness and first kisses. That's not the kind of thing I'm talking about.

I don't mean to say *my* world ended the day I turned 15. I don't mean that it was turned upside down by something that happened to me.

No.

I mean it when I say it: the world ended.

Ended.

It's kind of strange to think back on it now. The old world, I mean. The whole thing seems like it was a dream I woke up from that day. Or maybe a dream someone else had. A dream where you had family and friends and where you laughed at stupid things and couldn't explain later why they were so funny. Or where you argued with people you loved and said mean, hateful things and tried to make up for it later. It was a dream world where people went to work and drove on freeways and got married and had kids and grew old and died. Some people had everything they needed and some people had so little they couldn't even imagine all the luxuries they'd never know.

And it mattered so much.

It all mattered so much.

The littlest thing that went wrong would put such a kink in your day and you'd cry about it or fight about it or find a way to try and fix it. And the next day it would be something different, and all those things that had mattered so much the day before were just forgotten...blown away like dust or pollen. Or spores.

I knew a thing or two about things being blown away. My family, for one thing. We'd all been together when I was little: my mom and dad, my older sister Anna, and me—Scarlett. But then had come the divorce and my dad's new house and new wife, and before long I had new brothers. I remember it had all felt so weird, like my family—my *real* family—had died, and this new, split-up version had stepped in to take their place. By the time I was 14, I was done being sad and done being angry, done acting out and done trying to make my parents feel bad for not being able to fake it for Anna and me. I guess I'd come to accept it without really meaning to, my sister and I realizing somewhere along the way that our mom was going to fall apart if we didn't step up and make the best of things. There were times when it felt like we were the parents watching out for her rather than the other way around.

So when my mom told me I'd be spending my fifteenth birthday with my dad and his family, I didn't put up a fight. Mom hadn't planned a party, and I hadn't begged for one—had just assumed she'd let me hang with my friends and that they'd spoil me for an evening. That was what I really wanted anyway, so it was kind of disappointing to know I'd be going to a Dodger game with my dad and his new family. Still, I went along with the plan, knowing that my dad was at least trying, in his own way, and that fussing about it would just give my mom another reason to say she had a migraine and retreat to her room.

The day came—a Friday. I went to school, and my friends *did* spoil me with little presents and promises to do all sorts of things in the weeks to come. And at times during that day I forgot about the game coming up in the evening, forgot that I *had* to go rather than do what I wanted.

But the school day ended, and I went home and then it was get ready and go.

"Happy birthday, Scarlett," my dad said as I climbed into his Jeep. He leaned over to kiss the top of my head.

"Thanks," I said and hugged him for a second before putting on the seat belt.

We drove to his new house—bigger and fancier than the one my mom and sister and I were able to live in—and we switched over to my step-mom's car. Angie, my dad's wife, was nice enough to me and Anna, but I always had the feeling we made her uncomfortable, like she was faking her smiles for my dad's sake. She wished me a happy birthday and made sure her little boys did, too, but it didn't seem sincere, and I felt like my dad was the only one in the car who truly wanted to be there.

Dodger Stadium was this huge place—maybe still is—built into the sides of a ravine right next to downtown Los Angeles. I'd been there maybe ten times before this, so it was nothing special. It had been a hot day, and the sun was still high in the sky but dipping down in its arc toward the west when we got our seats. I wished for shade and knew the heat would turn tolerable once the sun dropped a little lower. For now, though, I sat uncomfortably in the plastic seat and looked down at the field far below.

The crowd filled in. It was all so ordinary. So sad to think about now. All those people, none of them with any idea what was about to happen. To them, it was just another game, another evening in Los Angeles, a little diversion from the everyday things they wouldn't be able to get away from the next day. That's what they thought, anyway. If they'd only known, I wonder if they would have traded what was to come for just one more average day filled with things they didn't really want to do. Actually, I don't wonder about that—I know it for sure. They'd have traded anything and everything for just one more day. I know I would have.

Two rows down from us sat a big man wearing a Dodgers shirt and hat. I noticed him only because he was such a big guy—probably six feet five inches and kind of overweight. I just remember thinking I was glad he wasn't *right* in front of me or beside me. He didn't appear to be there with anyone else. Later, that's what they said on the news, and I remember thinking I'd been right about him. Not that it mattered.

The game went the way games did: some activity, some excitement, and lots of waiting in between for something else to happen. My dad bought me a hot dog and soda. My half-brothers argued and had to be separated. The sun slid toward the horizon and the lights came on in the stadium. And every once in a while I'd catch my dad looking at me with a smile or a wink and I'd smile back. It was like we were having a little secret, just the two of us among all those thousands of people. I couldn't tell you now what the secret was or what it was supposed to mean. I suppose it was just that we were there, together, and that it was all right, or at least the best that it could be under the circumstances with me and him having to be apart so much and that for just this one evening we could act like it was all okay, like we were in a real family again.

The seventh inning came around. The other team was up and the batter hit a high fly that was just barely foul and the crowd got all excited for a few seconds and then settled down again. All except the big man two rows down.

4

"Foul ball!" he shouted, and I looked down at him. He was nodding his head vigorously, like he was signaling impassioned agreement with something more important than baseball.

"Foul ball!" he shouted again a few seconds later even though no other ball had been hit down on the field. This time, just about everyone else around him turned, giving him looks of annoyance.

I couldn't see his face, couldn't see how he responded. He just kept nodding.

"Foul ball!" he shouted a third time, even louder than before, and I saw the man next to him turn and say something, but quieter so I couldn't tell what he said from two rows away.

And then the big man shouted again, far louder than before. "FOUL!! BALL!!"

People from several rows began yelling at him to shut up and calm down, but the big man was oblivious.

I glanced at my dad and saw that he wasn't watching the game anymore either. His eyes were on the big man and the people around him. He looked worried, and I saw him shoot a glance at my step-mom. He caught me looking, and his expression turned from concerned to fake happy. The smile he gave me was supposed to make me feel like everything was all right, but I knew he was expecting trouble.

Like just about every other uninvolved observer, my dad was probably trying to decide if he should call security before things got bad. He even had his phone out. I saw maybe a dozen other people with phones in their hands, too, but none of them were calling anyone. They were shooting video, probably thinking they could upload to the Internet and go viral if a fight broke out.

Now, with all eyes on him, the big man seemed to notice the attention he had drawn. He turned and scanned the faces, and when he looked at me two rows above, I knew there was some-thing seriously wrong with him. His eyes were bouncing in their sockets and his lips twitched. He looked like he was fighting back the urge to laugh or cry; I couldn't tell which.

"You never paid me!" he yelled, his voice erupting without warning. "Never!"

The shouts were directed at no one now. He seemed to be imagining people around him who weren't there.

"Sit down!" and "Shut up!" and shouts of far worse things came from the people all around us, people who had been happily enjoying the game just a minute or two before. I don't know what was scarier—seeing this man have his mental breakdown right in front of me or watching everyone else around us getting angrier and angrier at the sight of him.

To be honest, I was angry, too. I know now that I should have felt compassion for the man, and I think when I replay that day in my mind I make myself out to be worried about what was going to happen—to the shouting man and to the people nearby who wouldn't have fared well if he'd started swinging those big fists. But I don't think I was really feeling that way, not in the moment. Before I figured out that there was something wrong with the man, I thought he was just acting like an idiot. And when I did see his face and saw that something bigger was going on, it was too late; I was already upset and scared, and the anger of the crowd swept me up so I wanted to shout, too.

"Darryl, do something," Angie said from two seats away, me and one of the boys in between her and my dad.

He glanced at her and then back at the raving man.

"You never paid me! I'm owed! I'm owed big!" he shouted at no one in particular.

I suppose it wouldn't have been long before the scene got ugly, but two of the stadium's security men showed up in the aisle just then, and the rest of the crowd stopped shouting when they saw the uniformed officers approaching. Not the big man, though. He kept raving as the officers got the nearby fans to leave the row. One of them shouted at him to calm down, and seconds later he doused the big man with pepper spray.

I winced as the man screamed louder, put his hands over his face and fell straight into the security officer, both of them hitting the concrete floor between the rows of seats. Shouts rose from the crowd, some frightened and others just surprised.

In seconds, the other security officer had joined the struggle, pulling the big man off the one he'd fallen on. Now he was screaming incomprehensibly, flailing his arms. At first I thought it was from the pepper spray, but the screams got worse.

"Killing me! Killing me!"

He was no longer yelling, but screaming in a high-pitched, frantic voice, desperate to be saved.

Four more security guards and two Los Angeles police officers had arrived by then, but before any of them could drag the man into the main aisle, he suddenly went quiet.

Passed out, I thought. And then, with a chill up my back and neck, another thought: *Or dead.*

My heart was pounding, and again I looked to my dad. This time he didn't catch my glance. His eyes were fixed on the spectacle, and it drew mine back as well.

And that was when it happened.

It's a moment that I'll never forget till the day I die, a sequence that's practically burned into the backs of my eyes.

One of the security officers was talking on his radio, probably calling for medical help. People in the crowd just stared. Several still had their cameras pointed at the afflicted man. I remember looking at one woman who stood right behind one of the crouched security officers. She was blonde, probably in her twenties, and she held a beer with one hand and her purse with the other. Her blouse was white cotton.

And then there was a popping sound. Not loud. Kind of a muffled cracking noise. I wasn't even sure I'd heard it.

And the woman's blouse, so bright and white and standing out from the darker clothes of the people around her, and the black uniforms of the security guards—that white blouse was spattered with red. The same was true of her face and her hair.

And the people around her.

All of them screaming, shouting. Unintelligibly.

Some turned their heads away.

Some tried to shield their faces, but it was too late.

Two of the security officers who'd been crouched over the prone man now fell back into the legs of the people around them, knocking some over. I saw their faces covered in blood.

I didn't want to know what had happened, but at the same time I did.

People began stumbling over themselves to get away from the scene they'd just been crowding into seconds before.

And in between the chaos of panicking bodies, I glimpsed the man who'd been so loud and seemed so dangerous just a minute before. I'm sure much of his face was gone, but it was all just blood, and I couldn't make out anything in the second or two that I had a clear view of him.

But in that second, I did see the other things, the things everyone would be talking about for the rest of the night. Two small white stalks stuck out of the opening in the man's face, maybe four inches high. I didn't need to know what they were; it was clear enough that whatever they were, they'd pushed their way out of his skull, breaking him open like an eggshell. I can't say for sure if I saw the little bulbs at the tip of each stalk, the little caps that were the real problem, but I saw enough of them later, and it all kind of blends together in my memory.

We were in a car wreck once, before the divorce. I was maybe six. All four of us were in the car, passing through an intersection. Another car ran the red light and slammed right into the side of our car, spinning us around before we stopped against the curb. I remember how everything seemed to happen so slowly even though it could only have been a few seconds from the impact to when we stopped and my dad started asking if we were okay. But in those seconds, everything seemed so clear. I knew what had happened. I knew we were spinning out of control. I had time to think about how loud the crash had been, to feel the seatbelt grab onto my shoulder like it was some kind of monster that would never let go, to smell the burnt sulfur as the airbags deployed. I didn't know if I was hurt or if anyone else in the car was, but I seemed aware of everything else. I had only a few seconds to process the accident, and I did, cramming more information into those seconds than seems possible when I think back on it. Maybe it's just a trick of memory, but I don't think so.

That day at Dodger Stadium, I felt the same kind of thing. Everything slowed down as I saw those stalks sticking out of the man's head. All the yelling and screaming seemed like it was coming from much farther away than ten feet in front of me. I couldn't really even feel my body. It was like I was nothing more than eyes and ears taking it all in.

And then the illusion of slowed time shattered.

Someone blocked my view of the man, and all the sounds and the chaos rushed back into place as though a floodgate had just been opened and water was pouring through the channels it had been kept from.

A second or two later, there was another popping sound and I expected to see more blood, but there was nothing. People gasped. And then what appeared to be a cloud of dust rose into the air around the stricken man. Some people nearby knocked others down to get away from the scene. More people turned away. More people yelled.

As for me, I think I was in shock. I could say or do nothing. I just stared.

And then I was moving, my feet shuffling forward without my thinking about it. My dad had grabbed me by the shoulders and started pulling me toward the aisle. Confused, I looked past him, wondering what had happened to my brothers and step-mom. They were already in the aisle. Angie was hustling them away, trying to shield the boys from looking back at the spectacle of the dead man in the aisle.

My dad's grip on my shoulders felt as tight as that seatbelt had in the accident. He wouldn't let me slow down, wouldn't let me turn to get another look. I wanted to tell him I was okay, but words wouldn't come—like in a dream where you want to scream, where you *have* to scream, and no sound at all will rise from your throat.

I felt numb as he pulled me up the steps and toward an exit, barely noticing the people running past us, some in uniforms, others not. And all the shouting. Maybe something else had happened down on the field. I don't know. I never found out.

I think I came close to passing out then. I found out later that a lot of people had fainted at the sight of the dying man and what happened to him there in the aisle. I felt all the blood leave my head, and for a few seconds I was dizzy and nauseous. I stumbled, but my dad had me so tight that I didn't come close to hitting the ground. He just held me, half pulling and half dragging me.

I don't remember leaving the stadium. It's funny that I'd remember everything but that. Maybe I did pass out. Maybe my dad had to carry me part of the way.

All I know is that when we got to the car and I piled into the back seat with my brothers, I put on the safety belt and then started crying inconsolably. My tears were contagious, or maybe frightening. At any rate, my brothers were crying too. My step-mom hit the gas, and we left Dodger Stadium behind forever.

CHAPTER TWO

Someday, when all the electricity comes back on again and people rediscover all the technology that's been lost, someone is going to find a way to tap into all the servers that held all the data from cell phones and emails and texts, and everything that was broadcast on TV and streamed on the web.

It's embarrassing to think about that as our legacy. All the stupid junk that people wrote about and fought about and scandalized each other over. I actually hope it never gets dug up again, that it's the part that gets forgotten by future archaeologists or is irrecoverable and has to remain one of the mysteries of a lost civilization. Because we were really ridiculous.

I was just as guilty as everyone else. That day, my mom had forbidden me from taking my phone to the game—*quality time with your father*, she'd said. That had been the only reason I hadn't pulled my phone out at the stadium to text my friends about how bored I was by the game or how I wished I could be doing something different with my birthday.

And I honestly don't know what I would have done if I'd had a phone in my hand when the man two rows down started yelling about the foul ball. Or what I would have done afterwards. Would I have filmed it? I'd like to think not. That may not have been the case, though.

At any rate, several dozen people who'd been in the same part of the stadium didn't second guess themselves when the man had his attack, and none of them had mothers who'd made them leave their phones at home.

I'm sure that within minutes of the incident, people had begun uploading their videos to the web. By eight o'clock it was on the local news, preceded by warnings from the newscasters that what they were about to show was extremely graphic and might be disturbing to younger viewers.

Like they cared.

My step-mom had driven me back to my mom's straight from the stadium, the boys and I silent in the backseat while my dad called my mom to tell her we were on our way. I could tell she was giving him the third degree, trying to figure out why were coming back so soon, but he didn't want to tell her over the phone, didn't want us to be reminded in the backseat of what we'd just seen and couldn't shake no matter how understated he tried to make everything sound. In the end, he lost it and shouted at her. "Damn it, Deena! Will you just believe me when I say Scarlett's fine—no, we're ALL fine—and just let me explain when I get there? Okay?"

I wanted to yell back at him, to tell him to leave her alone, that it wasn't her fault. But I kept quiet. Mostly because I *wasn't* fine. I sat in the back of that car with Randy and Mike, and I trembled, squeezing Randy's hand—something I'd never done before—and feeling for the first time like they were my real brothers, not half, not living reminders of the divorce. I probably would have held anybody's hand just then, just to feel someone else alive and near me.

When we got home, I ran past my mother without a word, straight to the bathroom and threw up. I hadn't had any clue that it was going to happen, but the instant I walked in the door there was no question. Over the sound of running water, I could hear raised voices in the living room and then silence.

By the time I came out of the bathroom, my hair now pulled back in a loose ponytail and feeling almost normal for the first time in an hour, I saw my dad standing in the open doorway, my mom a few feet away. He just stared at me, trying to look reassuring. My mom turned, her hand up over her mouth and tears in her eyes. Then she ran to me and threw her arms around me and squeezed, pulling my face into her shoulder as I squeezed back.

My dad left a few minutes later after giving me another hug, shorter than my mom's, somehow awkward now in this house. Then, hesitantly, he hugged my mom, too, just briefly. When he stepped away from her, he gave this funny little wave he always had when he didn't know what else to say, and he was out the door.

I watched through the window as the car pulled away, my two little half-brothers' heads barely high enough to be visible in the backseat. Seeing them go made me feel suddenly worse again. I wouldn't have been able to say why.

Neither my phone nor the computer could pull me out of my mood, so I didn't touch either one—just sat on the couch with my mom while she fretted over me, not thinking at all about checking my Facebook or texts for birthday messages or any other distraction. I didn't want to think. I didn't want to talk.

After a while, my mom said I should get a shower. It helped.

By the time I went back downstairs, dressed now in loose shorts and a soft old t-shirt, Anna had gotten home from her part-time job, got the short version of what had happened, and turned on the TV.

The incident at Dodger Stadium was on every local channel.

At first, I didn't want to see, but after they'd shown it a dozen times from different angles, I got used to it, kind of numb to it. It was like watching a video of one of your nightmares, inexplicably captured in more detail than you could have remembered and at more angles than you'd have thought possible. The newscast blurred out the most gruesome parts, but that didn't help me any; my memory filled those parts in without me even trying. Blocking those images wasn't even an option. I saw the details so vividly in my mind's eye that now, even though I know the real images were blurred out, when I play that night back in my memory, I remember it wrong, remember them showing the full uncensored version that I actually played in my head.

After getting used to the surreal images, and my mom's and sister's gasps as we watched together, the weirdest part was seeing myself in the background of some of the videos. People who'd been a row or two below the dying man had filmed the whole thing, and there I was, two rows up beside my dad. A few minutes into the coverage, I began watching myself on the screen more than the spectacle of the dying man. I knew that I was the blonde girl standing next to her father, wearing the red t-shirt and jeans, but at the same time it was hard to believe that girl was me. She looked so scared and confused by what was happening in front of her. She cringed and clung to her father's arm and turned her head away a few times as the man went through his final moments. I didn't remember doing any of that, but there it was on the screen for anyone to see. No arguing with video.

Along with endless variations of the scene, the newscast included several interviews with witnesses. They made me glad my dad and step-mom had hustled us out of there so quickly. I was glad not to have been one of those nervous, freaked out people with cameras and microphones in their faces. After that, the news switched to "experts" and medical correspondents and other people speculating on what had happened to the man.

This I wanted to hear, but it was difficult because our phone had started ringing.

"Reports are that the victim has been positively identified, but his name has not yet been released pending notification of his family," said the newscaster, an overly sincere brunette who'd probably practiced her catastrophe face before going on the air.

"She's okay, yes," my mom was saying in the background. A friend of hers had called after seeing my dad and me on TV.

"The Los Angeles County Coroner's office has announced that an autopsy will be performed and that there will be a news conference tomorrow morning."

"I don't think so, no," my mom said. She sounded annoyed, wanted to be off the phone.

"Our medical correspondent"—I forget the man's name—"joins us now to try and shed some light on this horrific scene."

"I will. Thanks," my mom said and hung up. The phone rang again before she'd been able to put the receiver back on its charger.

"It's difficult to know exactly what took place at Dodger Stadium this evening based solely on the images we've been seeing," the medical expert was saying.

"Hello? Yes, yes, it was her."

"But the evidence suggests that the victim was afflicted with some sort of parasite. The erratic behavior before his death would indicate that the parasite was putting incredible pressure on parts of his brain."

"No, she's fine."

"Have you ever heard of anything like this?" the anchor asked.

"Really. No, I don't think she should. But—"

"Not in my experience, no. But we have to remember that there are countless new discoveries every year of insects and microbes and all manner of things. This could be something we've known about previously, but in a mutated form."

"I have to go now. I'm sorry. Yes, yes I will. Bye."

"And it could be something undiscovered up to now, maybe the kind of thing that doesn't normally attack human beings."

The phone rang again. My mom unplugged it and then gave my knee a squeeze. I tried to smile.

"Frightening," said the anchor. "Have health officials made any announcements about any danger posed to fans at Dodger Stadium who may have been exposed to the same parasite?"

"No official word yet, but it would still be a good idea for anyone who witnessed this incident to get checked out by their doctor as soon as possible."

For the second time that day, I felt all the blood drain out of my face. The television was still on, but now it sounded like I was listening to it with pillows pushed up against my ears.

I looked at my mom. Her mouth was moving. Anna was at my other side, and I felt her take my hand. Then my mom stopped moving her mouth and looked at me with real worry, like she had just figured out that I wasn't processing anything she'd said.

She put a hand on my cheek.

And it was like she broke a spell. Sound came rushing back at me, and now I could really feel my sister's hand in mine, could feel the fabric of the sofa against my legs.

I collapsed into my mom's arms and cried. I'm not ashamed to say it. I cried and cried like I was just little again, and she held me and told me it was going to be all right, told me we'd get to the doctor tomorrow and that it would all be fine.

Her words and the feeling of her arms around me made some of the fear go away, but not all of it. I was going to die. I knew it. With luck, it wouldn't happen tonight, and I wouldn't start shouting about foul balls before it happened, but I knew that I'd go a little bit crazy soon and then it would all be over.

The newscast had moved on to an entertainment report, something about a movie premiere in Hollywood. I remember pulling away from my mom and turning to see an actress in a backless red dress smiling for the crowd as hundreds of flashbulbs went off. It was such a contrast to what they'd been showing a minute before that for a moment I thought it couldn't be real.

I got off the couch quickly.

"What's wrong?" my mom asked, alarm in her voice.

I just shook my head, trying not to look at the television.

"What if I go crazy like him?" I said, my voice trembling.

"You're not going to go crazy. You're fine."

"You don't know that!" I shouted, and instantly I feared the sound of my own voice, feared that this was it.

"Sweetheart, you need to calm down. It's going to be all right. If there was even a chance that something could have been contagious, they wouldn't just be speculating on the news. The Health Department would be giving instructions right now. Don't let it get to you. Anna, shut it off please."

My sister did as she'd been asked, and I felt a little better, but I still worried that I was about to go crazy. I questioned every one of my thoughts, trying to determine if they were normal or not.

My mom stood up and took both my hands in hers. "You maybe need some rest. You want me to go upstairs with you?"

I shook my head. "I'll be okay," I said, just above a whisper.

She kissed my cheek, and I tried hard not to flinch. As quickly as I could, I let go of her hands and walked to the foot of the stairs.

"Mom? Anna?" I asked with one hand on the rail. They both looked at me expectantly. "Will you promise me something?"

"Sure," my mom said, and my sister nodded. They both seemed so sincere that I found myself not wanting to believe them, but I went on anyway.

"If I start…going crazy…doing things or saying things that just don't seem right…"

"You're not going to," my mom interrupted.

"Stop. *If* I do, then stay away. Don't try to help me. Just…just get out of here. Okay?"

They both stared silently. I knew they were weighing what they wanted to say against what they thought they *should* say instead.

"Okay?" I repeated, more insistently.

"Okay," my mom whispered, tears in her eyes.

I raised an eyebrow as I looked past her toward Anna.

"Okay," she said.

There wasn't much point in saying anything else, so I just nodded at them and turned to walk up the stairs. I hoped I'd be able to make it to my room before the sobbing started, but I was only halfway along the upstairs hallway when the choked sounds reached me from the living room, mom crying first and then my sister with her. My chin quivered at the sound, but I clenched my teeth and wiped at both eyes with the back of my hand. Then I was in my room, shutting the door and leaning hard against it. It felt like I was trying to shut the whole world out, to lock myself away from it, but I knew it wouldn't work. It wasn't the first time I'd used my room as such a refuge; the door had never worked before when it came to keeping the world away for long, and I knew the same would be true tonight. Still, I felt a strange sense of comfort standing there and feeling my shoulders and back against the solid door, the sounds of my mother and sister crying now muffled and almost indistinguishable from the other sounds of the night.

Almost.

CHAPTER THREE

After a while, I stepped away from the door. Downstairs, my mom had suggested I get some rest, but I wasn't tired. That hadn't been my reason for leaving the living room. My real reason had been to get away from them, to put some distance between myself and the people I might hurt if I really did go berserk like the man at Dodger Stadium.

So instead of undressing and getting into bed, I pulled my phone from my back pocket. How many times in the past had I pulled the phone out the second I closed the bedroom door, walking across my cluttered floor without noticing where my feet fell, my eyes not drifting from the screen? For a few seconds that night, it was like old times. The unanswered texts were in the double digits, and I started thumbing through them as I made my way to the bed. I sat cross-legged and began reading and responding.

The texts were all from friends asking if I was all right. Some sounded scared for me. Others tried to be macabre and joke about it, but I knew they didn't really find any of it funny. They'd all seen me on TV or YouTube. Most of the videos had gone viral, none of them edited the way they'd been on TV. People sent me links by the dozen as the night wore on. I didn't want to click on any of them.

The later it got, the more surreal it all seemed. I almost could have convinced myself that everything that had happened at the stadium had been a dream and that all the texts and Facebook messages were just part of it. But even though my friends helped take the edge off of what had happened, there was still a part of me—a big part, I guess—that was terrified and in denial and wanting desperately for the distraction to work just a little bit better.

My phone had been chirping at me every time I got a new text, so when it actually rang around 11:00, I jumped.

Jen was my closest friend. We had three classes together that year and had known each other well since eighth grade. Of all the people who were texting and messaging me, Jen was the one whose words helped the most that night, the one person who didn't joke at all about what had happened and who seemed to get just how serious the whole thing might have been. She was the one who I knew really meant it when she said she was worried about me.

Now a silly picture I'd taken of Jen filled my phone's screen and a clip from her favorite song played as her ringtone. Anyone else's call I might have ignored. Not Jen, though.

"Scarlett?" she sounded scared, about to cry.

"I'm okay, Jen," I said. It seemed a bit odd that I was the one having to comfort her, but I gave it only a second's thought. "Don't get so upset."

"Scarlett, you have to turn on channel seven. Right now."

"Why? What is—"

"Just turn it on! Oh my God!" Then she was sobbing on the line.

I had a TV in my room but hadn't turned it on in months. You'd normally have found me on the computer or the phone if you'd come into my room those days—that or doing my homework or maybe reading a book. So of course I couldn't find the remote.

"Jen, come on. You have to calm down," I said while turning over magazines and looking in my nightstand drawer. Jen gave only sniffles in response.

I finally found the remote on a shelf above the television and turned it on to channel seven. A press conference was in progress, a gray haired man in a rumpled suit talking before a bank of microphones.

"There is no way to tell what Mr. Kirby or his co-workers came in contact with, but the other deaths do point to the airport as the source of initial contact."

Other deaths? I thought, my heart pounding. *This can't be real.*

"As of now, all traffic in and out of Los Angeles International Airport has been grounded. Flights in the air that originated from this airport in the last several hours are being diverted from their schedules and landing as quickly as is safe. Anyone who has been to the airport today is urged to isolate him or herself completely and seek medical attention once it is determined that this is the best course of action. I can take a few questions."

I remember a moment's chaos then as all the reporters fought for the man's attention. The questions and answers that followed helped me fill in the details, all with Jen sobbing in my ear over the phone.

The man who'd suffered the attack at Dodger Stadium had been named Harmon Kirby, and he'd been a baggage handler at LAX. The gray haired man insisted that it wasn't accurate to describe Kirby as "patient zero," but I didn't quite know what that meant. Apparently, Kirby and other baggage handlers had been exposed to something coming off a plane—no one knew for sure what, or which plane, or how long ago. Kirby's shift had ended early, but three other baggage handlers had died this evening, all the same way, all at the airport. Several planes had taken off before the Health Department had shut the airport down.

I remember a reporter asking with some outrage if the gray haired man knew whether any planes had landed elsewhere without the passengers being notified, and the man in front of the microphones had just stared at him for a second before answering. "It is highly likely," he said quietly. Then, amid the stir of voices and shouts from reporters that followed, he tried to calm everyone down, tried assuring them that every effort was being made to track every plane and every passenger that had passed through the airport that day and in the days before.

I knew as well as those reporters and everyone else watching that it wasn't likely to make a difference.

"Have they said what it was?" I asked Jen. "What killed them?"

She sniffled for a few seconds, and then I heard her catch her breath. "They don't know for sure. They were talking before, before I called you, saying they think it might be a kind of fungus."

"Fungus?" I repeated, incredulous. I'd never heard of a fungus that could do something like this. Mushrooms were a kind of fungus. And athlete's foot. Fungus didn't kill you, didn't make your head burst open. "How is that possible?"

"I don't know," Jen said. "They're just guessing, though. Said the spores were inhaled and then it grew in the sinus cavity and eventually built up so much pressure that…that…"

And then she was sobbing again.

I don't know why I wasn't. Too scared, maybe. All I could think of was the cloud of dust that had emerged at the stadium when those little pods had burst open at the ends of the stalks poking from the dead man's face. Spores. Probably millions of them. Microscopic little seeds that would spread on the air. And be breathed in by anyone nearby. The woman with the blood-spattered blouse had probably thought herself infected with something when she'd been sprayed, but she'd really been fine at that point. But after the stalks popped up and the bulbs burst…

"Scarlett?" Jen managed to choke out.

"Yeah?"

"I don't want you to die."

I said nothing. I had no words.

"Get your mom to take you to the emergency room."

"They said to isolate yourself if you've been exposed."

"Don't listen to them," Jen said. "Go."

"I don't know," I said, my voice just above a whisper. "I don't know."

All I could picture was my face breaking open and two white stalks popping out while my mom drove me to the hospital. And the car filling with dust as the bulbs burst open. And my mom breathing them in.

"I have to go," I said.

"To the hospital?"

"I just have to go."

"Scarlett?"

"Yeah?"

"Just be okay. Okay?"

"Okay," I said and clicked off. The phone's screen went dark, its picture of Jen blinking into blankness.

I watched the press conference for a few more seconds, and then dialed my dad's number. It was late, but someone should have answered. The phone just rang and rang, each ring seeming to make my heart jump a little in my chest as I listened for that slight change in the silence that would precede someone saying hello. It never came, not even the answering machine. They were probably on the phone and ignoring their call waiting, maybe even trying to call me at the same time I was calling them. I hung up and waited a few seconds before trying my dad's cell. Voice mail kicked in almost right away.

"Daddy, it's me. I just wanted to make sure you were all right...you and the boys and...everybody. I'm okay. Just scared. There's a lot of stuff on TV about what happened. It's... Just call me back. Okay? Love you."

I stared at the phone for a few seconds, willing it to ring, but it stayed silent in my hand. So I clicked it back into life and called my mom's phone downstairs. It rang twice before she picked up, and as it rang I walked to my bedroom door to twist the lock.

"Scarlett?" my mom said, panic in her voice.

"I'm okay, Mom." I tried desperately to sound calm, and I think I pulled it off. "Are you still up?"

"Yes. Why?" She sounded like she'd been crying and may still have been when the phone rang. Now she was pulling it together for me, but just barely.

"You saw the press conference?"

"We did."

"You should leave."

"What? No!" Now the panic rose again, and the tears, too.

"Mom, you should leave," I insisted. "You and Anna need to get in the car and go somewhere...go to a hotel or something."

"Absolutely not! We're not leaving you alone. Not now."

"But they said anyone who's been exposed should—"

"I don't care what they said! I'm not leaving you. We're taking you to the doctor in the...no, we should take you now. Are you still dressed?"

"I'm not going to the emergency room, Mom. I'm not. I don't want you and Anna in danger."

"We're not going to be in danger. Anna can stay here. Or...or I'll call the paramedics! They'll take you. You'll be safe at the hospital." Her every word was a plea, and I had a hard time listening to her sound so desperate. But I knew I was right, and wasn't about to be talked out of it.

I took a breath. "I'm not going, Mom. If I've...if I've got it..." Bravery could hold out only so long. My voice cracked. "If I've got it, then I've got it, and I don't want anyone else to get it. Not you or Anna or some poor paramedic or doctor who never even met me."

We argued back and forth for a while. I expected at any moment to hear her pounding on my door, but she never did. I also worried that she might be writing instructions for my sister to use the other phone to call an ambulance, and I paced back and forth from the door to my window to listen for sirens or look for flashing lights, but none came.

On my television, the news conference had ended, and the harried looking anchors at the news desk were re-stating what had already been said. Then I noticed a pause in what they were saying and stopped listening to my mom for a few seconds as I focused on the screen. Behind the newscaster, the words "Mystery Illness" had been displayed in bold red letters. Now they were replaced with "Another Death."

"Someone else died," I said, cutting my mother off in mid-sentence.

"What? Who?"

"Just…just watch the news for a second, okay?"

She remained silent as I turned up the volume.

"—not yet confirmed, but this appears to be similar to the deaths of Harmon Kirby and the other baggage handlers. We do not yet have an ID on this victim, but there is video from the scene." The newscaster was a middle-aged man with perfect hair and a perfect voice, but right now he looked like he'd just bitten into a clove of garlic or a whole lemon. His face lost that measured composure he and others like him always had. Now he paused for a beat and then said, "I'm told this is raw video just received in our newsroom and is extremely graphic. But we're going to show you the scene."

Video filled the screen, showing a familiar enough scene for LA. Several people jostled against each other outside of a nightclub for a second or two, smiles on their faces. Then a commotion began at the edges of the crowd. Some people screamed; others just looked confused and alarmed. Within seconds, people scattered. The person holding the cell phone camera took a few steps backward and stopped as others ran past. And then the camera focused on a woman lying on the sidewalk just outside the velvet rope that had kept would-be clubbers on the street.

I knew what was going to happen to her but still winced at the image.

No one approached the woman as she lay there twitching.

They know, I thought. *Everyone's been watching the video from the stadium. They know what's going to happen as well as I do.*

And then it did. The woman's face, far from the camera and not clearly focused, suddenly turned into a red blotch. People in the crowd screamed, and the man holding the camera swore loudly.

My mother gasped. I'd forgotten for a second that she was still on the phone.

"Now the stalks," I said.

As though on cue, the white stalks popped out of the red mass that was the woman's face, curling up into the air and looking like stop-action film of flowers growing. Up they shot, extraordinarily fast, and when they stopped I knew the little bulbs would be at the top.

"She's dead?" Mom asked, her voice trembling.

"Yes."

I want to say I felt something as I said it, but I didn't. Maybe I was still in shock, or filled with disbelief. I can't really say. All I know for sure is I was numb to that woman's suffering.

Seconds later, just like at the stadium, the little bulbs burst and the air around the dead woman shimmered for several seconds as though a cloud of glitter had been loosed, only to be captured by the dozens of cameras all trained on the spectacle. I heard more shouts from the crowd, and more people ran to get away from the little cloud, but it dispersed almost immediately, the dust from the bulbs so fine that even the motion of people running caused enough disturbance in the air to send the particles this way and that way until it wasn't a cloud anymore, just a memory burned into my mind.

The image switched back to the newscaster, clearly as shaken by what he'd just shown as anybody would have been from watching it on TV. "I'm being told we have audio from a telephone interview conducted with a young man who was at the scene we have just shown you. He wishes to remain anonymous."

A still image of the woman lying on the ground, her face still intact, filled the screen as the interview played over it. A man's voice, high pitched, came from the television speakers. He sounded like he'd been crying.

"I don't want to say her name, but I knew her. I was here with her and some friends. She seemed fine, and then she just started talking about her dog, how she had to get back to her dog, how it needed to be walked. We all thought she was just fooling around, but then…"

A woman's voice, probably someone at the TV station, said, "Do you know if the deceased woman had any connection to Los Angeles International Airport, or to the baggage handlers there who have died under similar circumstances?"

"No. No, but…"

"Yes?"

"She was at the Dodger game today. She saw what happened. That's why we took her out…to get her mind off it. I didn't think…She never…" The man began to sob; then there was a click. The interview was over. The image of the dead woman stayed on the screen a second more and then cut back to the newscaster.

"Oh God," my mom was saying, her voice shaky.

For myself, all I can say is that I sat there trembling, convinced I'd just watched a preview of my death. She'd been at Dodger Stadium today. So had I. Who knows how close to Harmon Kirby she'd been? But it didn't matter. I'd been close. Two rows away. Close enough to see it all. Close enough to be infected. I didn't need a news analyst or a doctor or some other expert to tell me the dust from the ends of the stalks was the source of the infection.

27

What sort of infection…whether fungal or something else…that I didn't know. Or how many others would die. Or how long it would take. The details didn't matter.

I was going to die.

The strangest part is I actually felt relieved, like a weight had been lifted off me, a weight I hadn't even known I was carrying around. It had been holding me down since Dodger Stadium…fear of the unknown. And now it was known. And with that knowledge, the weight lifted. The feeling didn't last, but for those first few minutes the unburdening was almost euphoric.

The same can't be said of my mother. She began crying harder. "We have to get you to the ER right now!" she said through her sobs.

"No," I said, my voice calm.

"Don't be ridiculous, Scarlett!"

"I'm not being ridiculous, Mom. If I go to the hospital now, who knows when I'm going to…when it's going to happen to me? I'm not going to get you or Anna sick, too. If it's going to happen, it's going to happen."

"We'll call a taxi then!"

"No! Don't you get it? I don't want *anyone* to die because of me. Not you or Anna or some taxi driver or an EMT. No one."

"But we can't just sit here and…wait."

"I know. And I don't want you to." Still calm, knowing I had to be. I wouldn't get what I wanted by throwing a tantrum. "Mom…we don't know what this is or how widespread. But I know there's a good chance I've got it. Dad, too. And the boys." It was hard not to get choked up as that realization hit. "And if we do…if any of us do, then anyone who's around us when it happens is going to be sick, too."

"I just want to help you." She sounded so small, so frail as she said it. Like a little girl. Like I was the parent all of a sudden, and I had to tell her she couldn't have what she wanted.

"I know. But if I'm sick, I don't think you can help." Reasoning with her now, breaking it down the way you would with an upset child, letting her know the options and steering her toward the only obvious conclusion. "And if I'm not, then it'll all be okay, right? We don't know how many people are sick, though. I mean, all those people at the stadium, and whatever else happened before then at the airport."

"So what are you saying?"

I took a deep breath. "I'm saying that you need to leave."

"Scarlett, I won't! I can't!"

"You have to. And not just to a hotel like I said before. You have to get out of the city. You and Anna both."

"That's ridiculous! I'm not going anywhere without—"

"You have to!" I raised my voice to cut her off, then repeated more calmly. "You have to. Mom. For me. You and Anna have to be okay. If something bad's going to happen to me, the only thing that's going to help me is if I know you guys are okay."

Silence on the line for a moment. Then she said, "But I can't" in the same tiny voice as a moment before. The situation we faced and the things I was saying were all just incomprehensible to her, and it reduced her almost to nothing.

It was like she was beaten, hit by waves from all sides until she couldn't stand anymore and had only a feeble "I can't" left as her defense.

"You can," I said, my voice quiet and calm. It killed me to have to talk to her like that, to hear my mom so scared and to be the one to offer comfort instead of the other way around, the way she'd done with me when I'd been little. "You can," I repeated. "It's not going to be easy, but I need you to do this for me, Mom. I need you to be okay. It's the only thing I can hold onto here. Please?"

A long pause followed, during which I could still hear her breathing and every now and then sucking back a sob. Finally, she said, "Where should we go? Where, if it's as bad as you say?"

Tears of relief welled up in my eyes, and I had to choke back my own sobs before I could answer. "Go to the cabin."

"Big Bear?"

We'd had the cabin in the mountains since I was little. My mom had gotten possession of it in the divorce, but we'd been up only three or four times since my dad had left.

"You should be safe there."

"I can't. It's too far."

But I knew she didn't mean that. From the second she'd asked where I thought she should go, I'd known she was resigned to it, if only to save one of her daughters.

"You can. You'll be fine," I said, still feeling like I'd become the parent. "But you should go now. Other people are going to start getting the same idea. People are going to run. You'll be in traffic all night if you don't start now."

"Oh, Scarlett!" More tears then.

"There'll be time for that later. Call me when you're driving. Just go. Now."

Another long pause. "Okay. Okay, baby. Okay."

I hung up, and then I went to the door to listen for sounds of her and Anna leaving, maybe packing a few things. It didn't take long for her to knock on my door.

"Are you ready?" I asked.

"Mm-hmm." Barely audible through the door.

"I can't hear you, Mom."

"I said we're ready." Her voice quavered, like she'd spent the last several minutes crying while she gathered everything she needed and had only just now pulled herself together. "Are you sure?"

"Yes, Mom. You have to go." I paused. "And I have to stay."

"I don't think I can do it, Scarlett. You're my baby."

"I'll always be your baby, Mom. Maybe I'll be okay. But you can't help me if you stay. You know? If you go…that'll help. That's all that'll help. Please?"

Another long pause from her, and then, "I love you, sweetie."

"I love you, too. Is Anna there?"

"Right here."

My sister sounded strong, together, resigned but not falling apart like our mother. I knew Anna would drive when they left, my mom sitting in the passenger seat with her arms folded tightly across her stomach. She'd spend most of the miles between home and Big Bear just looking out the passenger side window and trying not to cry.

"Take care of Mom, okay?" I said.

"I will. I wish…"

"I know. Me too. Maybe it'll be okay, though."

A pause. Then, "Maybe."

"I love you."

"Love you, too," she said.

I couldn't remember the last time we'd said that to each other. It wasn't like we weren't close. We didn't fight much. We just didn't feel the need to talk about how we felt about each other. I've felt sorry about that ever since that night.

"Bye, Scarlett," my sister said.

"Bye."

"I won't say goodbye," my mom said. "I won't. This isn't goodbye."

"All right, Mom. That's fine. Be safe."

"You too, baby. You too." She was about to lose it again, and I could picture Anna having to lead her away from my bedroom door and toward the stairs.

I listened for the door into the garage closing but never heard it. I only heard the garage door rolling up and went to my window to look out and watch the car back out into the driveway. In the dark, I couldn't tell if I'd been right about Anna driving, but I thought I could see someone waving from the passenger seat and so waved back. I didn't cry, didn't want them to see me cry, to have that be their last memory of me.

It turned out that my mom was wrong.
It really was goodbye.

CHAPTER FOUR

I'd thought myself terribly brave as the car pulled away. So it kind of surprised me how hard I began to cry when the taillights passed out of my line of sight. It wasn't fear of what was to come that got to me. It was just missing my mom and sister and knowing I'd probably never see them again.

I hadn't completely calmed down yet when I tried my dad again. Just thinking about being able to talk to him made me feel a little better. This time I got the answering machine and left another message. His cell went to voicemail right away, so I knew it was turned off. I hung up and the tears came back.

The rest of the night passed slowly. Once I stopped crying, I went back to the TV, then the computer, and finally back to my phone. I texted and called and emailed. None of my friends were asleep. We spent all our time being horrified by what we were seeing and then slowly, oddly becoming desensitized to it.

After a couple of hours I had watched enough video of people's faces exploding to feel as though it was nothing more than special effects in a movie or TV show. There was more video from the airport, from Dodger Stadium, from the nightclub, and other reports from all over the city where people had died without having cameras pointed at them. There were reports from hospitals, police headquarters, and city hall.

All the news was bad.

Some of the victims did horrible things before they died. Some attacked other people with guns or knives or fists. Some could be linked directly to one of the baggage handlers. And some couldn't.

After a while, I realized that most of the friends who were connecting with me through the phone or the computer were hanging on my words, trying to engage me, commenting just to comment though they had nothing to say. At first, I thought it was sympathy, that they just wanted me to know I wasn't alone, that they still cared. But then I realized it was morbid curiosity. They were expecting me to start freaking out over the phone, to lose my mind and die. As simple as that.

I started saying and sending my goodbyes and then stopped replying to everyone but Jen. She didn't seem like the others. She commented on what we were seeing or asked me questions no different than she would have asked me the day before, and that was it. Same old Jen.

A little after four, the call waiting beeped.

"I have to go, Jen. It's my dad," I said after checking the number on the screen.

"Okay. Call me back later if…you know, you need to."

"I will."

I expected my dad's voice. I expected wrong.

"You little brat, Scarlett!" my step-mom shouted as soon as I said hello.

My heart instantly racing, I said, "Angie? What are—"

But that was as far as I got.

"You always hated me! Always! And I knew you were trying to get him to go back to your mother! You never gave me a chance!" She was yelling as loudly as she could, and I didn't know what to say. I wanted to yell back, to argue, to defend myself, but the words wouldn't come—partly because there was the littlest sliver of truth in what she accused me of.

But then her voice grew quiet, and through her tears she said, "I'm not so bad, Scarlett. I'm really not."

"I know, Angie," I ventured. "I know. You're not bad at all. You're a great mom."

I was going to go on, telling her how awesome she was with my brothers. She cut me off, though, venom in her voice.

"A great mom? You don't know what the hell you're talking about. A great mom! Would a great mom..." A whimper then, almost a giggle, before she went on. "Would a great mom do what I did tonight?"

I thought of all the terrible things I'd seen on TV in the last few hours.

"I want to talk to my dad," I said, willing the tears back.

She laughed, horribly.

"Angie, I want—"

The phone went dead.

And I knew that along with all the other people who had died tonight, my dad was dead, too.

My brothers also.

Angie had done something to them. Something terrible. She'd gone crazy like the others and would be dead herself any minute.

I felt numb.

Absently, I clicked on my phone and dialed 911. It rang and rang and rang. Finally, a recording came on, apologizing about all the operators being busy and to please hold or try back later.

I clicked off the phone. Then I turned off the TV and the computer and the lights and fell onto my bed. I don't know why I didn't cry. I don't know why I didn't scream or break things. Shock, I guess. I just lay there, hugging a pillow. Looking up at the darkness of my room, I told myself it would be my turn soon, and there'd be no one here to see me lose my mind under the pressure of the stalks growing inside me.

In the quiet of those early morning hours, with all the electronics off and no one left to talk to, I noticed that things really weren't quiet, not outside, not like it should be. I could hear sirens, lots of them—some far away and some getting closer. And shouts, raised voices reaching through the walls and windows. Maybe people panicking. And maybe people losing their minds before the pop of the stalks.

I put my pillow over my head to drown out the sounds and imagined holding it down so hard that I could smother myself, do myself in before the inevitable. But it was just a stupid, desperate fantasy. I knew that if I could actually manage to make myself pass out, my arms would relax right away and I'd start breathing again.

There were other ways. My mom had some pills, or there was always a knife from the kitchen. But then I thought of my mom finding me like that…if she ever made it back here again. For some reason, the idea of her discovering me dead by my own hand seemed so much worse to me than her coming across my body with those stalks growing out of my skull.

Maybe in the morning, I'd change my mind.

If I lived that long.

For now, I was satisfied with using the pillow to block the rest of it all away.

* * * * *

I wouldn't have thought it possible to sleep under those circumstances, but I must have. I woke up with the gray light of dawn coming through my window and the smell of smoke in my nostrils. In seconds I was up and stumbling to my window, rubbing the sleep out of my eyes and absently reaching for my phone as I went.

I remember thinking I'd gotten a better room than Anna's since mine faced the street while Anna's window opened onto the back yard. I could always see what was going on in the neighborhood or know who was pulling up to our house before anyone else in the family.

That morning, my first full day of being fifteen, I looked out the window not with anticipation or curiosity, but with dread. My phone gave off a series of chimes to let me know I had messages, but I didn't even look down at it.

A house on the next street over was fully engulfed in flames. It was a house I'd only been able to see the back of, as it butted up against the neighbors directly across the street from us. Orange flames and black smoke poured from the house, from the windows on the second floor and even from a hole in the roof that the fire had already burned through.

I could see no firefighters, had heard no sirens. The man who lived across the street—I remember his name was Jennings, or Jenkins—had climbed onto his garage roof with a garden hose to try and fight the fire and keep it from spreading to his house. He must have been seventy and had no business up on the roof, but there he was in boxer shorts and nothing else, trying to do the right thing.

No one else was helping, not from where I could see anyway. I thought of going out myself, but again the thought of spreading the disease I'd been exposed to kept me planted right there at the window. It surprised me, though, that no one was doing anything to save the house or to help the old man with the garden hose.

And then a car drove by, and I understood. It was a small sedan with a family inside it, a child's face pressed to the back window. The trunk was halfway open, held secure with bungee cords to keep everything from falling out. Suitcases and boxes had been crammed inside the trunk, and a baby stroller was strapped to the roof, all folded up the way it would have been if the family inside had packed it for a trip to the zoo or the beach.

They weren't going anywhere like that, though.

They were just going.

The same way I'd told my mother and sister to go the night before.

A few more seconds passed, and then another car followed, similarly overloaded. This one practically flew where the other had simply been driven with purpose.

Not long after, a dog loped down the street, barking desperately. Which of the two cars it followed, I couldn't have guessed.

The man across the street was having a terrible time with the fire and his ridiculous garden hose. I could hear him yelling, though at whom I didn't know. Maybe his wife. Maybe the people who lived in the burning house.

I thought of calling for help, but remembered what had happened during the night when I had dialed 911. It would be more of the same, I knew. I could hear sirens now, though none seemed to be approaching, and when I looked to the horizon the air seemed gray. This wasn't the only fire burning.

Thinking about calling for help drew my attention back to my phone, and I thumbed through the texts I'd received during the last few hours. They were goodbyes. My friends all thought I was dead.

Scarlett? Plez text back

Goodbye Scarlett I'll never forget u

RIP Scarlett

U always made me laugh. Wish u still could

RIP

Ur lucky in a way. This is all gonna b so much worse soon

Dont b gone Scarlett plez plez plez

The first and last were from Jen. I almost dialed her number but stopped. Something else was wrong.

There should have been a text from my mother or sister. They would have checked in on me. Even with a traffic nightmare, they would be at the cabin by now. My mom would have called, would at least have left a message to let me know they'd made it.

But there were no missed calls from her or Anna.

I tried both their phones. Nothing. We hadn't kept a landline at the cabin, not since we'd stopped going regularly.

I told myself they just didn't have service where they were, maybe wouldn't have it till they came back down from the mountains.

There were other possibilities, of course, all of them terrible, and though I told myself not to think of them, the images flooded my mind regardless: my mom and Anna in a terrible accident, in some psycho-filled traffic jam trying to make it out of the city, or dead in the front seat of the car, white stalks poking through their faces.

I thought of the way my mom had hugged me when my dad had brought me home. I was bound to have had the spores on me. And my dad had hugged her, too. That had been it; that had been enough. Others had already died from less direct contact with the infected. I couldn't get the hug out of my mind, and for several seconds I thought I was going to throw up again.

Tears in my eyes, I called Jen.

It took her only seconds to answer, and then a full minute to stop crying.

"I thought you were dead," she kept repeating through the sobs. "I thought you were dead."

"I'm not dead," I said through my own tears. For some reason, it made me want to laugh, and I giggled while I cried. For a second, I thought I was finally going crazy, that this was the end, but then the feeling passed, and I just cried with Jen on the phone for a few minutes.

"Are you okay?" I finally managed.

"For now."

"What do you mean?"

"Haven't you been watching the news?" she asked.

"I was asleep. I…think my dad's dead. I mean, I'm sure he is. Probably my mom and Anna, too. I just had to…shut down for a while. You know?"

"I know. I'm sorry, Scarlett."

"What have they been saying?"

Jen took a breath and seemed to hold it for a few seconds. "It's bad. The whole city's been quarantined. They've shut down every freeway out of the whole LA area. The airports are closed, the trains. Everything. People are going crazy to get out."

"So what are people supposed to do if they think they've been exposed?"

"I don't know. I don't think anybody knows. It seems like anyone who's exposed is dying. I thought *you* were dead, Scarlett. All our friends did, too. The hospitals are filled with people who were at that game last night. They're all dying. Or already dead."

I just sat there on my bed and tried to make sense of what she'd just said. Across the street, Mr. Jennings or Jenkins had given up on fighting the fire and climbed down a ladder in his boxer shorts. He was running around his front yard now, looking like he was shouting as he waved his arms in the air.

"What do you mean by *all*, Jen? How many?"

"Different channels are saying different things. But it's thousands, Scarlett. They don't know where to put the bodies. And now there are doctors and nurses dropping dead with those things popping out of their skulls. And just…people. People who didn't seem to have any connection to the Dodger game."

"My God," I said. "What is it?"

"They don't know. They're still calling it a fungus, but no one really knows anything. There's all these rumors and…"

"And what?"

"And stories about how it's already spread to other cities. There are videos on YouTube showing people dying and they say they're in San Francisco and Phoenix and one even says it's in New York. I think they're hoaxes, but…what if they're not?"

"It doesn't make any sense."

"What?"

"If all this is happening, why am I not dead?"

Silence for a few seconds and then, "Maybe you're the cockroach who the pesticide doesn't kill."

"Like in Biology?"

"Maybe."

"That's ridiculous," I said. "There's got to be a better explanation. These people can't all be dying. The news has got it wrong."

"I don't think so. You should watch for a minute and look online. It's crazy, Scarlett. It's…"

"What?"

Then she was crying again. "I'm so scared, Scarlett. I don't want to die. I'm just fifteen. I don't want to die. I don't want my mom and dad to…"

I let her sob. There was nothing I could do. Across the street, the neighbor had dropped to his knees and had his arms over his head, looking up at the sky like he was asking God or something else to save him. And then he fell forward onto his face.

I turned away from the window.

It was unreal.

Your neighbor who you didn't really even know just collapses across the street, and your response is to turn around and not watch because you know he's about to die and there's nothing you can do for him.

That wasn't the world I lived in.

At least that's what I was telling myself.

Well, it hadn't been the world I lived in. Not the day before.

But that had been a world where I had parents and a sister and step-brothers, a world where the police or fire department came when you called them, a world where the Dodgers played the Giants and the only thing people said about the game the next day was whether it had been any good or not.

It wasn't a world where people's faces burst open from parasitic fungus that grew so fast you didn't even have the chance to say goodbye, didn't even have the chance to know you were sick.

But the old world was gone now, and a new one had swooped in to take its place. And here it wasn't just the fire department or the police who wouldn't be able to help you. It was also your parents and your friends and your neighbors.

I was on my own.

Not even Jen could help me.

She couldn't help herself.

But maybe I don't need the help, I thought. *Maybe I am* the cockroach who survives the bug spray.

"Jen?"

She was still sobbing.

"Jen, you need to pull yourself together, okay?"

She tried, taking deep breaths. The sobbing grew a bit less intense.

"Do you think you've been exposed?" I asked.

"How can you tell?"

"I don't know. But you haven't been outside since it started?"

"No. On the news they said to seal the houses, so my dad tried."

"How?"

"They said to put plastic and duct tape on all the windows and doors. He used trash bags. Everything looks so dark. I just want to see outside."

"You probably don't," I said.

"What do you mean?"

"It's horrible outside." I turned back to the window, my eyes drawn to the man face down on his lawn across the street. "People are dying. People are running away. Things are…"

Mr. Jenkins' or Jennings' house was now on fire. The house behind his was completely engulfed, and I could feel the heat coming through my window even though I was at least three feet away from it. The palm tree across the street had begun to smolder, and several bushes in front of other houses were burning as well. I could also see now that another house on the street beyond had begun to burn, and more neighbors had come out with hoses. Several wore masks—flimsy painters' masks most of them, but some had more heavy duty ones with filters that made them look like aliens from some bad movie.

"What is it?" Jen asked, a new level of panic in her voice.

"Things are on fire," I said quietly, incredulously.

Glowing embers were touching down in my own yard now, and when I went closer to the window to get a better look, I backed away again immediately. I felt like the window would burn me if I got too close, even if I just looked through it.

"What's on fire?"

"Houses. Trees. Everything. Jen?"

"Yeah?"

"I think I'd better go."

"Don't! Scarlett? Please!"

"I'll call you back. I have to go."

I clicked off and looked around my room, telling myself not to panic. For all I knew, the roof of my house was already smoldering from embers that the breeze had blown across the street, or just from the heat of the other fire. I was scared to look left or right outside my window for fear that our palm trees had already turned into torches with black smoke trailing into the sky and blazing chunks falling down onto our driveway and lawn.

I didn't know what to grab. I hadn't thought I'd need to leave. Our house had always been safe. Even now, with all this horrible stuff happening on the news, happening to my parents and brothers and sister, the house had seemed like the one safe place to be, a place where I could ride out the crisis until it passed, until order was restored and people figured out what had happened. And what to do with fifteen-year-old girls who'd been orphaned.

But not now, not any more. I had to go.

I dumped my backpack onto my floor, spilling out my notebooks and math homework for the weekend, and threw my laptop and charger into it. My phone went into my back pocket. Glancing around, almost spinning, I couldn't think of what else I'd need. Then I bolted for the door, stopping halfway there to open my closet and grab my heaviest coat. I hadn't worn it since February, but when I thought of running outside in my t-shirt and shorts, embers falling all around me, I knew I'd be glad for the jacket then.

I don't remember going down the stairs. I must have taken them three at a time, and it's surprising I didn't break my neck. I just remember going into the kitchen and pulling my mom's biggest butcher knife from the wooden block that held it and sliding it into my backpack. Then I opened the utility drawer and found my mom's little hammer and a utility knife with a retractable blade.

I slammed the drawer shut and then opened it again immediately, memory driving me as I scanned the jumbled contents. I couldn't see what I was looking for, so I pulled the whole drawer out and let everything fall onto the kitchen floor. Seconds later, I saw the Swiss Army knife my mom had teased my dad about using, saying it was the tool he'd grab for any occasion—that and a roll of duct tape. I grabbed the knife and tossed it into the backpack and then, for good measure, opened the bottom drawer and found the half used roll of duct tape that had been there forever. Into the backpack it went, too.

From the fridge, I grabbed two bottles of water.

From the pantry, three protein bars and a jar of peanut butter.

And then I ran into the living room, looking around frantically for anything else that might be useful, expecting to hear our smoke alarms going off any second.

On the mantle was a framed photo of our family, the family that had been ours before the divorce and all the ugliness and the split visits and the new wife and half-brothers. Me with big dimples and blonde braids and Anna in braces, standing in front of Mom and Dad, big smiles on all our faces. We'd gone to the Griffith Observatory in the hills above Los Angeles for a Sunday outing, and in the photo the city spread out behind us as we stood on one of the observation decks. I remember my dad asking a tourist to take the picture, and I'd been embarrassed about posing in front of some stranger, but the smiles had been real. At least they'd seemed real. I didn't know about the fighting and accusations yet, but a month after the picture had been taken, my dad had moved out. I kind of hated that picture, and kind of loved it, too. It had always surprised me that my mom had kept it out for everyone to see, a reminder of what had been lost.

Of course, I didn't think any of those things now. I just grabbed the photo and stuffed it into my backpack without wondering why or what good it would do me.

I knew there was a good chance I'd never make it back to this house, this neighborhood. And that if I did come back, it would be a miracle to find the place standing or for there to be any record of the family that had once lived here and then fallen apart.

Back in the kitchen, I pulled the spare key ring off its little hook and then yanked open the back door. Out of habit, I twisted the lock and pulled the door closed behind me. And then I ran to the driveway without looking back.

The street was in chaos. Flames shot from every window in the house across the street, and the houses on either side were burning as well. No one had done a thing about the body on the lawn. I could hear dogs barking, people shouting, and the roar of the flames. On this side of the street, several trees were already on fire, and when I looked up at our house, I could see smoke beginning to rise from the roof, maybe only from embers that had landed there, but maybe not.

The heat was terrific, and I slipped my jacket on, pulled the hood up, and ran toward Anna's second-hand Nissan parked at the curb. She'd let me drive it up and down the driveway a few times, but I'd never actually driven a car on the street. That wasn't going to stop me, though. I'd known when I was still inside the house that taking my bicycle would be a terrible choice. Driver's Ed was going to start right now.

I almost started crying when I got into the car, my backpack on the passenger seat and my jacket all bunched up between me and driver's seat. The tassel from Anna's high school graduation dangled from the rearview mirror. Such a simple thing, but it said everything about my sister, everything she'd been and done and wanted up until yesterday. Such an innocent, stupid little thing, just hanging there. And now all her dreams and everything she'd worked for…everything. It was all up in smoke like the houses around me.

I resisted the urge to yank the tassel off the mirror. Instead, I carefully removed it and let it drop into the cup holder on the console.

"Okay, then," I said, wiping tears away with the back of my left hand while I slid the key into the ignition with my right. The car started right away, and then I took a few seconds to think about the steps. Brake, gear, let the brake up, and then a little gas.

My fingers gripped the wheel tightly as I felt the car roll forward. I didn't step on the gas even though I wanted to get away, as fast and as far as I could from the smoke and the flames and shouts and screams and the dead man on the lawn across the street.

But I kept my calm and just let the car roll forward for a few feet, forgetting to check the mirrors before pulling out into the street and then remembering in a panic at the last second. Of course, no one was coming. No cars, and certainly no fire engines.

A dog ran across the street right in front of the Nissan, and I punched the brakes in panic even though it was gone before I'd had time to react. If I'd been going faster, if I'd stepped on the gas the way I'd wanted to, I probably would have killed the dog, so I was glad for that.

I let the car roll on slowly past a couple more houses and then gingerly pushed on the gas. The little Nissan picked up speed, and I told myself I'd get the hang of this quickly.

Three houses down, a woman I recognized but had never spoken to was standing on her lawn, her hands over her mouth as she looked in horror at the burning houses behind me. She turned toward me as I drove past, and I saw a look of anger come over her.

I was abandoning the street, the neighborhood. I was running away. It filled her with rage, not any kind of reaction a normal person would have, but probably something you'd think if you were sick, if you had a fungal growth pressing on your brain. Her rage would likely have come out over anything, or anyone, but it came out over me driving by in my sister's car, barely doing ten miles an hour.

When I saw her turn and start running across her lawn toward the street, an incomprehensible bellow coming from her still-open mouth, I didn't hesitate, but punched the gas and felt the little Nissan leap. In seconds, I was beyond her reach and driving away as fast as I thought was safe. If she hadn't come after me, I might have forgotten to look in the rearview mirror for one more glimpse of the street I'd grown up on. And as I did, I saw no trace of the good memories I had, just an angry woman standing in the middle of the street, waving a fist impotently at me as I sped away, burning houses on either side of the street behind her.

CHAPTER FIVE

I didn't know where to go at first.

The police station, I thought. Or a fire station. Or a hospital. Any of those places made sense, but when I pictured myself walking in and asking for help, I imagined how many others would be there wanting the same thing and decided against it.

Then I thought about my school. The last place a fifteen-year-old girl would want to go voluntarily when she didn't have to, but somehow it also seemed a safe place at the moment. Still, the thought of the empty halls and classrooms now made me shudder.

So, for lack of anywhere better, I ended up at Jen's.

It felt strange pulling up to the curb in a car I was driving, not being dropped off by my mom. It felt like I was some time-warped version of myself, arriving the way I would a few years in the future if everything hadn't gone so horribly wrong.

Stranger still, though, was the way the house looked with green plastic trash bags taped up inside all the windows, almost like the house had been blasted with holes where the windows had been.

I stopped the car, careful not to hit the curb, ending up almost two feet into the street. It didn't matter. I got out and looked around. Almost every other house nearby had the windows covered, too, some with white trash bags, some with clear plastic.

Behind me, dark columns of smoke reached into the sky. My neighborhood going up. Jen's neighborhood was separated from mine by about a mile and a half and one major street that I doubted the fire would jump. Still, it gave me a little peace of mind to hear sirens approaching. The neighborhood might not be saved, but at least the fire could be stopped from spreading to others.

I knew not to knock on Jen's door. No one would answer. And I wouldn't have wanted them to. Still haunted at the thought of the hug I'd given my mom, I didn't want to do anything to endanger Jen or her family or anyone else. But I knew they were inside, and I was out. It would stay that way, and I'd be safe here, as safe as could be anyway. And they'd be safe from me.

I gathered my jacket and backpack and locked the Nissan. My car now. And then I headed for the gate on the side of the house. I would have hopped it if I'd needed to, but it was unlocked, so I slipped into the backyard and walked around the pool the way I'd done a hundred times before, only now there was no laughter, no barbecue, no anything. Just me and the still water and the smell of smoke in the air.

Jen's room was on the second floor, and her window looked out onto the pool. I glanced up at it now, not surprised to find it covered in the same plastic as all the other windows in the house. Calling up to her wouldn't be a good idea—would only get the attention of her parents and brother, too. I knew her dad wouldn't want me back here, would be afraid of what microscopic dangers I was carrying. He'd kick me out for sure, if he had the nerve to come outside. Still, I didn't want to risk it. If I just stayed quiet, I could wait here until I figured out what else to do.

The backyard looked no different than it would have on a normal day—lounge chairs scattered around the pool, a glass-topped patio table with a folded umbrella poking through its center and padded chairs around it, the covered barbecue near a sliding glass door. I quietly pulled a chair away from the table, sat down, and began removing my things from the backpack, laying them all out on the table before me. It wasn't much, not enough to survive on. I should have grabbed more food, I told myself, but there was no going back now. There were bound to be Red Cross centers up already; I just needed to find the nearest one and then try to figure out what I was going to do next. What do you do when you've turned fifteen, become an orphan, and had your house burn down all in twenty-four hours? I wondered how the Red Cross would handle that one.

The Waverlys had an outlet in a neat little box sticking out of the lawn right near the table, so I uncoiled my laptop's charger and plugged in, just to make sure I had 100% battery life by the time I had to leave—whenever that turned out to be. Then I logged onto Jen's Wi-Fi and opened my Facebook. I could see from the chat icon that Jen was online; so were a couple of our friends, but I didn't care about them right now.

Jen? I typed.

Seconds later. *OMG! Where r u?*

Ur back yard

What?

U gonna make me type it again?

What happened?

I dont wanna go into it. I need a place to stay. Can I hang out here for now?

I think my p wont like it but I wont tell.

K

U all rite?

For now. U?

Scared.

Not sick?

No. Not yet.

K. Call me when its safe.

K

I logged off then and just looked around the yard, listening to the sound of helicopters not far away and wondering if they were part of the effort to save what was left of my neighborhood. I suppose I was in shock, as I didn't think at all about everything I'd lost in the last few hours or the final blow to my old life that the helicopters and billowing smoke signaled. Realizing I hadn't eaten anything yet, I unwrapped one of the energy bars and opened the peanut butter. Then I went to Google and tried to figure out what was going on.

The disease was definitely a fungus, authorities claimed.

Others claimed it was a virus.

The sites that claimed it was aliens or the wrath of God, I didn't bother clicking on.

All the pages with theories included pictures of people dying from the growths. I'd seen it so many times by that point that it was no longer shocking. If I'd thought about my parents or brothers or Anna, I don't think I could have handled it, but I suppose my mind had begun compartmentalizing everything, so I just didn't go there, didn't think about it in context with what I was reading on the computer screen.

The disease, whatever it was, had been contained within the Los Angeles area.

According to other pages, people were dying in Arizona and San Francisco.

The National Guard had been called out to the California border to enforce quarantine of the state.

People were dying in New York and Miami, Tokyo and London.

All air traffic in and out of the US had been stopped.

But not before a lot of people had traveled.

The Mexican government was welcoming refugees.

The Mexican government had called out their military, and they were shooting anyone trying to cross the border from the US.

A thousand people had died in Los Angeles County alone.

Ten thousand had died.

A million.

Ten million worldwide.

No one had died. It was all an elaborate hoax.

It was the Chinese.

It was the anti-Christ.

It was the Earth taking its revenge on our species for all we had done wrong.

It was the latest in a series of mass extinctions dating back millions of years, part of a natural cycle. All that remained was to hug one another and say goodbye to the fantasy that humans had been the dominant species on this planet and would stay that way forever.

It couldn't all be true. And yet some of it must have been. Which things were legitimate and which were the lies…I had no way to know.

I gave up, pulling the laptop's lid closed and resting my head against the back of the chair. I closed my eyes and listened to the helicopters, the distant sirens, the dogs barking, and the faraway shouts and cries of people who would be dead soon.

Why not me? I thought. *Why no headache, no nosebleed?*

But then I asked myself why I was even wondering about these things. Did I wish myself dead? Did I want to go out the way all these others had?

No.

But did I want to be alone—no family, no friends, nothing left that I'd ever been able to count on?

No to that as well.

So where did that leave me?

Not wishing for death, but not sure how to live in this new world I'd woken up to.

After a while, I checked my phone. Jen hadn't texted back yet. Thinking about why she'd remained silent made me nervous, and I got up from the table to wander around the backyard. Leaves and a few dead bugs floated in the pool, and I watched everything move on the current that the filter created, wondering if I should try calling Jen or just leave her be. She knew I was out here. If she needed me, she'd call. But what could I do in that case? Nothing.

The Waverlys had a changing room for the pool with a toilet and shower inside. I went in for a minute, used the toilet and then looked at myself in the mirror. I looked awful, no makeup, hair half pulled out of the ponytail I'd slept in, dirt smeared on my face from where I must have wiped at tears. If I'd smiled, my dimples still would have been there, about the only thing recognizable in the mirror, but I didn't feel like smiling.

"Oh well," I said to my reflection. "Forgot to pack makeup and a curling iron."

Back outside, I decided I couldn't wait any longer and sent Jen a text.

U still ok?

No reply.

I just looked at the screen and waited for some sign of life from inside the house.

None came.

I began texting other people, friends I hadn't checked in on since the night before.

No replies at all.

Maybe later, I told myself. Maybe their phones were off, or they were asleep, or had headed out to the desert or somewhere else with their families, somewhere without cell service.

Or maybe not.

By the early afternoon, I was telling myself I should go, that there had to be a better place, a proper place for kids without parents to look for shelter and be registered or gathered up by the authorities. Maybe there were places that were giving out vaccinations. Maybe someone would be interested in examining a girl who seemed to be immune. At any rate, hanging out in your best friend's backyard, lazing around her pool and waiting for more people to die…that probably wasn't what I was supposed to be doing. I wondered what my teachers would say, if any of them were still alive. And I couldn't imagine a single thing that would come out of any of their mouths.

And still I stayed, practically frozen to the spot, scared to move, scared to leave, scared to stay. Eating another energy bar dipped in peanut butter and drinking a bottle of water and trying to stay off the Internet. Trying harder not to check my phone, wondering if a text had come in that I'd somehow not noticed.

But of course every time I looked at it, always telling myself I shouldn't, there was nothing there.

Finally, I gave up and called Jen's cell.

Straight to voicemail.

Her phone was off.

I called the home number.

Mrs. Waverly's pleasant voice asking me to leave a message after four long, agonizing, empty rings, a muffled bit of which I could hear from outside by the pool.

"Hi, it's…" I hesitated.

They're all dead, I thought and pictured my voice playing inside that house, calling out like a lost little child hoping someone would come and save her. And no one would hear. The dead didn't listen.

But I talked anyway, probably out of a sense of hope that I didn't think I still had, but it must have been there anyway, under the surface all the time like an instinct rather than something I could really have identified.

"It's Scarlett," I said. "I…I wanted to see if you were all okay still." My voice cracked and a tear ran down my cheek. "I wanted…"

There was nothing else I could say. There were all sorts of things I wanted, but none of them came into my mind; none of the thoughts were strong enough to push past the idea that the house I sat here and looked at, the house I'd spent so much time in, laughing and just *being*…that it was now a house full of dead people.

I clicked off.

"Jen?" I called out, trying to aim my voice up toward her covered window. As loud as I could, "Jen? Are you still in there?"

Of course she was still in there. What a stupid thing to ask. It didn't occur to me then.

"I'm still out here. Can you just let me know you're okay?"

The tears that had started when I was on the phone kept coming now, and it was hard to choke out the words and get them loud enough to be audible to anyone still alive inside the house.

"Please?" I begged.

And then I dropped back into the chair.

And I cried, and I cried, and I cried, my head in my hands as though I was ashamed of my tears and trying to hide myself from anyone who might see or hear me.

I think I cried for it all then…for my parents and sister and brothers, for all my friends, for Jen and her family, for the people who'd died in front of me and died on the news, and died, and died, and died. And I cried for myself, for all the things I'd hoped life would bring, for graduation and college and falling in love and getting married and having babies, for all the things I'd ever thought I'd see or do, none of which I could have articulated that afternoon, none of which was specific. It all just came pouring out of me in a deep gray wash of agony and loss and emptiness that I knew I'd never fill no matter what the people who survived were going to do with orphans like me, no matter what sort of life I could piece together out of what was left around me. And I cried because I was scared, really scared of being alone with nothing and no one to count on.

I cried because I didn't want to die. By that point, I think I'd come to accept the possibility that I really might be immune to the disease, but that wasn't the kind of death I feared. Instead, I think I was terrified of being just fifteen and not really knowing a thing about how to take care of myself. I knew I was going to have to figure everything out on my own, and with every decision I made about what to eat or where to sleep, I would run the risk of messing up, of poisoning myself or putting myself into a situation that wouldn't have been dangerous in the old world, but in the new one, this one where I was on my own…who could say? There'd be a thousand ways to die every day, and as I sat there and cried, I worried that there was so much unknown.

After a while, I stopped. I'd cried myself out and just sat there with my head on my folded arms, completely drained. My face ached from sobbing, and tears and snot had run past my lips once I'd given up on wiping them away. Jen's dad could have burst out of the house, yelling at me to leave, and I don't think I would have lifted my head—not for him, not for Jen, not for anyone. I was done, spent.

Exhausted, I actually fell asleep then.

When I woke up, it was late afternoon. I wiped at my eyes and re-did my pony tail. Then I checked my phone for messages— nothing. The same with email on the computer. None of my friends were active on Facebook, nor had they been for hours.

I pushed the chair back and took a deep breath.

I was hungry, and I didn't want more peanut butter.

The Waverlys' back door was just across the yard with its plastic-covered window and shiny brass doorknob. I let out a sigh and said, "Brave new world." Then I walked around the pool and began looking for something to break the window with.

I decided on a ceramic snail in one of the planters, hefting it for a moment before approaching the door. The snail was about ten inches long and weighed maybe a pound. I wondered if it would break before the window did, but decided to give it a try.

I knocked first, loudly. "Hello?" I called out, my mouth as close to the window as I could get it. "Jen? Mrs. Waverly?"

I put my ear to the glass. No signs of life came from inside the house.

I called out, knocked, and listened again, and then a third time. Then I looked up once more to Jen's window, half expecting to see her waving down at me with the plastic pulled away from the glass.

"All gone," I said. "Sorry, Jen."

I drew back the snail and swung it at the window, remembering to close my eyes at the last second. There was a crash, and I felt my hand passing through the window, opening my eyes a second later to see that both the snail and the pane had been smashed. Carefully, I pulled my hand back, checking for cuts and relieved to find none.

Angry with myself, I realized I'd just run up against my first chance at serious injury, all my own fault. There had to have been a dozen different ways to break into the house, none of which would have had me running the risk of slicing open a vein in my arm. Fortunately for me, I'd been lucky, but I resolved not to make hasty decisions from now on.

I dug the Swiss Army knife out of my backpack and went back to the window, slicing away at the plastic on the other side of the broken glass. It already had little cuts in it from the glass and the shattered snail, but not enough for me to reach inside. Carefully, I cut at the plastic and moments later had cut a hole that would give me access to the locks on the other side.

There had been no reaction from inside the house when I'd broken the window, so I knew there was no point in calling out again. Instead, I reached inside, watching the edges of broken glass to make sure I didn't cut my upper arm. Seconds later, I had the door unlocked.

Jen's cat, Cisco, bolted past me as soon as I had the door opened a few inches. I turned to watch him run around the edge of the pool and then jump to the top of the block wall with no effort at all. He walked a few feet along the top of the wall and then jumped down the other side, not looking back once. "Good luck,

Cisco," I said, hoping for lots of mice and birds in his future. There'd be no more gourmet cat food for him.

I ventured inside, steeling myself for what I'd see. The Waverlys' kitchen had always been neat, like something out of a magazine. It looked mostly like normal now—with the exception of a few cupboard doors left open and some dishes in the sink. And a pair of legs on the floor, blocking the entryway into the dining room.

I knew it was Jen's mom, her feet still in the casual sandals she wore all the time.

"Mrs. Waverly?" I said, just above a whisper as I slowly approached the body. I knew there was no point in whispering, no point in calling out at all, but I did it anyway.

When I got to the entryway, I just stood there for a moment and nodded. She'd gone like all the others and was lying there on her back, arms splayed, face a bloody mess, and two obscene stalks rising up from where her nose had been. The little pods at the tips had already popped, spreading their spores throughout the house and probably through unseen cracks in the walls and gaps in the plastic that covered the windows.

How were you exposed? I thought. It certainly hadn't been at the Dodger game or a nightclub or anything like that. I didn't know at what point Jen's dad had covered the windows with plastic, just that it had been too late.

I thought about how I'd seen the little cloud of dust that had burst free from the stalks on the "foul ball" man at the stadium. For the spores to have spread so far and so fast, and to have been able to slip inside houses sealed in plastic, to get past the masks I'd seen people wearing online and on TV, they must have been microscopic. And yet I'd seen them burst out of the pods after the stalks had sprouted out of the "foul ball" man at the stadium. For things so tiny to look like a cloud of dust...there must have been millions if not billions of spores in each pod. And within hours the infected had succumbed, and pods of their own had popped into the air, spreading billions more.

Infecting everyone but me.

Or so it seemed as I stood there looking at the body of my best friend's mom. Jen and her dad and her brother could be anywhere in the house, all in similar states. I didn't want to have to see, but I couldn't just leave either.

Mr. Waverly was in the living room, absurdly planted in his recliner, the stalks that emerged from his face pointing at the ceiling. He'd been watching television, and it was still on, an enormous flat screen mounted to the wall.

Trying to ignore the corpse, I picked up the remote from where it had fallen beside the recliner and began flipping through channels.

The locals were what I really wanted, but they were all dead. None had been broadcasting their normal programming. Each channel was running the same thing, a simple static image of the station's news desk. Chatty anchors and overly made-up weather girls should have been at the desks, but there was no one. On one channel, I could see a pair of stalks waving in the air on the other side of the desk, some poor broadcaster or station employee having died on camera. But the rest all looked abandoned, whether from massive panic in the studios, or sudden deaths, or the employees all leaving their posts to rush home to the illusion of safety.

The emergency crawl was pretty much the same on all the channels: We Are In A State Of Emergency. All Citizens Are Urged To Stay Indoors. Do Not Call For Emergency Services. Resources For Survivors Will Be Allocated Once The Crisis Has Passed. Stay Tuned To This Channel For Updates And Instructions. We Are In A State Of Emergency. All Citizens Are Urged...

It just looped like that.

That was all they'd had to offer: stay inside and watch TV and don't change the channel whatever you do. I wanted to laugh, but it would have been too cruel in front of Mr. Waverly's corpse.

The cable news channels offered a bit more. Things must not have been as bad yet in Atlanta and New York. There, people wearing masks still spoke to the camera, but you could barely understand them through all the filters.

If I'd had any doubt that it was the end of the world, it left me that afternoon staring at Mr. Waverly's giant television screen. CNN showed image after image of streets filled with corpses and crashed cars, buildings on fire, and people dying not just here but all over the world. They called it a plague, an outbreak, and an apocalypse, and it had struck in Europe, Asia, Africa, and South America. During the time I watched, there was no mention of Australia, and I began to wonder about islands, or people doing research in places like Antarctica or out in the ocean on submarines or cruise ships. There had to have been people who hadn't been exposed yet, and surely there would be some of those who could find a way to keep safe.

And there had to be others like me, who were immune. Or at least slow to show signs of infection.

But how would I find them?

I thought about going into downtown LA to City Hall or finding the nearest police department in Pasadena, reasoning that any other survivors might try the same thing. Part of me thought it sounded like a good idea. And part of me wondered who else would be there. Police, I hoped. But what would make them so special? The people in charge, the people you could count on, the good people…they weren't somehow more likely to have survived this long. But who then? Other people like me? I wanted to find them. And at the same time I thought of the woman who'd lived down the street from me, the one who'd looked at me so strangely as I'd driven away from the fire. There might well be people who'd survived this far through luck or genetics and who were not at all happy about it, not at all ready to embrace other survivors.

I gave it a minute's thought and then clicked off the television, setting the remote neatly on the coffee table and leaving the room as though everything was normal.

At the foot of the stairs, I tentatively called out, "Jen? Are you up there? It's Scarlett."

There was no reply, no movement, no sound. I could have walked upstairs and found her; I told myself that maybe I should, that it would be the last thing I could do for her, the last friend I'd have the chance to say goodbye to. But I turned from the stairs instead. There was no point in climbing them. I'd just have to come back down again. My tears for Jen had fallen outside by the pool. I wasn't about to let them start again.

Back in the kitchen, I began looking for proper supplies, not just the kinds of things you grab when you fear the house will burn down around you if you don't get out fast enough. Jen's mom had re-usable canvas grocery bags in the utility closet by the back door, and I filled them with canned food after finding a hand-operated can opener in a drawer. Mixed vegetables, tuna, pineapple, beans. I tried to remember nutrition class and the things I'd need most, but it was all a blur, and I grabbed whatever made sense.

One cupboard held four gallons of water, and several liter bottles of more expensive "designer water" as my mother had called it. Those all went into canvas bags, too.

I also found three flashlights, only one of which worked, and a package of batteries with enough in it to get the other two powered up.

I grabbed more knives and tools, and from a hallway closet I pulled three blankets and a quilt and a pillow.

It took a couple of loads to get everything to the front door. Using a knife, I sliced through the plastic that Mr. Waverly had used to try to save himself and his family. It seemed so flimsy, such a futile thing to try. Then I unlocked the door and carefully cracked it open, peeking outside to see if anyone was around.

The neighborhood looked as empty as it had hours before when I'd arrived. A couple of crows flew past. A dog barked distantly. The air still smelled smoky, and the sky was hazy from the fires, but I no longer heard sirens or helicopters.

There was no one around, no one to come up and ask me why I was taking things out of the Waverlys' house. Of course, I was paranoid about having to explain myself even though I knew I wouldn't have to. The world had only just ended. The old rules hadn't been forgotten yet. You didn't just gather supplies from a house that wasn't your own and cart it all away in your sister's Nissan. You got things from the store. You paid for them. That was the way things were supposed to work. Even though they didn't work that way any more, I still couldn't shake the sense that I had to be on guard, ready to justify my actions.

It was like being in a dream where nothing makes sense and yet you somehow know exactly what you're supposed to do…only no one else in the dream seems to know what's going on or why you're acting the way you are.

A deep breath, another look up and down the street, and then it was out to the car with my first load. I packed the car methodically, thinking about what I'd need most, what I should hide in case other survivors got curious about what I was carrying, what was most valuable, what I could do without if it came down to that.

When I was finished loading the car, I went back through the house and got my computer and other things from the backyard. Then I left Jen's house without looking back, without even closing the door behind me. I might think of something else I'd need later. If I came back and found the door closed, I'd know someone else had been there—I wouldn't know who, and I wouldn't know if they were still there, but at least I'd know the house had been visited. I seriously doubted I'd be back, and doubted even more that the door would be anything but open just as I'd left it.

CHAPTER SIX

It didn't take me long to realize how impractical Anna's Nissan was going to be, or how I'd pretty much wasted all that time loading the car so carefully. There'd been a few cars in the middle of the streets in Jen's neighborhood, but they'd been easy to avoid, with me driving slowly and cautiously, still feeling shaky behind the wheel. But when I got out on the main street, with the intention of getting over to Colorado Boulevard, I found it to be just about impassable.

Cars were everywhere. Not parked. Just there. Some had crashed into each other. Some had gone up onto the curbs and sidewalks or crashed into homes and businesses. Some were just abandoned in the middle of the street.

There were dead people in many of them—men and women and children with stalks growing out of their faces. More dead people lay in the street.

At first, I just stared in disbelief. There were so many of them. And no one was around to do anything about it.

No one was around.

Just me.

Some people hadn't died from the disease. I saw more than one who must have died in crashes before the disease had gotten them. They were just dead, sitting there behind their steering wheels. I hadn't been ready for that, ready to see dead people who were…regular, like me. Had some of them been immune, too, and just unlucky? I tried not to think about it, tried just to watch the road in front of me and thread my way through the cars and bodies.

After a few blocks, I gave up, having already driven across one lawn and cutting through two parking lots to try and get through. There were just too many cars.

I navigated into a parking lot and brought the car to a stop.

Now what? I thought.

I was in front of a dentist's office. There were probably dead people inside. There would probably be medical supplies, too, but I didn't know what I might need or what to do with any of it, so I put the thought out of my head.

Even though I was all alone out here, I decided to protect all the supplies I'd gathered, popping the trunk and then moving all the canvas shopping bags I'd filled at Jen's. The quilt and pillow I left in the backseat. Then I locked the car and headed out, intending to walk the mile or two to Colorado Boulevard with only my backpack and phone. I wondered about taking one of the knives from the backpack and holding it close as I walked, but everything was so quiet that it didn't seem necessary.

I hated that walk, hated being so close to all those people who'd just been trying to get away. How many more streets were there just like this one? How many bodies? And in how many other cities could the same thing be found? And what were the odds that some other survivor was wandering out there, thinking the same things?

That was what I hated most—thinking. I hated wondering if I was all of a sudden the only person left alive. Anywhere. I trembled at the idea, more than at the sight of all the bodies.

I didn't want to believe it, knew that chances had to be good that people on other continents were fine, or at least some people. There had to be people on islands, sailors on submarines...people who were immune or just lucky, people who hadn't been exposed yet and now knew to avoid contagion.

That was what I hoped, what I had to believe. What choice did I have?

I didn't have much of a plan beyond making it to the main boulevard. I'd had a vague sense of what to do when I'd struck out from Jen's house, but the impassability of the streets had changed that. There was no point in planning anything that had to do with driving. That new skill I'd only just started playing with was now useless.

When I finally reached Colorado Boulevard, I realized that if I'd somehow managed to make it this far by car, I'd have needed to abandon the Nissan then. The street was clogged, cars pushed together, some still running with their owners dead behind the steering wheels. Even the sidewalk was blocked in places, cars' front ends pushed through storefront windows. These I had to walk around or climb over; in most cases, climbing was easier. I didn't want to start walking out into the street and the maze of cars, fearful that I'd find my way blocked. The last thing I wanted was to be hemmed in among the smashed fenders and dead people.

As I walked, I couldn't help thinking about where I'd spend the night. It was early evening now, and though I still had at least another hour of daylight, I knew the time would pass quickly.

After walking a few blocks, I glanced across the street and saw three things in quick succession. The first gave me a little hope. The second brought a rush of elation. And the third terrified me.

The first thing was simple enough—a sporting goods store. I thought of tents and sleeping bags and all sorts of outdoor and survivor gear. Food even. Lanterns, batteries. Everything I'd need if I was going to be on my own for a while.

With one foot off the curb and heading for the store, I stopped, stock-still.

I was no longer alone.

A woman was walking along the other side of the street, having almost reached the sporting goods store. Why she hadn't seen me moving along ahead of her, I couldn't say. Maybe she'd only just started down the street. Maybe she'd just come out of a different store or restaurant or some other place where she'd been hiding. And maybe she'd been so focused on what was in front of her and on weaving her way among the dead bodies and crunched cars that she hadn't thought to look more than a few feet in front of her.

At any rate, she was there. I wanted to call out and wave. But I worried that I might scare her away. She looked to be in her twenties, in jeans and a pink t-shirt, her blonde hair a mess. She looked like she'd been through hell. I probably looked the same. She moved along slowly, warily, and I knew a call from me would make her bolt. Then where would I be? I certainly didn't want to have to chase her through the streets just to have someone to talk to. But what choice did I have?

"Hey?" I called out, hoping the word came out softly, not threatening or surprising. My voice sounded feeble and squeaky.

But before I could get up the nerve to call out again, I saw the third thing. A man came up fast behind the woman, running full speed across a clear stretch of sidewalk. I don't know how he moved so quietly and quickly at the same time, but he did. Neither the woman across the street nor I had any clue he was coming until he was right on her, tackling her.

The woman fell with her attacker, barely able to gasp out a scream before he was on top of her.

I screamed as well. "No!" Then I shot into the street, dodging around cars and hopping over a few to try and get to the other side, not sure of what I'd do when I got there.

When I reached the sidewalk, I saw the man had one arm around the woman's throat and the other under her stomach. He held on tight as she tried to wrestle her way out of his grip, attempting to thrash from side to side, but he didn't show any sign of weakening.

"No…. no," the man kept saying while the woman writhed beneath him.

She said nothing, just grunted in her struggle to free herself.

"Hey!" I shouted, not sure what good it would do, hoping just to scare him off.

The man barely glanced my way, hardly even seeming to see me. Then he buried his face in the woman's hair and kept saying, "No…no."

I'd never really been in a fight before. I'd never taken karate class or anything like that. I'd never hit anybody in real anger or self-defense.

Even so, I didn't think twice. I took another three steps, planted myself right beside the struggling pair, and then I placed a well-aimed kick right in the man's side.

He shouted then and half rolled off his victim but still didn't let her go.

My toes hurt where I'd kicked him, but I saw my advantage and did it again, this time getting him in the stomach before he had the chance to roll back down and protect himself.

Again, he shouted and grimaced in pain.

"No!" he yelled.

And now the woman under him managed to break his grasp and wriggle out from under him. She barely looked at me and then started running.

It was the last thing I had expected. I'd just saved her life, and now she was abandoning me to face her attacker on my own.

Thinking back on it now, I guess I might have done the same thing if I'd been in her position.

I didn't know what to do besides run after her, so I kicked the man again, getting him in the ribs this time and feeling his body lift just a little with the blow, and then I tore out after the woman.

Half a block along, I started catching up to her, and when she had to run into the street to get around a delivery truck that had run up onto the sidewalk, I cut around another car behind the van and was right at her side.

"Wait!" I said with barely enough breath to get the word out.

She looked at me for a second, nothing but fear in her eyes. I knew she wanted to bolt again, but she was just as winded as me. So I was relieved when she just stood there regarding me and breathing hard.

Blood streamed from her nose, and her chin had a nasty scrape on it. Her t-shirt had been torn at the collar in the struggle, a big flap hanging down across her chest. She stood up straight and tried pulling the flap up, but it just fell again.

"You're bleeding," I said.

The news didn't seem to surprise her.

Slowly, so as not to scare her, I slipped my backpack off and looked inside to see if I had anything she could clean herself up with. The only things useful for something like this had been left back in Anna's car. I shook my head incredulously when I saw the kitchen knives I'd taken from home at the bottom of the backpack. It hadn't even occurred to me to pull one on the man. I still wonder if I would have dared use it. Even so, I promised myself right there not to be caught off guard again.

There were other survivors, and some of them were going to be dangerous.

"I'm Scarlett," I said.

"Debbie."

"Are you okay?"

I kept waiting for her to thank me for saving her, but she must have been too shaken up for gratitude to have gotten past her fight-or-flight filter.

"I think so."

"Did you know that guy? Was he following you?"

She shook her head. "No. I mean...I don't know. I didn't even see his face."

I looked back in the direction of the sporting goods store, half expecting the man to be pursuing us. There was no sign, but that didn't give me much comfort. Rather than running after us, he could have been stalking us, prowling along among all the cars.

"He was probably sick," I said. "You know? Like, getting sick in the head from the...fungus."

"Probably," Debbie said. "Or maybe he was an angel. They have wings, you know?"

"I..."

And then, there was just nothing more to say.

I wanted to cry as I watched the blood flow from Debbie's nose.

I thought I'd found someone, someone like me, another survivor.

But she wasn't bleeding because that man had hurt her.

She had the disease, was just a few hours behind Jen's family and all these other people who'd been trying to get somewhere safe on Colorado Boulevard. She had been wandering along on her own, having hallucinations or delusions about angels when she'd been attacked. *As good as anything else to spend your last moments thinking about*, I told myself.

I'd saved her from one thing, saved her from having her last moments being spent in agony and fear and victimization.

But I couldn't save her from this. There was no arguing with the blood.

"Do you want to rest?" I asked. "Maybe catch your breath in one of these cars?"

She considered it for a moment and then nodded.

I glanced around, looking for a car without a body in it. There were several. A lot of people must have just abandoned their cars when they saw the street was jammed. Some lay in the road. Others had wandered off to who knows where. They'd all ended up the same.

I chose a black BMW with its driver's door hanging wide open. The back doors were unlocked, and I got in first, sliding over to let Debbie get in with me.

"Only for a minute," she said. "I need to find the angels."

"Okay," I said. I looked down at her hands and saw a wedding ring. "You're married?"

She glanced at the ring. "I think so." Then her eyes shifted back up to me. "You're not…you're not an angel, are you?"

I smiled. "I…I don't know what I am. Would an angel know she was one?"

"I think so. But maybe not."

She looked both sad and hopeful.

I felt terrible for several reasons. One, I knew I was about to watch Debbie die. Another, I could maybe make her feel better in these last moments, but it would mean lying to her. And lying to her about being an angel was something I felt really bad about. Finally, selfishly, I felt awful because I was about to be alone again. I hate to admit it, but that was the main reason I didn't want Debbie to die.

I took her hand. She seemed to have no inclination to get out of the car again. Squeezing my hand, she smiled at me, no trace of fear on her face now. I hoped she had no memory of the man who'd attacked her.

"Are you an angel?" she asked again.

"I think so," I said.

She smiled broadly. "I knew it," she gasped. "I knew it." Tears rolled from her eyes now. "I didn't want to be alone. I knew you'd come."

I squeezed her hand back. "You're not alone," I said.

Her tears kept falling.

"Does it hurt?" I asked.

"Some."

"I'm sorry."

"Can you make it stop?"

"I'll try."

"Okay," she said. Then her eyes opened wider. "Oh! Oh! It's working."

Her head dropped forward and her hand went slack.

"Sorry, Debbie," I whispered.

I opened the door and scooted across the seat, leaning over toward Debbie and then pulling her so she could lie on her back. Then I folded her hands across her stomach and got out of the car, turning back to pull the torn shirt so it covered her as much as it could.

I took out my backpack and closed the door, leaning against it with my back and waiting for the popping sound. I didn't want to see it. But I didn't want to leave Debbie, either. I'd told her she wasn't alone, after all.

When it was over, I took a deep breath and walked away from the car, trying not to think about it.

* * * * *

The whole time I'd been sitting there with Debbie, I'd been listening for any sign of her attacker. There'd been nothing. With luck, he was already dead. The way he'd kept repeating "No, no," told me he'd been fixated on something, just as Debbie had been with angels or the man at the stadium with foul balls. Physically, he'd been attacking Debbie, but with the growth pressing up on his brain, who knows what he'd been imagining as he wrestled the poor woman to the ground? It certainly hadn't seemed like any kind of sexual attack. At any rate, I wasn't about to let the possibility that he might still be lurking on the street keep me from the treasure trove that was the sporting goods store.

The sun had set and streetlights were coming on, but it wasn't dark yet. I looked in my backpack and pulled out a flashlight, shoving it into my back pocket. Then I selected the Swiss Army knife and pulled out the biggest blade. It might not be as lethal as one of the kitchen knives, but it was more easily manageable. Besides, I didn't really think I'd need to use it.

I headed back along the sidewalk, reaching for the flashlight pretty quickly and shining it into every shadow I approached. If the man was still alive and still functioning well enough to stalk me, he wasn't going to be so easy to spot, and more likely would be somewhere out on the street skulking among the cars and waiting for the opportunity to strike at me. But he might just as well have been in the last stages of the disease and holed up in one of the shadowy spots along the sidewalk, not really a danger to me, but not something I wanted to be surprised by.

A little farther along, I saw him. I just stood there for a few seconds, barely letting myself breathe. My grip on the knife relaxed just a bit.

He lay on his stomach, his arms stretched out in front of him. The stalks poked out from under his face, reaching along the sidewalk toward his hand like another set of limbs. Seeing him dead like that, I felt sorry I'd kicked him, sorry his last moments had been spent hurting because of me while I'd helped make Debbie's at least a bit peaceful. I knew my regret didn't make any sense. I'd had to kick him, had to get him off Debbie. In the end, they'd have ended up the same way regardless of my presence here on the street. But I hadn't known that then. I'd thought I was saving a fellow survivor, starting on a new path in this new world. Now it was just the same as it had been—terribly quiet with death all around me.

I walked past him, not bothering to prod him to make sure he was dead. There wouldn't have been any point. Then I walked into the store, still holding the knife but shoving the flashlight back into my pocket.

It was weird, like I had walked into a different world. Outside, all was chaos and silence. Inside was the world as it had been. Florescent lights still burned, music still played over hidden speakers, and the smell of new things just about overwhelmed me along with all the bright colors of the shirts and helmets and kayaks on a rack along one wall. Maybe the weirdest part were the advertisements and promo posters—huge images of smiling, energized faces peering out at me from high up on the walls and atop just about every rack of clothing, people biking and swimming and playing soccer, doing all the vibrant, exciting things the store promoted and living the happy, active lifestyle all the images and products promised. And now they were all gone, their smiling faces on the posters and signs like gaudy memorials for nameless people who'd go unremembered now and forever.

I looked around at all the survivor gear: water-purifying tablets, hand-cranked flashlights, thermal blankets. There were maps of all the local hiking areas and others of Yosemite and the John Muir Trail. There were also more energy bars and supplements than I could even consider. The teenager in me liked the gadget displays—the GPS systems and all the gear for phones and tablets; there was even a little satellite system so you could get a signal out in the middle of nowhere. It had cost thousands of dollars the day before, but it was free now. Everything was.

There was a gun counter, but the idea of using a gun made me uneasy; plus I knew that to get good with a gun would mean lots of practice, and that would mean making lots of noise that might draw out other people like the "no no" man on the sidewalk. Still, I figured I should have one. The guns were locked up, though, and I guessed that there'd be an alarm set off if I broke the glass countertop to get to them. Even though there wouldn't be any police to respond to the alarm, I still didn't like the idea of listening to its braying and so left the guns for later.

The archery section appealed to me more. I could practice with a bow and arrows or crossbow and not make much noise at all.

I looked at all the camping equipment, too, considering different tents and sleeping bags and portable gas stoves.

The bicycle display made me think of pedal power to get myself around the city. I liked the idea, but then I started wondering: what about a little motorcycle? It would be just as maneuverable as a bike, and I could get a lot farther a lot faster. A motorcycle would be superior to a bicycle if I needed to get away from someone or something. The only problem was that I had even less experience with motorcycles than I did with cars. Still, I thought, now there was time to learn. No school on Monday.

At the back of the store, I passed through a door marked "Private," opening it slowly. Relieved to find no one living or dead, I began exploring the manager's office. I went straight to the controls for the store's music, twisting the volume to zero. Right away, I felt more at ease, telling myself I'd be able to hear now if someone else entered the store. An old computer took up much of the desktop, and I pushed it to the edge to make room for my laptop. Flipping it open, I plugged it in, liking the feeling of keeping it fully charged as often as possible. Then I pulled open the drawers and was pleased to find a ring of keys in the center one. I would have bet that one of them would unlock the gun case.

The store had a secure Wi-Fi setup, but taped to a corner of the desk was a square of paper with the network's name and password. Seconds later I was pleased to find myself online again. The websites for the major cable news networks were all down, just a blank screen with a crawl along the bottom advising viewers to gather at local police stations and city halls for disaster instructions.

I tried other searches but just got the same speculations and rumors I'd seen while sitting beside Jen's pool. I decided to limit my search to posts from within the last hour and got things from Australia and New Zealand. If the disease had reached those places, then it hadn't yet devastated them.

So I searched for an Australian television station that streamed its broadcast and found one in a few keystrokes. The stream had to buffer ever fifteen seconds or so, but I kept with it regardless. The image of the newscaster took up a quarter of my screen, a sandy-haired man wearing a high-tech respirator that covered his whole face.

I just looked at him, dumbstruck. His delivery was so muffled that I could barely understand a word he said. But from what I could piece together, Australia was one of the last places to be struck by the disease, and the Australians had been able to prepare themselves a bit because they'd known it was coming. The news station showed footage of people—very few people—walking the streets of Sydney wearing apparatuses similar to the newscaster's.

"Citizens are advised to keep contact with others at a minimum," the man said, "until further information on the outbreak becomes available. Scientists are scrambling to find a cure or an inoculation, while others examine the cause and the possibility that the disease will run its course and the infectious spores will lose their potency once they no longer have hosts to invade."

He went on to report on measures the Australian government was taking to protect their people, but I began focusing more on the crawl when these words flashed by: "Reported survivors in Europe, Asia, and Africa indicate natural immunity among a small percentage of the population. Possibly these 'survivors' are hoaxes."

Thank God, I thought. There were other people like me, other people who could go on without having to wear masks and filters and worry about dying if the respirator failed. People who would go on. I wasn't the last person on earth, and I wasn't going to be. The thought brought tears to my eyes.

"Okay," I said and leaned forward to navigate around the website. They had a contact button that brought up an email form, and I filled it in, writing, "My name is Scarlett and I'm still alive in Los Angeles, California. I think I'm immune. I haven't found anyone else yet who is." I almost hit the *send* button, but then wrote one more thing: "What should I do?"

I clicked the button and waited. I imagined a room full of people monitoring email, hoping for further proof of survivors, imagined them erupting with applause when they got my message the way people in the space program used to go nuts when a probe sent back images from Mars. They'd write back immediately, of course.

But they didn't.

I checked the webcast again to make sure it wasn't just looping. I hated the thought that the man I'd been watching was really dead, his last words put on the web to play in a circle until the power went out. But it didn't appear to be a loop as he read new stories and played new video.

And then I saw this in the crawl: "New survivor reported in United States."

That's it? I thought.

The email chimed and I checked it. A simple message had come back, but at least there was some humanity to it. "Good to hear from you, Scarlett. Take good care of yourself. Maybe you can check back in a few days to let us know you're still there. I hope we're here to get the news. Good luck to you."

It wasn't signed.

I wanted to write back, wanted to tell them everything I'd been through and to ask what they thought I should do next, wanted to tell them I was only 15 and could use a little help here. But then I thought of what they were going through, whoever this nameless, faceless person was on the other end of the email. This would be someone like me, trying to stay alive, trying to process all the death and loss, trying not to go crazy with grief and fear. They didn't have time for a pen pal.

So instead of pouring my heart out, I just wrote, "Thanks. I'll check in when I can. Good luck to you, too."

I closed the screen and left the computer to charge again. Then I tried a few phone numbers just to torture myself: my mom, Anna, my dad, a few friends. No one picked up.

I spent the next hour or more gathering supplies, selecting some nasty looking hunting knives and testing different backpacks and sleeping bags. I tried out my archery skills on a mannequin and found that I was going to need a lot of practice.

Then I used the keys I'd found to open the gun case. I squatted before the display, just looking. I didn't know the first thing about guns or ammunition, and hoped more than anything that I'd never need to use one. Still, I knew it would be foolish to let this opportunity go, so after a minute or two of pondering I picked up a shiny handgun and hefted it for a few seconds. Not liking the feel of it, I set the gun down on top of the glass counter and then looked for a box of ammunition to match the caliber. Beneath the display shelf was a storage space with empty boxes for the guns, and I found one that matched the weapon I'd chosen, pulling the paperwork from the box and setting it along with the gun and bullets next to the pile of supplies I'd already gathered.

There was plenty of food and drink for sale in the store—most of it geared toward camping—so I had no problem finding something to eat and drink. It was late, and I was tired, so I decided to take a sleeping bag and a foam mattress back to the manager's office and call it a night, but not before locking the glass doors at the front of the store. Another survivor would have no problem smashing the glass to get inside, but I'd know about it if something like that happened. What I wanted to avoid was someone wandering inside the store while I slept unaware, either a survivor or someone infected and unstable. I wondered how many more people like that were still around; all I knew for sure was that I didn't want to run into any of them.

In the office, I set up a little nest, checked my phone one more time, and then got ready to turn out the manager's light. I had a rough plan of going to look for a motorcycle shop the next day, but beyond that, I didn't know where I'd go or what I'd do.

I didn't like how quiet it was even though I'd had some time to start getting used to it, but once I shut the lights off the quiet seemed so much worse. I lay there and tried not to think about it, tried to think of other things, but there were so many images in my head, so many terrible things I'd seen just since this morning when I'd woken up to find my neighborhood about to go up in flames.

A quick succession of recent memories flew through my mind then, and I sat up, reaching for my phone to use it as a flashlight. The phone in one hand, I dug through the backpack, sifting through as though the things in it were in geological layers. Underneath the things I'd taken from Jen's house were the few items I'd taken from home, and under all that was the photo of my mom and dad and me and Anna that I'd taken from the mantel.

There we were—all four of us, happy, with the whole city spreading out behind us from our vantage point outside the Griffith Observatory. I looked at it not out of nostalgia, not because I was looking back at the world that wasn't there anymore. No, this time I was looking forward.

Holding onto the frame, I lay back down and turned off the phone's light. I remember that I fell asleep almost right away then, exhausted but also relieved because at least now I had a plan.

CHAPTER SEVEN

The road to the observatory twisted up the hillside, mostly free of abandoned cars or those occupied by the dead. With just a few clouds in the bright blue sky and a little breeze coming through the trees, it would have been easy to mistake the day for any other where cars filled with tourists and hikers and families out on picnics would have been threading their way along the road, a typical SoCal day in paradise.

We had had it so good, and sometimes had even remembered to be grateful. But even when you didn't take the time to appreciate what you had, it was still okay: short of a major earthquake, everyone knew that California would still be there the next day with its beaches and mountains, Mickey Mouse and all the beautiful people. There was always more time to be thankful, more time for everything.

But the beautiful people were all gone now.

And some of them had started to smell.

I'd spent the last couple of days in Pasadena, finding a motorcycle shop and learning to ride after studying eHow and YouTube videos.

I'd picked out a little Honda, not one of the big ones and nothing fancy. I just wanted something that could maneuver through the jammed streets and get me out of trouble if any found me. It hadn't been too difficult learning how to ride; figuring out how to time the clutch had been the hardest part. Before long I'd mastered the motorcycle shop's parking lot and the alley behind it, working out a little obstacle course of abandoned cars and bodies on the ground. I even picked out a helmet, letting myself go the silly route by opting for gaudy purple with big pink flowers.

When not practicing on the bike, I'd spent time gathering and organizing supplies in the sporting goods store, working on my archery skills, and planning my move to the observatory. It wouldn't be possible to bring everything I'd need in one trip, so I loaded a backpack with the essentials, and then loaded three more with all the rest of my gear in order of descending importance. After some thought, I packed the gun and ammunition into the high priority pack even though I hadn't yet found the nerve to fire the thing. Then, telling myself I'd be back as soon as possible, I headed out one morning and actually felt a little sorry to go. The store had come to be like my new home, the manager's office my new room.

I had studied the maps in the store and brought one with me, having memorized several possible routes to get me from Pasadena to Griffith Park but expecting that I'd need to make adjustments to my plan along the way. I must have looked a sight on that little bike with my oversized backpack and flowery helmet, a bow and arrows bound to the back fender with bungee cord, and a respirator strapped to my face. The mask had nothing to do with spores but rather with the smell that had begun on my second full day alone.

The people who'd died from the fungal infection weren't so much the issue. I'd had the chance to observe quite a few bodies in various stages of decay, and it looked like the fungus didn't just stop when the host was dead and the spores scattered on the wind. The host bodies began to shrivel and dry out, like the fungus was taking all the moisture from them, and they didn't seem to smell at all. I realized soon enough that the bodies were being eaten, and by the time I set out on the motorcycle, it wasn't unusual to see some of the dead people's limbs reduced to bone and more stalks sprouting randomly from the bodies as the fungus reproduced and reproduced again.

The fungus made short work of its victims. It was the other people who were a problem, though. The ones who'd died in accidents or were the victims of infected people who'd turned violent before dying—those were the bodies that stank. Them and the people who'd died naturally from heart attacks and other ailments in the hours of crisis when emergency services had been unable to help everyone. And, of course, the suicides.

I'd gone into a restaurant in Pasadena after practicing on the motorcycle for most of one morning, hoping to find something canned that I could eat quickly and then head back to the sporting goods store. A man had hanged himself in the main dining room, a belt around his neck and the other end tied to a ceiling fan. Flies buzzed around the body, and the smell made me gag. I turned and ran, no longer thinking about food.

After that, I noticed the suicides more readily, having seen them previously but not having noticed the difference between them and the corpses that the fungus feasted on. The first several, I contemplated for some moments, wondering about what these people's last minutes had been like, how lonely or scared they must have been. That their corpses hadn't sprouted stalks told me they hadn't been infected before taking their own lives, and I wondered at the possibility that some of them could have been like me, immune. If so, they'd just given up before learning they could have survived. Or maybe they'd already figured that out and had opted to die rather than go on alone in a world without friends and family.

Which made me wonder why I hadn't killed myself, too.

Honestly, the thought hadn't occurred to me once since I'd left my house. I'd been too busy trying to figure out what I was going to do to stay alive to start pondering the possibility of bringing it all to an end.

The suicides made me angry. The odds were that one of them, *at least* one of them, could have survived like I had, given me someone to talk to and make plans with. I know I was thinking just about myself then, not about the suffering or fear all these people had gone through before making their final decisions. But I'd had fear and suffering, too. My decisions had just been different.

At any rate, they all smelled, and by the day I left the sporting goods store, I needed a respirator to keep it from getting to me. I suppose I would have gotten used to it before long, but I also worried about disease. I didn't know what sorts of illnesses I could pick up from being around so many dead and decaying bodies, and I didn't want to find out. That was another reason to get to the observatory. I'd still be around millions of dead people, thousands upon thousands of whom had died from things other than the fungus, but at least I'd be above most of them and maybe able to breathe a little easier. Still, I knew I couldn't stay in the city forever; the observatory would just be my next step, one of many I'd have to make along the way, and all of them made on my own without any help or supervision.

When I'd come here before with my family, the road had been lined with parked cars and mini-vans and SUVs. Now it was just about empty, a narrow strip of pavement winding its way up the hill with views of the city spreading about below me when I'd round some of the turns. There were a few cars to navigate around, and I told myself I could come back later and move them out of the road. At the top of the hill, the parking lot was also mostly empty—but only mostly, and I put on the brakes as soon as I hit the flat expanse of asphalt.

I hadn't been the only one to think of getting up above all the chaos. There were five cars parked here—all looking random and nothing to worry about. And there was also a medium-sized motor home, an old Winnebago, all angular and oxidized with no hubcaps but still the big "W" logo on the striped sides. It sat at the edge of the parking lot, not in any of the marked spots but rather blocking the road, its front tires up against the curb. Someone had parked it there with no regard for anyone else coming up the hill, and I knew that meant they'd been assuming no one would be coming—either because the occupants had gone a little crazy from the fungus pressing into their brains, or because they were immune like me and had set up their base camp here in the hills.

I killed the little Honda's engine and flipped down the kickstand. Climbing off, I slipped the straps of my backpack over the handlebars and carefully unfastened the bungee cord that held the bow and arrows to the fender. I wasn't ready to shoot anyone with it, doubted I had good enough aim to even hit the side of the motor home if it came to that, but I was counting on anyone still inside the Winnebago not being willing to take a chance on my accuracy.

Notching an arrow, I walked slowly toward the old camper, listening intently for any sign of life. Up here, all was silent, but a cool breeze blew up from the city, and it made enough noise to mask any sounds that might be coming from the motor home. I was approaching with the wind at my back, so if I made a noise, the breeze would carry the sound to anyone inside, but if they made a move I wouldn't be likely to hear it. I should have stopped, backed away, and approached from the other side of the parking lot. But I was here now, and there were no signs of life yet, so I kept on, maybe a bit foolishly.

Ten feet away from the hulking old camper, I stopped. Someone sat in the driver's seat, looking out at the view. I just froze, holding the bow tightly and waiting for something to happen, waiting for a sign of life, waiting for the head to turn toward me.

Nothing happened, so I inched closer, reminding myself to breathe and trying not to blink. A few feet closer and I relaxed just a little, letting out a long breath and loosening my grip on the bow just a bit. Stalks protruded from the driver's face.

The motorhome's main door was open, but a screen door was closed. I approached, reached for the handle, and just listened for a few seconds. Then I pulled at the respirator so it dropped below my chin. "Hello?" I said quietly. "Anybody in there?"

No reply, no movement, no rustling.

"I don't want to hurt anybody. I just want to know if I'm alone or not, okay?"

Still nothing.

"I've got a weapon," I added, hoping I sounded believable.

The door opened with a squeak after I clicked the button on the screen door's handle. Then I climbed the steps and went in. It was dark inside, all the curtains pulled shut with the only light coming through the windshield and the driver's compartment. I just stood there for a few seconds to let my eyes adjust. When I could make out faux wood cabinets and a stovetop and fridge, I turned toward the back of the motorhome.

The body was where I thought it would be, sitting at the little table all the way at the back, slumped forward. The table would fold down, I knew, to form a bed out of the seat cushions. That would have made a more comfortable final resting place. As it was, the woman who'd died here had her arms under her head, her upper body halfway across the tabletop, the stalks poking out toward a window. When I got closer, I could see that she'd been old—gray-haired and wrinkled, probably somebody's grandma.

I left her and went to the cab. The old man sitting in the driver's seat had died with his seatbelt on and the Hollywood sign in full view on the next hilltop. A perfect place for tourists to meet their ends. I wondered which one of them had died first. *Probably the wife*, I thought. Maybe here, maybe down below. And then the old man had sat and looked at the Hollywood sign and the trees and the hills until it was all over.

Leaning over him, I saw the key still in the ignition and gave it half a turn. The instrument panel lit up showing three-quarters full on the gas tank. That was good. I immediately started thinking about loading the motor home with the supplies I had gathered in Pasadena and using it to head out of the city when the time came. It was a good idea, but it would be hard to find a route out of Southern California that wasn't already clogged with people who'd died trying to do the same thing. On the way here, I'd passed Interstate 5, now literally a parking lot filled with cars and corpses.

Still, I thought, there might be some use for the Winnebago. I took the keys and left the old couple there, planning on coming back later to drag them into the bushes. Then I went back to the motorcycle and rode the rest of the way across the parking lot, up onto the sidewalk, and past the statue of James Dean that my mom had gone on and on about.

Before me were the steps leading up to the entrance, and at their top an ornate black door hung open, ready for visitors. From the bottom of the steps, I could see that the lights still burned inside the building. That was good. I didn't like the thought of searching it with a flashlight. Taking another deep breath and gripping the bow and arrow once more, I walked up the steps and poked my head through the door.

All was quiet, and no bodies lay on the floor in the main hall. Glad of that, I walked in and carefully toured the first level, ignoring all the educational displays about gravity and the phases of the moon and looking instead for any sign that I wasn't alone. The place wasn't that big, and after a few minutes I'd covered both of the ground floor wings; I remembered that there was a downstairs with more exhibits and a cafeteria and that upstairs were observation decks and access to the dome and the telescope. If anyone was hiding in here, it would be downstairs or else in some of the employee-only areas.

But to get downstairs meant going back outside, and when I slipped out one of the rear doors, I found myself on the lower observation deck...the same one where I'd posed with my family for the picture now in my backpack. No other tourists crowded against the rails now; no little kids begged for quarters from their parents so they could look through the big telescopes at the city that spread out as far as anyone could see. It was just me and the breeze.

I felt like a ghost, returned to some earthly haunt, stuck there and confused at the changes all around. A ghost might not have understood that the change was in itself, that it had passed on and no longer belonged here. In my case, I understood the change, and it was hard to take. *Ghosts are better off,* I thought as I walked to the wall at the edge of the deck.

The city went on forever...the skyscrapers downtown, the freeways clogged with cars, the grid of streets, some running straight as could be for miles and miles. In the distance I could see the ocean, and I made a guess at where the Santa Monica pier was. Smoke from several fires rose into the air. And all was silent—no traffic, no jets in the sky, no distant voices or laughter, no sirens.

I nodded at the view, telling myself I'd have plenty more time to look later. Then I turned away to continue exploring the hilltop.

On the observatory's top deck, I found a single dead man. He'd dropped to the concrete not far from the entrance to the dome, and I squatted next to the body for a moment, noticing that it had already begun to shrivel as the fungus consumed it. I thought about dragging the body off to a corner where I wouldn't have to deal with it anymore, or possibly hefting it over the rail and to the ground so I could move it off into the bushes later, but for now I decided to just leave it be.

Downstairs, I found the cafeteria and more exhibits, also several back rooms for employees, but no more people, no more bodies.

"Just me," I said aloud as I sat in one of the plastic chairs in the dining area with a bottle of cold milk in front of me.

The place would do, for now. I needed more of a plan for the future, but at least I would be safe here for a while. The thought of those fires burning in the city below made me nervous, as there was no one left to put them out, and it wasn't hard to imagine them spreading, maybe even as far as the Hollywood hills and Griffith Park. Though the high ground of the observatory brought me safety from a lot of things, it also made me vulnerable with all the vegetation in the hills. Who knew what could happen? The best thing I could do was to stay vigilant and keep the motorcycle gassed up.

I drank the milk, wondering how long the power would stay on. Before long, I knew, luxuries like cold milk would be just a memory. I decided to enjoy it while I could, so I added ice cream for lunch.

After that, I found the security office and a set of keys. Soon, I had the place locked up tight, every exit door on every floor. Then it was time to head back to Pasadena for the rest of my supplies.

* * * * *

I made three runs by the end of the day, and that was enough. On the last one, I added a trip back to Anna's Nissan to recover anything else from Jen's house that I didn't want to have to replace through scavenging in the mansions on Los Feliz just below the observatory.

Each time I returned to my hilltop sanctuary, I approached the parking lot with caution, trying to spot anything that looked different from when I'd last left. I also carefully circled the outside of the observatory to look for other visitors, but there were none.

After I'd gotten my last load stowed away in the entrance hall, I went back out to the dead tourists' motorhome. I didn't like doing it, but I pulled the bodies out and dragged them behind the restroom at the edge of the parking lot. Then I started the Winnebago and backed it away from the curb. It took some maneuvering and quite a few failed efforts, but eventually I got the motorhome situated right at the edge of the parking lot so it completely blocked the way. Anyone coming up here in a car would have to stop and walk the rest of the way to the observatory; a motorcycle could get by, but the rider would have to slow to a crawl to get around the front of the motorhome. I wasn't expecting anyone, of course, but I still wanted to be cautious. Facing someone on foot wouldn't guarantee that I could best them, but I felt it would still give me the upper hand if some other survivor had to abandon his car to get to the observatory.

It's not that I expected a fight. If there were any other survivors, I figured they'd be as thrilled to find me as I would be at being found. But at the same time I relived my memory of the man who'd attacked Debbie in Pasadena. There might still be some people messed up from the disease but not dead yet. And there might be survivors who'd been bad people before the outbreak. Being among the last humans on earth wouldn't necessarily change their temperament. It might even make it worse. Not to mention the thoughts some men might have at finding the last female in California waiting up here for them. I thought of Rapunzel in her tower as I walked back toward the big dome with the sun setting beyond it.

The breeze had shifted since morning, and now I heard a new sound. It frightened me at first, and then it made me sad. The Los Angeles Zoo was just over the hill on the other side of Griffith Park. The animals were probably starving, and the breeze carried their cries and roars toward me. I could hear elephants and either a tiger or lion pretty distinctly, but there were other sounds, too— maybe the gorillas, or birds. It was too hard to tell.

For just a second, I imagined myself trekking to the zoo and releasing the animals so they could fend for themselves in this new wilderness. But I knew the idea was ridiculous. If I could even figure out how to do it, my kind-heartedness would get me nothing more than attacked by a hunting jaguar in a few weeks' time. No, if the animals could get out on their own, so be it. I couldn't involve myself in their plight.

This got me thinking of other animals, though. I knew there were coyotes in these hills, and maybe even bobcats or mountain lions. If not in these hills, then in others, and before long the wild animals would move down into the city to take it over. There'd also be dogs and cats that would go feral now that their owners were dead and no one else was around to open a bag of kibble. Not to mention all the pets trapped inside houses, many probably starving already. Again, I knew I could do nothing for them. Freeing the thousands of dogs and cats—and hamsters and rabbits and whatever else—would be well intentioned but foolish. I was already going to have to worry about territorial German Shepherds and Chihuahuas; adding to their ranks would be asking for trouble. The downside, of course, was that there was going to be a lot more death and decay, and with that perhaps more disease.

I stood at the rail of the observation deck thinking about it as the sun slivered its way past the horizon and the flames from the still burning neighborhoods and factories in the distance grew brighter with the coming night. The city was dead, or dying. Beyond saving. And I was like the last parasite trying to suck just a little more life out of my host.

I couldn't stay here, not for long anyway. I had my supplies and relative safety, but the security of my fortress wouldn't last. If it wasn't brush fires or disease brought on the breeze by all the death around me, it would be something else. Coming to the observatory hadn't been a mistake or a waste of time or resources. It was better than staying in Jen's house or the sporting goods store. I could gorge on ice cream and potato chips in the cafeteria, eating enough to remember what those things tasted like in the years to come when food wouldn't be so easy to get. And the parking lot would be a good place to learn to shoot a gun and a bow; I should also practice my driving skills. If I played it right, I could come down from the hill in a month or so a much different person, someone ready to light out for parts unknown and make a new life for myself. Maybe even find a boat in the marina that would get me to Australia or New Zealand or some little island with just a few other people on it…people who'd welcome me.

Or fear me.

I shook my head and turned my back on the view. It was all too much to think about now. I headed inside to unpack my gear and get my little fortress all set up, telling myself I wouldn't be able to hear the tragic sounds of the zoo once I was inside the building's thick walls. In the morning, I'd start planning what to do next.

Right now, I just wanted to sleep and forget.

* * * * *

I awoke with a start, nearly panicking.

Everything was dark. *Everything.*

I'd set up my sleeping mats and sleeping bag in an office behind the cafeteria on the lower level of the observatory. Before turning in, I'd left on the lights in the hallway outside and kept the office door open a crack. It had been just enough light to sleep by.

But now I couldn't see anything, literally couldn't see my hand in front of my face. How long the lights had been out, I couldn't know, but I had the feeling it had been only a few seconds, that the sudden darkness had been the thing that woke me.

I sat up in the sleeping bag, staying perfectly still, just listening.

And then a light came on in the hallway, much dimmer than it had been when I'd gone to sleep.

Someone was in the building. Someone had to be. I could think of no other explanation.

I'd gone to sleep with my backpack beside the sleeping bag and the gun under it. Somewhere inside the pack was one of my flashlights, and now I cursed myself for not thinking ahead to have it more easily accessible. Still, the gun was reachable without much effort, and I snaked my hand outside the sleeping bag to grope for it beneath the backpack, all the while listening for the sound of footsteps or anything else in the hallway or beyond.

Crawling out of the sleeping bag, I was conscious of every noise I made, and I held my breath, tensing myself for an attack from beyond the door. None came. Soon, I was at the door, peeking out the narrow opening and hoping I wasn't making myself visible to whoever was out there. I had yet to hear a noise and began wondering if I hadn't just dreamed the darkness and was now simply imagining that the light in the hallway was dimmer than it had been when I went to sleep.

Finally, I found the courage to pull the door open just a little more. When I heard nothing more beyond it, I opened it all the way, poked my head out with the gun held tightly before me. After a quick glance in both directions, I let my breath out and lowered the gun.

I had my explanation. The main lights were out, but the emergency lights mounted at either end of the hallway burned dimly.

The power had gone out. After the few seconds of total darkness that had awoken me, an emergency power system had kicked in, maybe a generator or two somewhere in the building coming to life when the main source of electricity switched off.

It was still possible that someone had tampered with the observatory's power, but I doubted it.

Going back for the flashlight and keeping the gun with me, I made a search of the lower floor and then went outside to head upstairs.

On the observation deck outside the cafeteria, I decided there was no point in a trip up to the next level. The city below me was almost all in darkness. I guessed that there were some other places with generators, as a few electric lights still shone in places. Several fires continued to burn across the city, but everything else was blackness for as far as I could see.

The power was out, the electric plants having shut down now that there was no one left to run them. While I felt some relief at knowing I was still safe here in my fortress, the darkness extending to the horizon made me uneasy. The city was dying, plain and simple. It might sustain me for a while as I lived off whatever I could scavenge from houses and businesses, but it wouldn't last forever. The gas and water would stop soon, too—no more heat, no more toilets, no more drinking from a tap. I couldn't guess at what else I'd soon be without, and the thought made me sad: not because I'd miss the comforts of modern life, but rather because I knew I'd have to move on sooner than I'd thought necessary. I had just wanted the chance to collect myself, to use the safety of the high ground to get used to my new life.

"That's the way it goes," I said to the darkness and turned back toward the building, trying not to think of what I should do next, but knowing I couldn't *not* think about it. Sleep wouldn't come easily again, I knew. Resigned to lying there and waiting for it, though, I went back inside, resolved to keep a flashlight handy from here on.

CHAPTER EIGHT

I kept myself busy for the next couple of weeks: making myself more comfortable in the observatory, calculating how long the cafeteria's bottled water supply would last, and practicing my marksmanship and archery in the parking lot. Books on camping and outdoor survival from the sporting goods store showed me how to pick a good spot for a latrine and how to dig one. And the houses in the neighborhoods next to Griffith Park provided me with the supplies I hadn't thought to gather in the first days of my new life.

Going into the homes was a bit unnerving at first, as I warily crept in and surveyed the rooms for any sign of living occupants. I got more used to it after the first couple of days—though I still forced myself to focus before each entry. It would not do to become complacent. At first, I considered the dead when I went in, looking them over and wondering about their lives and deaths. After a while, though, it got to where I would just pass the bodies without thinking about them, like they were part of the abandoned furniture or no different from the houseplants that had been left behind.

It was worse when there were pets in the house. The starving cats would tear out of the doors the second I cracked them open, just like Jen's cat had done. But the dogs were a bit tougher, torn between defending their territories and getting out to find something to eat. Usually, they only tried staring me down for a few seconds before deciding I wasn't worth the trouble. I doubted any of the dogs had ever had a gun pointed at them, but they all managed to figure it was something formidable and backed down after a bit of barking, slinking past me and out of the houses—much to my relief.

I didn't find much that was worth my time in any of the houses. I did raid a couple of people's libraries, carting a small stack of books back to the observatory and setting up a lounge chair on one of the observation decks. There, I worked out an absurd imitation of the California Dream: lying in the sun with a book and a million dollar view as the days wore on around me. All that was missing were the servants and the millions of people in the distance going about their daily grinds.

The generators at the observatory had died by that point, and I was surprised when I walked into one hillside mansion to find the power still on, a big chandelier still shining its light on the expensive furniture. At first, I didn't get it, but when I walked outside again, I noticed solar panels on the roof, which also explained the few sources of light I could make out when I looked down at the city at night.

On the ride back up to the observatory, I toyed with the idea of moving down the hill and using the solar house as my home base instead of what I'd come to think of as my hilltop fortress. Before I was halfway up the winding road, though, I'd decided against it; I knew nothing about solar technology, what it took to maintain it. For all I knew, it would last for years, and then again it might crash in another day. I was fine where I was. If I needed electricity for some reason, it was an easy trip down the hill to access it—at least for now.

That afternoon, before cracking open the copy of *To Kill a Mockingbird* I'd been reading, I stood at the concrete wall of the observation deck and tried to find the solar powered house with my binoculars. They were pretty high end, and I could see a lot of detail as I scanned the area. After a couple of minutes, I gave up; there was too much in the way for me to spot the house or even be sure of the exact area it was in.

I set the binoculars on the wall and looked out at the city. Some fires still burned, but nothing else seemed to have changed. It was like I had a panoramic photo of Los Angeles to stare at every day.

And then I snatched the binoculars up again, almost knocking them off the wall before getting a grip.

I'd seen something move down in the city. Not just the movement of a tree swaying in the breeze or the shadow cast by a passing cloud. Something more deliberate than that. Something manmade.

It took me a few seconds to orient my vision with the binoculars and pinpoint the area where the movement had been, lifting the binoculars to my eyes and then pulling them away again as I checked and double-checked the area. It had been several miles away, the details lost in the haze of the smoky air, but I would have sworn there'd been a vehicle moving through an intersection.

"What the hell?" I whispered, desperately scanning left and right to find the trail of the thing I'd seen.

And then, faintly, I picked up the sound of an engine almost lost on the breeze, but there nonetheless. Faint and far away and probably growing more distant.

The desperation that overcame me then was stronger than anything I'd felt for a week or more. I wanted to shout and call out, wave my arms like people used to do in shipwreck movies when a freighter would show up on the horizon. We'd read *Lord of the Flies* in school, and I kicked myself now for not having thought of setting up a signal fire for just such an occasion.

Turning impotently, I started a frantic search of the observation deck for something, anything to get the attention of whoever was down there in the city I'd thought of as dead or dying for days now. Of course, there was nothing. I could have run into the building and found the gun and fired it, but it would be impossible for someone down below to connect the distant gunshot with the Griffith Observatory. I wished for a flare gun, but even that wouldn't have driven someone's gaze up here.

"Damn it!" I shouted and kicked over the lounge chair.

Then I turned back to the wall and picked up the binoculars again, my cheeks wet as I held the lenses to my eyes. I think I scanned the city for at least an hour before giving up. The sound of the engine had long faded to nothing.

I didn't feel like reading after that. I didn't feel like anything— not eating or even sleeping. I just wanted to be turned off, wanted to forget everything that had ever been and not think about anything that was to come.

Inside the observatory, I took one of my flashlights and went into the planetarium, moving through the dark with my beam of light before randomly choosing a seat along one of the aisles. They were soft and reclined almost all the way back. Visitors used to crowd in here several times a day to watch the laser show on the rounded ceiling. Since moving in, I'd considered using the planetarium as my bedroom; the seats were more comfortable than the mat and sleeping bag I used in the office behind the cafeteria. I'd decided against it though, feeling a little wary about being too comfortable when I slept. I told myself it was because I needed to stay vigilant, but really I think I worried that I might wake up and, for a fraction of a second, forget where I was. It wouldn't do to wake up and think I was home again, like Dorothy after Oz, only to find that it hadn't been a dream after all.

Now I didn't care about that. I just lay back, shining the light up at the ceiling for a few seconds before turning it off and letting the total blackness of the planetarium swallow me up. If there were ghosts of ushers or scientists or James Dean in that place, they would have heard me crying in the dark for a long time.

* * * * *

Before going to sleep that night, I put three powerful battery-operated lanterns along the wall of the observation deck and let them blaze into the night. It wasn't as good as a signal fire, but it was something, and I remember sleeping decently, even hopefully.

The next day, though, brought a little perspective to the situation, and I took the lanterns down; their batteries had died, but I didn't even want them glinting in the sun. With the new day, I realized it might have been a good thing that I hadn't been able to get the attention of whoever had been driving through the city. That there actually had been someone, I was sure of. No hallucinations here. Not yet anyway. What I was unsure of, though, was how trustworthy any other survivors might be.

In my heart, I wanted to believe that anyone who found me would be a good person. Odds were that it would be an adult, someone ready and willing to help out a teenager in trouble. But what if it wasn't? What if I'd gotten that person's attention and it had put me into the middle of a bigger nightmare than the one I was living now? What if I'd run into someone like Jack from *Lord of the Flies*? It was tough to imagine, and I didn't really want to believe it, but I had to acknowledge that it was possible. No, I finally told myself, it was better that it worked out the way it had—with me aware of someone else in the city and them clueless about me. I had the upper hand this way. Any meeting would be on my terms, my decision, my timetable. I regretted those lanterns now and hoped no one had seen them or thought anything of them.

I ate in the cafeteria and then gathered a few things before heading out. I'd learned how to siphon gas from the Winnebago's tank to keep the motorcycle going, and now I hopped on with a backpack full of supplies. Kicking the engine to life, I rode across the grass, the parking lot, around the motorhome, and then down the hill. Within a few minutes, I was navigating around dead cars and dead people to work my way back to the solar powered house from the day before. It hadn't taken me long to learn how to get around the area, practically having memorized all the macabre obstacles in the streets and thinking no more of them than I would have considered stop signs or railroad crossings.

When I got to the solar house, I went in and made myself at home, setting the backpack on the bar at the end of the kitchen and pulling up a stool. I'd only brought a few things: my phone, my laptop, and the satellite Internet system I'd taken from the sporting goods store, still in its box. I found a cold soda in the fridge and then opened the box, pulling out plastic-wrapped components and pages of instructions. It was confusing, but I read through it all and began connecting parts together with the cables inside the box.

As I worked, I had only real goal: to try and check in with the Australian TV station again to see if the disease had hit that continent as hard as it had hit everywhere else, or if they'd been at least partly spared thanks to being one of the last places the spores had reached. If things didn't look safe there, I'd try New Zealand, and after that I'd search for smaller islands. Somewhere, *somewhere*, there had to be people who'd been spared, groups of people, people who could still make a go of it and move on into the future. I wanted to find them.

And if I did, it would be off to a library or bookstore for me. Just as I'd learned to ride the motorcycle, I told myself I was going to learn to sail. Every day as I looked out at the city from the observatory's deck, my eyes eventually went to the strip of ocean at the horizon. I thought of the email I'd gotten from the Australian and looked at the water, knowing there'd be good-sized boats just waiting for me. I didn't know a thing about boats, but I knew kids younger than me had sailed solo around the world. All I needed was to teach myself what to do and how to do it. It would be dangerous, I was sure, but I was up for it. As I'd been thinking since getting to the observatory: LA couldn't take care of me forever.

But all my big plans for overseas communication fell flat when I got to the section in the satellite instructions on setting up an account. You couldn't just transfer data from the satellite; you had to have everything set up beforehand. In the old world, a wealthy camper would have established an account and then gone off into the middle of nowhere, hooked up the equipment, and then been charged a ridiculous amount of money per byte downloaded. I had no doubt that I could have set up an account with a dead person's credit card, but I needed the internet up and running to be able to set it up. And that wasn't going to happen without the satellite account in place beforehand.

I could have kicked myself for not thinking to try this when I'd first found the equipment, when the phone systems and everything else the Internet ran on was still functioning. But it was too late now.

I slammed my fist down on the countertop and then threw the half-full can of soda at the wall, screaming as soda sprayed across the kitchen.

"Damn it!" I cried. "How could I have been so stupid?"

I almost picked up the laptop to slam it down, too, but somehow stopped myself. There might still be something I could do, something I hadn't figured out yet. Destroying the computer and then finding out I still needed it would just be one more reason to hate myself, one more mistake I'd regret. So far I'd been lucky: none of the mistakes I'd made had gotten me into serious trouble. One of these days, though, I knew my luck was going to run out. Why help the bad luck along by doing stupid things?

So instead of throwing a bigger tantrum, I took a few deep breaths and began re-packing my backpack.

Call it old training, but I felt bad about the mess I'd made with the soda. The kitchen looked awful now, so instead of leaving I grabbed a sponge from beside the sink and wet it, taking a quick minute to wipe most of the splatter from the tiles and cupboard doors. Then, more old training, I rinsed the sponge, turning on the hot water the way I'd always done, just automatically.

In a few seconds, it was running warm, and then hot. I hadn't had running water at the observatory in days, and forget about anything warm. The water heater in this house must have run off of solar power like everything else. While no new water was likely flowing into the pipes, there was still water in the tank. I dropped the sponge and went to find the bathroom.

Minutes later, the room was steaming, and I was having my first hot shower since the crisis had begun. On the bathroom counter, I'd found a dock and plugged my phone in; now my music blasted into the bathroom as I washed my hair and conditioned it and then just stood under the shower, letting the water pour over me. It felt luxurious, indulgent. The nicest thing I'd done for myself in…forever, it seemed. The moment I felt the water begin cooling, I turned it off, not wanting to ruin the memory of hot water on my skin. With the faucet off, I just stood for a moment, listening to the sound of the last bit of water dripping from the showerhead. Such a simple sound, one I'd never thought needed appreciating before. But I hadn't heard it for a while now, and I doubted I'd hear it again for a long time, if ever.

Then I got out and dried off, got dressed, and found a blow dryer for my hair. That felt weird: using some dead woman's blow dryer and brushes and mirror to make myself feel close to normal one last time. But not weird enough to stop me. When I was finished, I wrapped the cord neatly around the handle and set the dryer down on the vanity counter. Looking in the mirror, I saw the same old me. I gave myself a half-smile, letting my dimples come to life again, and headed out, telling myself I'd be back. It's funny what you assume sometimes.

I was only a block along Los Feliz, heading back to the road into Griffith Park, when I realized something was seriously wrong.

Some of the cars left in the middle of the street—cars whose positions I'd just about memorized while zipping around on my little Honda—had moved during the time I'd been at the solar house. I don't mean they'd *moved.* I mean they'd *been moved.* Violently.

I sat on the Honda, the engine idling under me, and looked at the black marks on the road where the tires had rubbed, looked at the dents and scratches in the fenders where the cars had been pushed...but by what? Turning my head, I could make out what looked like a cleared path of cars along the street for a good distance behind me. In the other direction, the path continued, stopping at the entrance into the park.

Trembling, I thought about the flash of movement I'd seen from the hilltop the day before and the lanterns I'd foolishly set out on the wall overnight. A beacon. It had drawn something, all right. Something powerful. Someone had a powerful vehicle or some other force to be reckoned with, and they'd used it to come looking for the beacon, to come looking for me. The solar powered house had only been a block below Los Feliz, and I should have heard the commotion from there with everything else so quiet...but maybe not with the shower running and the music blaring and the blow dryer blasting hot air and a stream of noise at my head.

Mistake after mistake after mistake. Tears of frustration filled my eyes as I thought of the observatory and everything I had stored there, set aside to get me through, to ensure my survival for just a little longer. Someone was going through it right now, some-one with enough power to get rid of obstacles, a fifteen-year-old girl included. The thing I was most upset about losing—because I *did* think of it as lost now—was the framed photo of my family. I imagined someone picking it up, looking at it, and tossing it down, the glass cracking.

The thought made me so angry that I kicked the Honda into gear and sped down the road toward the park entrance. Not worried about stealth or safety, not concerned about someone on *my* observation platform watching me through *my* binoculars or even through the scope of a high-powered rifle, I tore around corners, going up and up the winding road I'd gotten so used to over the last few weeks.

I slowed as I neared the top, though, and thought about walking the rest of the way up to the Winnebago and beyond. It wouldn't do to go flying headlong into an ambush. Nothing good could come from that. But at the same time, I knew that if someone was up here, they'd come expecting to find the observatory occupied. With the place empty, they'd be counting on my return at some point, and the sound of the little Honda's engine would have carried up here from a long way down. They knew I was coming. If I tried switching to stealth mode now, it wouldn't do any good.

Even so, as I cleared the last corner and caught sight of the motor home at the top of the hill, I did stop the bike for a few seconds. The Winnebago looked untouched, unmoved.

Maybe I'd been wrong. Maybe whoever or whatever had rammed those cars aside down on the street had just kept going, passing the entrance to the park and moving on toward Hollywood. All the cars that blocked the road to the observatory had already been moved out of the way—by me. So there hadn't really been any sign of another person or a moving vehicle since I'd turned off Los Feliz. Maybe I'd just assumed they'd come up here after pushing all those cars aside. Or maybe they had found the Winnebago too big an obstacle, and then just turned around and went back down the hill. I'd missed the whole show during my luxurious shower, and now they were going to leave me alone, all because of the blockade I'd stuck at the top of the hill.

I didn't really believe that, but there was still a moment's hope.

Giving the Honda more gas, I finished the climb and then got off the bike when I reached the motorhome. Pulling the gun from my backpack, I looked carefully at the old camper. It hadn't been moved, and no new dents had appeared on its side. Whatever had pushed the cars aside down below had left the Winnebago alone, and I was grateful for that. Still, I decided it was best to walk the rest of the way to the observatory.

Ducking around the Winnebago, I just stood and surveyed the area for a moment. Nothing seemed changed. There was no sign of people; nothing had been moved in the parking lot. And yet I felt vulnerable just standing there, knowing there was still a chance someone had gotten into the building before me. So, sticking close to the edge of the sidewalk that rimmed the hilltop, I started running, trying to duck as I went to make myself a smaller target should someone with bad intentions be watching from inside the observatory.

Still no signs of life from the building. I stopped at the statue of James Dean, hiding behind it for a moment and waiting, listening. Nothing. Maybe they really had chosen to leave me alone. I couldn't believe it, though. The old Winnebago across the road couldn't have been *that* intimidating.

I decided not to go up to the main entrance. That might be what anyone who'd just gotten here might expect. No, I ran down the stairs along the side of the building and into the cafeteria area where I'd made my base. Again, all looked undisturbed. I went back to the office where I'd been sleeping, quickly surveyed the scene, and then slipped the photo of my family into my backpack after determining that no one had been here either.

The same held true for the rest of the building. For almost an hour, I swept through it as carefully as I'd done on the first day, checking every room and hallway, cautiously rounding every corner inside and out with my gun in my hand and telling myself I might actually have to use it.

Nothing. There was no one there. Just me.

I sat down on my lounge chair after completing my search and took some deep breaths. Feeling worn out from being on such high alert the whole time I'd searched the building, I wanted nothing more than to sit, to be able to read my book and feel the breeze and have everything be like the day before, but I knew I couldn't do that.

Someone else shared the city with me, someone who'd figured out how to harness a powerful vehicle where I'd opted for a little trail bike, someone who pushed things out of the way where I went around them. And that someone knew I was up here. Of that I was still certain. Maybe they hadn't opted to raid my fortress, but they'd been nearby and hadn't been worried about keeping their presence a secret. Maybe they'd leave me alone. But I doubted it. I felt like I was now a player in a huge game of chess; the rearranged cars on Los Feliz having been my opponent's latest move. And now I was left to figure out what it meant, what the strategy could be, how the next three or four moves would go and how best to counter them.

I had no idea how to start figuring this out, though: I'd always been lousy at chess.

"Hello?"

The voice came from down the hill, a man's voice calling out.

I wanted to jump to my feet and run to the edge of the observation deck so I could peer over and see, but I forced myself to stay planted to the lounge chair.

"Anybody up there?"

My heart pounding, I slid off the chair and into a crouch. With the gun held tightly in one hand, I slunk my way over to the wall, careful not to expose myself to whoever was coming up the hill. Several hiking trails led up to the observatory, and I guessed that my visitor was on one of these. My position above him and behind the thick wall that bordered the observation deck gave me a complete advantage over the man, but that didn't make me breathe any easier.

"I don't want to hurt you or anything. Not trying to scare you, okay? You want me to go, I'll go."

To call out, or not to call out? Let him know I'm here, or make him keep guessing?

I couldn't decide, which was a decision itself. Stuck between choices, the result was not calling out, keeping him guessing.

"I saw your light last night."

He sounded young, not threatening. I knew that didn't mean anything, though.

The longer I waited, the closer he'd get. Whichever trail he was on, it would end at the top of the hill soon enough, and then he'd be exploring the observatory. I wouldn't know where he'd be. Right now I did know. I decided to hang onto whatever advantage that gave me.

"What do you want?" I called out, still keeping myself below the top of the wall.

There was a moment's pause from him, during which I had to wonder if he'd heard me, if I'd been loud enough. Then I heard him say, "I just want to find out who's up here. I thought I was all alone till I saw your light."

"There are other lights left on. You go looking at every one?"

"No. Yours is the first new one I've seen, though. The first new anything I've seen. You must have thought someone would come looking."

He had me there.

"I wasn't sure," I called out.

"What's your name?"

I didn't want to say. Not that it made a difference. I could have given him any name I wanted. I just didn't like him knowing anything about me. Or thinking he knew.

"You first," I yelled.

"Chad," he said right away.

"Chad what?"

"Chad Maxwell," he answered without hesitation. Probably not a lie.

"Are you alone?"

He actually laughed at that.

"Well, yeah, I'm alone," he said after a second. "Never been more alone in my life."

"How'd you move all those cars down below?" I asked.

"Cars?" he asked. "I came on foot."

"You didn't have anything to do with it?"

"I don't know what you mean."

I didn't like that answer. Could there really be two people who'd seen the lights? This Chad person and someone else who had the power to move those cars out of the way on Los Feliz? It seemed doubtful to me.

"Where have you been staying?"

"I found a house with solar power and got enough bottled water and canned food out of a grocery store to get by on. Not as good a spot as what you picked."

"So what now? You want to try and take it from me?"

"No." He sounded confused, maybe even hurt. "I just wanted to see who's up here. I mean, we're neighbors now, right? Even if I'm half a city away, we're still neighbors. I figured it made more sense to see if we could maybe help each other rather than both of us just going it alone. You know?"

Slowly, I stood up, just high enough to be able to see over the wall and ready to duck again if anything seemed wrong. He stood on the bare hiking trail not far below the deck—not a man, I saw now, but a kid, like me, with sandy hair and a scruff of beard, cargo shorts and a striped t-shirt with a hole in the sleeve. His hands were empty, but he had a backpack on his shoulders.

"What's in the bag?" I asked as I held my gun up for him to see.

He put both hands out in front of him, palms facing me in an effort to keep me calm. "Just some supplies," he said, trying to sound reassuring.

Slowly, with one hand, he slipped the pack off his shoulders and bent to open it.

"Don't shoot me, okay?"

I didn't say anything, just watched, glad he wasn't taking an aggressive tone.

From the backpack, he drew a bottle of water, a hat and sunglasses, and some small packages, probably energy bars. Their foil wrappers glinted in the sun. Then he tipped the bag upside down and shook it gently to show me that nothing else was coming out.

"See?" he called. "Just supplies. Nothing scary. I promise. I didn't come up here to try and hurt you. Or take away your...observatory."

I thought about it for a few seconds, then nodded. "All right. Come up."

Trying to keep an eye on him, I watched him re-pack his things and begin up the trail again as I went along the edge of the observation deck toward the side of the building that had access to the main entrance. I wanted to be out front when he got to the top of the trail.

It took him several minutes. The trail didn't come straight up to the observatory but must have deposited him somewhere near the road and the Winnebago. When he rounded the side of the old motorhome, I tensed a bit and gripped the gun a little tighter, wondering if I could actually use it if I felt threatened. So far, he seemed all right, but I couldn't be sure. He might have been telling the truth, and he might not have. The phrase *those cars didn't move themselves* kept running through my head, keeping me focused.

He must have read my mind, as he stopped halfway across the parking lot, raised his hands over his head for a moment, and then slipped off the backpack, letting it drop to the asphalt without giving it a glance. Then he started walking again.

Sweat beaded on my forehead, and I felt my palms grow moist as well. I didn't know what to do. Worried about all the mistakes I'd made until now, I wondered if my luck had finally run out, if I was making another mistake, a big one, that wouldn't be revealed to me until it was too late, far too late.

At the same time, I wanted desperately for him to be all right. Just seeing and hearing him made me realize how lonely I'd been, and I knew the silence of the observatory would be horrible if the next five minutes worked out badly and I had to send him away—or worse—and ended up alone again.

He had crossed the parking lot now and began making his way across the expanse of lawn. I stayed silent, just shifting my weight from leg to leg, watching his progress.

When he got to the foot of the steps, he stopped and smiled at me. He had kind eyes and looked sort of boyish in spite of the scruffy beard. Actually, the wiry hairs made him look more boyish, as it wasn't a proper beard; he needed a few more years for it to look right. His hair had probably needed cutting before the disease struck. Now it wanted to drop down in his eyes, and he casually pushed it aside so he could keep looking at me.

"Nice place you got here," he said, cracking a smile.

"Thanks."

"So…you gonna invite me in?"

I shook my head. "This is fine for now." I nodded toward him. "Why don't you sit down?"

He raised an eyebrow at me and then sat cross-legged at the base of the steps, looking up at me. I hesitated a moment and then sat down, too, keeping the gun in my lap, one hand on it.

"I still don't know your name," he said.

"Scarlett."

He thought about that for a second, then nodded. "Hi, Scarlett. Nice to meet you."

I still wasn't sure if it was nice to meet Chad or not. I wanted it to be, though, so I said, "Same here. How old are you?"

"Does it matter?" I just raised an eyebrow at that. He smiled, kind of foolishly, and brushed the hair out of his eyes before answering, "Seventeen. You?"

"I just turned fifteen. Before … you know."

He gave me a grim nod. "How long have you been up here?" he asked.

"Couple weeks."

"Almost since the beginning."

I nodded. "Have you seen anyone else?"

He hesitated a moment. "Since...?"

"Yeah."

He shook his head. "No."

"And you just happened to see my lights?"

"They were pretty bright. There hadn't been any lights on the hill before. From down there, it just looked like a big black wall at night. And then those lights last night. I had to come see. Why'd you decide to put them up?"

I didn't answer. "What about before?"

"Before the...disease?"

I nodded again.

"I lived in Hollywood. With my dad. Hollywood High, the whole deal."

"Your dad rich?"

He shook his head. "No. Yours?"

"No."

We talked for a while then, me pulling answers out of him and only giving him bits about myself when I felt like it. His story paralleled mine in quite a few ways. He talked about being out with his friends on Hollywood Boulevard the same evening I'd been at Dodger Stadium, about someone having an attack on the sidewalk in front of him, about how freaked out he and his friends were, about how he couldn't pull himself away from the Internet and TV all that night, and about how he was the only one out of his group who'd still been alive the following afternoon. He'd watched his father die that evening after they'd argued about staying in their apartment or trying to get out of the city. After that, he hadn't been able to bear the apartment and had left to try and find a new place. He'd opted for a mansion in Hollywood at the base of the hills and had set himself up with supplies not unlike what I'd gathered for myself.

"It's nothing like this, though." He looked past me toward the observatory's entrance and then glanced around at the wide expanse of lawn behind him. "Looks like you picked the best spot in the neighborhood."

I tried to read that, tried to tell if he was asking if he could come up here for good, share the space with me. I wasn't sure how I felt about that. The company would be nice, more than nice, but I still wasn't sure I could trust him.

"You been up here before?" I asked.

He nodded. "My dad and me used to come up here a lot when I was little. Haven't been here for a while, though. It's funny I kind of forgot about this place when I was looking for somewhere safe to stay."

"It is pretty safe," I agreed, not sure what else to say.

"Can I see your set-up?"

"Not much to see. I'm pretty much camped out in an office behind the café. And I've got a little patio set up on one of the observation decks. It's not bad. Nothing great."

He nodded, waiting for me to invite him in. Then he tipped his head toward me. "Any chance we could..." I blushed, sure he was going to proposition me. "...lose that gun?"

I'm not sure what my expression conveyed; maybe shock, maybe relief, maybe surprise or amusement at the absurd difference between what he said and what I'd been expecting. At any rate, I didn't know how to respond.

I picked the gun up from my lap, hefted it a second, and gave him a look. His eyes didn't leave the gun; he watched it expectantly, like a little kid who's asked for a toy or a dessert and now waits to see what the adult is going to do. Only now, he didn't want the toy; he wanted it to go away and waited eagerly to see what would happen. He looked harmless, completely harmless.

I popped the safety into place and leaned forward, tucking the barrel into the back of my pants. Then I stood up.

"For now," I said, smiling just a little.

He got up, too.

"Come on," I said.

Second-guessing myself the whole way, I led him around the side of the building rather than through the main entrance. We went down the concrete steps and were soon walking past the entrance to the café.

"That's Scarlett central?" he asked.

"That's it." I didn't want him in there, not now. I didn't feel comfortable yet being inside with him, or letting him see everything I'd gathered at the sporting goods store or since. Instead, I kept going, rounding a corner and leading him up another set of concrete steps to the deck where I had my lounge chair and book. I'd show him the view, I told myself, and where I'd set the lanterns the night before. I could offer him something to eat or drink and maybe we could talk a bit. But then I'd ask him to go. Just because we were the last two people in Los Angeles didn't mean we had to be instant companions. He could come back. Maybe eventually the idea of companionship or safety in numbers would override my uncertainty, but not yet.

He walked beside me up the steps, keeping our little conversation going, asking if it was creepy up here at night.

"Sometimes," I said, thinking of the bats that fluttered around just after dusk. But I never got the chance to explain.

With one foot on the platform at the top of the stairs and the other lifting off the last step, I was thrown off balance when he pushed himself into me, not just leaning hard but really knocking into me. For half a second I thought he'd just tripped, but then I realized it was a tackle.

I went down onto the concrete with him on top of me, hitting first my elbow and then the side of my face on the rough surface. I think I cried out, but I might not have. A thousand things raced through my head—about what he was going to try, about how I'd blown it again—but rather than panic, I managed to focus and fight.

Protecting and then reaching the gun: nothing else mattered. I tried rolling out from under him, shoving my arm and hand between us to reach the gun, but he was stronger than me and was turning me on my back with the gun underneath me. I managed to get my other hand up under his chin and tried squeezing at his throat, but he jerked his head away from me.

"Just stop it! Just stop!" he was saying. "I don't want to hurt you. I didn't want to do this."

I didn't answer, just struggled under him. He had straddled my stomach and was trying hard to pin both my arms to the concrete, but I thrashed under him and tried scratching at his face. Finally, I got him a good one, raking my nails across his cheek and watching the red marks trailing behind my fingers.

It really hurt him, and for a second I thought he'd let me go, but then he redoubled his efforts and actually bent down closer, getting his face right next to mine. Enraged, he shouted, "Stop fighting me! You don't know what you're doing!"

And then he had me, both arms down, my shoulders pinned to the concrete like they used to be when I played wrestling with Anna and she never let me win.

He got his wish. I stopped fighting him, just lay under him breathing hard and waiting for him to make his next move. Whatever it was, it wouldn't go easy. The second he relaxed his hold on one of my arms, I'd be swinging my fist at him again.

"Just listen to me," he said with heavy breaths. A bead of sweat dropped from his forehead onto my cheek. "Just listen. I'm sorry. Okay? I didn't want to do that. But I was afraid if I just told you...you'd have that gun on me again."

He paused, his eyes darting as he watched my face for a response.

"Told me what?" I said.

Donovan hooked the two handcuffs together with a short length of chain and a padlock. Barely glancing at me, he turned, picked up his gun, and went to the front of the bus, pausing for a moment to collect my backpack from Chad's seat and walking it back to me.

Then he climbed into the driver's seat, and the old bus's engine rumbled to life. It still had one of those chrome bars for the driver to shut the door without getting out of his seat, and now Donovan used it to seal us in. He put the bus in gear and then began down the hill, turning at the intersection to take us away from the Winnebago and the observatory. I turned my head a few times automatically, thinking I'd be able to see the last of the observatory out the window, but the windows were all blocked and sealed, even at the back of the bus. I knew that if I ever got another look at the Griffith Observatory, it would be from far away, just a big white building on a hill beside the Hollywood sign. It had been nice while it lasted.

CHAPTER NINE

"Where are you taking us?" I finally asked.

We'd come down the hill quickly as the sun set, and then I'd been able to watch through the windshield as Donovan navigated the bus along the path he'd already cleared on Los Feliz. Now it was fully dark out, and the bus's bright lights cut eerily through the night. Ever since the power had gone out, I hadn't been away from the observatory at night, and now it felt creepy to be down in the city with everything so dark, the headlights and those on top of the bus revealing new things in the distance that seemed to rise up out of the night without warning. Donovan drove slowly, but still it felt like we sped recklessly through the darkness.

Donovan gave no answer, no indication that he'd heard me.

I leaned forward, trying to get Dolores' attention. "What about you? Do you know what he's going to do with us?" I asked.

In the dark interior of the bus, I could see that she shifted her body in the seat and then turned as far around as possible with her hands chained like mine. I think she smiled. "*No se*," she said.

Spanish, I thought.

"You don't speak English?"

"*Poquito.*"

Just a little, I thought. *Great.* I'd had one year of high school Spanish and had struggled with it. I might be able to ask her where the bathroom or the library was, or to be able to say that Pedro's father is a doctor, but as far as anything practical...I had my doubts.

"Okay," I said. "Thanks. *Gracias.*"

She nodded and turned to the front again.

"What about you?" I said a bit more loudly so Chad could hear. I didn't want to say his name, didn't want him to think I'd forgiven him for helping Donovan. Honestly, I probably would have done the same now that I saw Dolores as a real person and not just an abstract idea I could write off in some survival-of-the-fittest fantasy. I could see how it would have been tough to run off into the wilds of Griffith Park and leave Dolores in Donovan's hands when he'd promised to kill her if Chad hadn't come back. Still...there must have been another way. He hadn't needed to be *so* compliant, could have found a way to trick Donovan, to use me and get himself and Dolores freed in the bargain. But maybe he wasn't that kind of hero. All he could really manage was to keep everyone alive. So far so good.

"Do you know where he's taking us?" I asked a bit louder when Chad didn't turn or acknowledge my question at all.

"East," came Donovan's muffled reply from the driver's seat. "Riverside, if you have to know. Now shut up."

There were a few lights burning in the instrument panel in front of him, and from their glow I could see his face in the wide mirror mounted above his seat. He glanced up now, staring at me for a moment in the mirror before turning his gaze to the road again. It was hard to read that look, but I would have described it as hatred. Donovan hated me and Chad and Dolores, hated us for being the real survivors, the genetic winners, where he had managed to survive only through luck and forethought and technology. He knew his fate and he knew ours, and he was doing everything he could to reverse that order, to force himself into the winning camp.

Too bad for you, I thought. Now all I needed to do was make sure I kept alive until he made a mistake. That had probably been Chad's plan, too. But knowing that still didn't mean I had to forgive him.

The bus rolled along. Donovan seemed to know his way well, even in the dark and even with the obstacles that blocked the road. Every so often, we'd come to a spot where cars blocked our path, and I wondered how that could have been if Donovan had cleared the way already. It wasn't like there were bunches of other survivors out, moving abandoned cars around to block the roads. I guessed that he was either taking a different route now than he'd taken on his way into the city, or that when he'd moved the cars the first time, they'd been left unstable and had fallen back onto the road, needing to be moved again. Either way, Donovan slowed the bus and used the plow attached to the front to push the cars out of the way, and before long we'd be back to the path he must have cleared before. It must have taken him days, I realized, to have made it this far into the city if he'd come from Riverside in the first place, a distance of maybe thirty or forty miles.

I tried sinking farther into the seat, slumping down and wishing I could shrink into nothing and just be gone, just have it over with. Since that wasn't possible, I told myself I should just go to sleep and maybe dream that I was somewhere else. But the seat was old and lumpy, and the springs poked at my butt and back, so there was no point in pretending I could sleep as the bus rolled along. Besides, new obstacles got in the way often enough to pull me out of any sleep I might get, the bus shuddering as it pushed a car or van out of the way.

Maybe two hours after dark, it began to rain. I looked up front to see the windshield wipers going. It was coming down hard, drops bouncing up in the road ahead of us as they splashed into puddles. Donovan had slowed down with the rain, and I could see him leaning forward over the steering wheel, peering into the night and the storm to watch for hidden obstacles.

He should stop, I told myself. *This isn't safe.*

As though he'd read my mind, Donovan slowed the bus even more, just creeping along the street. I had no idea where we were now; he'd found a pretty steady east-west route to make his way into the city, and followed it back out, cutting through industrial areas, then business districts, then neighborhoods and back to businesses. All I knew for sure was this was a part of the city I wasn't familiar with. If I could get away here, I could find my way back to the observatory easily enough, but what would be the point? Donovan would just come looking for me again. I'd be better prepared next time, though.

Next time.

A ridiculous thought.

I wasn't getting away from Donovan. Not tonight. And most likely not alone. *If* I could swallow my anger long enough to have a conversation with Chad, and *if* we could even find the opportunity to have such a conversation, then all we'd need to do would be to find some way to get away from Donovan, to subdue him, maybe even kill him, and with a little luck manage to get Dolores away in the bargain.

All long shots, I thought. *More than long shots.*

And then the bus stopped with a quick jerk and a squeak of brakes.

I looked ahead, past Donovan as he peered into the rain soaked street and saw the same thing he looked at, dumbfounded and doubting my own eyes. Chad appeared to be looking at the same thing, sitting up and leaning forward in his seat. Dolores, who hadn't seemed to move for the last several miles, also sat up straight now and craned her neck as though the extra inches would give her a better look out the wet windshield.

Standing twenty feet in front of the bus, her hands waving in the air in a signal for us to stop, was a woman, a very wet and very pregnant woman. The rain had plastered her brown hair to the sides of her head, and her shirt and pants already looked saturated. She stood there, rainwater dripping off her face, and when she lowered her hands—satisfied, I suppose, that we really were stopping—I could see that she was crying, maybe in fear, maybe in desperation.

Donovan set the bus's parking brake and reached for the radio, snatching the mouthpiece from its cradle and flipping a switch. He held the mouthpiece up to his mask and said, "Who's with you?" I could hear his tinny words echoing out into the night through the bus's P.A. system.

The woman looked even more desperate at being interrogated. She shook her head and arched her eyebrows, begging to be believed. I watched her mouth the words *No one.* Then she looked to her left and right, as if to show us that she really was alone, that there could be no one else here—in the dark, in the rain. She was alone and had been alone and probably thought she would have to have her baby alone. I couldn't begin to guess what she'd been going through, how much harder it had been than my existence. And here we were in this bus to show her how wrong she'd been.

You don't know what you're getting yourself into, I thought. *You were better off five minutes ago, alone. You think we're here to save you. You're so wrong, so wrong.*

Of course, I kept my mouth shut.

Donovan flipped another switch, turning on the banks of lights mounted on top of the bus. All I could see, though, was that more light came in from the driver's side window and the other windows in the accordion door. Donovan turned in his seat to look long and hard out his window; then he got up and went to the door to peer further into the night.

"Turn around slowly," he said through the P.A.

The pregnant woman hesitated a moment and then did as she was told. When she had her back to the bus, Donovan said, "Stop. Now get on your knees."

Again she hesitated but followed his instructions a few seconds later.

Donovan killed the engine and then walked up the aisle to Chad. With a rattle of chains and a click from the locks, he soon had Chad freed. "Same drill as before," he said. "Bring her back. You run, and I hurt the ladies. You think I won't?"

Chad gave no indication he'd heard the question.

Donovan shoved his shoulder, jerking Chad's body sideways in his seat.

"You think I won't?" he repeated, louder.

"No," Chad said, his voice bitter and just above a whisper.

He hates him, I thought, *hates what he's making him do.* It was the first time since Chad had tackled me at the top of the stairs that I got to see another real side of him, not the Chad who was scared of Donovan and did everything he was told. It was still hard to get past the way he'd lied to me so easily at the observatory, but the anger I could hear in his voice now made me start to feel a little better about him.

"Damn straight," said Donovan.

He must have had a case or duffel bag on the seat in front of Chad. He reached in and handed Chad something. "Tie her like you did the girl," he said, and I knew he'd given Chad more zip ties.

"She's pregnant," Chad said.

"You think pregnant girls can't fight? Tie her."

Chad said nothing, just took the ties and stood up.

"Nothing stupid," Donovan said, stepping aside to let Chad pass.

I watched as Donovan went back to his seat and pulled the chrome handle to open the door. His posture in the seat as Chad passed him told me he had his gun out and aimed at Chad as he went down the steps and out the door. Would he really turn the gun on Dolores and me if Chad decided he didn't want to repeat the adventure he'd had with me? Chad could easily decide to run, could easily decide against his plan of waiting to save himself along with Donovan's other captives and opt to save just himself instead. And where would that leave me and Dolores?

I didn't think about it at the time, but I wonder now what I would have done if Donovan had chosen me to go out and bring the pregnant woman back. Would I have cooperated? Or run off into the night to get back the freedom I'd lost only a few hours before? I want to say I would have complied, wouldn't have risked others' lives by calling Donovan's bluff—if bluff it was. But I don't know. I really don't. I might very well have lit off on my own, hoping for the best and gritting my teeth in anticipation of gunshots, of bullets whizzing past my head, of the terrible realization that they *weren't* whizzing past me and must have gone somewhere else instead. What would I have done if I'd known the bullets were thudding into Chad or Dolores as a direct result of my actions? I'm sure I would have run faster.

But of course, Donovan hadn't chosen me. He didn't know me well enough to know I wouldn't run, leaving people I didn't know or care about to face his wrath. He'd chosen Chad, the boy who still clung to the old world's idea of heroism and manliness, the boy who'd come back to chains rather than let the women get hurt.

Out he went into the rain and was soaked by the time he got to the pregnant woman. I saw him bend to speak to her and then try to grab one of her wrists, probably having told her to be still and let him bind her, that it would be for the best.

But she jerked her hand away from him and turned her head. She spoke, and it looked like she was shouting at him, then pleading with him. Chad took a step backward, the fear on his face looking like it might tear him in two.

I wondered what the woman could have told him, wondered if she was sick with the fungus, somehow having managed to avoid infection until now. But that wasn't it.

Chad hesitated a second and then ran through the rain back to the bus, only putting his head and shoulders inside the door.

"She won't come," he said. And before Donovan could protest or scold or shout, he added, "She says her water broke. She's in labor."

Donovan swore. For several seconds he just sat there, his head turning from Chad to the woman kneeling in the rain.

"There's a drugstore right over there," Chad said, hooking his thumb in the air to indicate a spot somewhere behind him. "She was going to try and have the baby in there when she heard the bus coming." He just looked at Donovan then. Our captor said nothing.

I couldn't believe what I was hearing or seeing, didn't know what to feel or think.

"What do we do?" Chad asked. He didn't mean just himself, or Donovan. He meant all of us, the woman in the rain included, and for a second seemed to have forgotten that one man among has had all the power over the rest.

"Sit down," Donovan said, waving his gun toward the aisle.

"We can't leave her," Chad said, and I wanted to say the same thing.

"Shut up and sit down."

Chad looked out into the rain for a moment and then complied. A minute later, he was locked in place again, and I expected we'd be on our way. Whatever plan Donovan had for the survivors he'd captured, three must have been enough; he could do without the headaches of a pregnant woman and the baby she'd be saddled with before long.

But instead of turning back toward his seat, Donovan approached Dolores and me.

"You two are gonna help her," he said, bending to free Dolores before me.

"How are we supposed to do that?" I asked. Other than my step-mom, I'd never really even been around a pregnant woman before, and when my brothers had been born I hadn't been in on any of the details.

"Figure it out," he said. "Can't be too hard. People did for thousands of years before hospitals. No more hospitals now." He moved farther along the aisle so Dolores and I could exit in front of him. "Hope your Spanish is good," he added.

I didn't reply, just got up after a moment's waiting. It wasn't that I weighed the possibility of defying him. I just didn't want him to see me get up as soon as he commanded me to.

Dolores went first, and when we got to the door, Donovan said, "You do anything stupid, and I'm gonna shoot your boyfriend here. You got it?"

I turned, looking from his face to Chad's. For just a second, Chad met my gaze; then he dropped his eyes to the floor. *Can't handle having your life in my hands?* I wanted to ask. I didn't need to. I knew it was true.

"It might take a long time," I said at the bottom of the steps. Dolores was already out in the rain, heading toward the pregnant woman.

"You got a watch on? Come back in two hours and check in. Don't forget."

Then I was out in the rain, too, hurrying toward Dolores, no thought at all in mind about running away. Not then, anyway. Everything I'd said to Chad before I ended up on the bus, all the posturing about not caring if Dolores died...I had meant it, kind of. But now there was a pregnant woman out in the rain. Leaving her there on her own just wasn't an option.

We got to the woman, and right away we helped her off the ground. Rainwater streaked across her face, but I could tell there were tears as well. She looked to be about ten years older than me.

THE GIRL AT THE END OF THE WORLD

"Please help me," she begged.

"Okay," I said. "Just…come on."

I didn't know what else to say. Dolores and I each took an arm and walked with her to the curb. I was thankful for the lights from the bus, could see the drugstore across a narrow parking lot. It was a chain store and looked no different than the one near our house where I'd gone countless times before with my mom and sister.

"Who are you people?" the woman asked as we crossed the parking lot. She sounded astounded that we'd found her.

"I'm Scarlett," I said. "This is Dolores. We're…"

I didn't want to tell her we were captives, that we were helping her because the guy who'd first come out of the bus was being held at gunpoint now, his safety contingent on our return. She could hear the ugly truth later. She had enough to worry about right now.

"We're traveling. Donovan…he's the driver. He had this bus before…the sickness. He found us one at a time." Then I added, "He saved us."

I counted on Dolores not understanding any of what I said, or if she did understand, that she'd play along and know my intentions as I lied to the poor woman.

"What's your name?"

"Alex. Alexandra. I can't believe you're here. I've been alone all this time, and now…"

"It's okay. We'll help you."

I didn't know what I was saying and certainly didn't believe it. How could I help a woman deliver a baby? I had no idea what Dolores could do, if she'd had kids before, if she knew anything about what to do or how to do it. But, ignorant and scared as I was, I knew Alex was more scared, more lost. What the last weeks must have been like for her, I couldn't imagine.

"Thank you," Alex said. "Thank you. Oh God."

A contraction must have hit, as she stopped moving and half bent at the waist, letting go of my arm to grab at her stomach. We were maybe ten feet from the store's glass doors, and I could see now that one of them had been smashed to bits, a thousand tiny crystals of glass on the ground around and inside the entrance. The electric opener hadn't worked anymore, and Alex had needed to get inside. I'd have done the same thing, though I couldn't see what she'd used to smash the glass.

Dolores gave her only a few seconds to deal with the pain and then began nudging her forward, gently pulling at her arm to lead her toward the door. Of course, the store's lights were out, but Alex had several flashlights burning. They didn't make it bright inside, but as our shoes crunched across the broken glass, I could make out the counter with the registers and the make-up aisle to my right. The pharmacy would be in back, but Alex had set up a little area near the front of the store where she'd planned to have her baby; now I was going to have to help, and I found myself shaking at the thought.

It wasn't the little kind of drug store that just sold things related to health and hygiene. It had a bit of everything. And far enough from the smashed door to be sheltered from the rain and the breeze outside, but not so far in as to be swallowed in the dark, Alex had arranged orthopedic pillows and some cushions from a cheap display of patio furniture. She had gathered several bottles of rubbing alcohol, towels, blankets, medical tape, a first aid kit, cotton pads, scissors, and several other things I couldn't identify at first glance.

"*Siéntate*," Dolores said as we approached the makeshift delivery room.

That was a word I knew, and so I followed suit, encouraging Alex to sit down on the cushions. The photo counter was right behind her, and now Dolores arranged pillows so Alex could lean against it.

"Just try to relax," I said.

Dolores put her hands on Alex's stomach, feeling the baby.

"Have you ever done this before?" Alex asked, apprehension in her voice.

Dolores didn't reply, just looked at me and said, *"Ir a buscar unos guantes."*

I had no idea what that meant and gave her a quizzical look, hoping my cluelessness didn't scare Alex.

She took her hands off Alex and mimicked putting on a pair of gloves, repeating, *"Guantes, guantes."*

"Gloves," I said. "Gloves?"

Dolores nodded, *"Sí."*

"I'll be right back."

Taking one of the flashlights with me, I went back to the first aid aisle and looked for Latex gloves. They were easy enough to find, and I went back to the makeshift delivery room. In my absence, Dolores had removed Alex's pants and underwear and now had her covered with a blanket. I watched as the older woman put on the gloves, prodded Alex to bend her knees, and then she pulled back the blanket.

At that point, I didn't want to watch any more, and so shifted my position. Kneeling closer to Alex's upper body, I reached for her hand, and when she squeezed back, it made me feel glad to be there for her, scary as it was.

"Has she ever done this before?" Alex asked again.

"I don't know," I said. "Maybe."

"Oh God," Alex said, tears not far behind.

"It's okay. I think…I'm pretty sure she knows what she's doing. At least you're not alone."

"Okay," she said. "Okay."

"Do you know if it's a boy or girl?"

She shook her head. "We didn't want to know."

I didn't want to ask who the other half of *we* was.

Then another contraction hit, a bigger one, and she tried to writhe with the pain, but Dolores held her knees and kept saying, *"No se mueven."*

"Hold still," I translated. "Try not to move around so much." And I put my hands on her shoulders, hoping to encourage her to be still without actually pinning her down. I didn't think I was strong enough to force her.

It took several seconds for the contraction to pass. When Alex stopped gasping and grunting through it, Dolores sat back and smiled. "*Pronto*," she said.

"Soon," I translated.

"Okay."

Sweat beaded on Alex's forehead. I found a small towel among the supplies she'd gathered and used it to mop her brow and wipe at the tears running down her cheeks. She smiled a little at that.

The contractions came and went, maybe for an hour. I tried talking to Alex, first telling about when my brothers had been born and how I'd gotten to hold them as babies, and then just moving on to things about my family, anything to keep her focused on something other than the pain and what I was sure must be her fear over something going wrong.

At one point, she said, "Do you think the baby'll be okay?"

"It'll be fine," I said. "I really think Dolores knows what she's doing."

She shook her head. "No, I mean after. What if it...gets sick? You know?"

She meant the fungus. What if the baby didn't share her immunity? I hadn't even considered the horrible possibility. To carry her child all this time, to go through the pain and risk of labor, to hold the new baby and love it...only to lose it in a day's time if it breathed in the spores and they infected it. I didn't want to think of an infant suffering the death I'd seen thousands afflicted with in the past weeks, but even so the image popped into my head, and it was hard to get it out.

"You just have to hope," I said after a few seconds. "Maybe it'll have your immunity. Or...who knows? Maybe the danger is passed. Maybe all the spores are out and gone and floated away. There may not be anything left to make the baby sick."

She nodded and gave a feeble smile, but I knew she was still worried.

The contractions got closer, and Alex's reactions to them more dramatic. She squeezed my hand to the point I thought it would break and then apologized when the pain had passed.

"It's okay," I said. "I'm tough."

She smiled, not so weakly this time.

"Have you ever taken care of a baby?" she asked.

"Not really. My brothers a little. Well...half-brothers. I wasn't around them that much."

She nodded. "Listen. Kayla if it's a girl. Okay? Michael if it's a boy. Michael Ramos." A distant look overcame her.

I almost asked why she was telling me this now, but then I understood. She wasn't just worried about the baby not surviving.

"That was...the dad?" I asked.

She nodded again, and then another contraction started. Alex writhed and cried out and at one point moaned in desperation, "I can't do this."

"You can," I said, still holding her hand. "You are. You're doing it."

When that contraction passed, Dolores got a pleased, almost beatific look and said, "*La cabeza.*"

She leaned back and waved me toward her. I was scared to look, expecting to see the baby's whole head sticking out, but when I leaned over the edge of the blanket, all I saw was Alex, her legs open. Dolores must have known what she was looking at, but I couldn't tell and didn't want to stare. I leaned back and forced a smile at Alex.

"Can you see?" she asked, tears and sweat running down her cheeks.

"I think so."

The next contraction started almost right away, and Alex screamed as she clutched my hand in one of hers and clawed at the floor with the other.

"*No gritar!*" Dolores said. "*Empujar! Empujar!*"

I didn't know what that meant and looked with panic first at Dolores and then at Alex, feeling completely useless.

Then Dolores made a pushing motion with her hands. "*Empujar. Empujar,*" she said again. She waved her hands in front of her mouth, opening it wide and making a face as though she was screaming with the same force as Alex. "*No gritar!*"

I got it. "Don't scream," I said to Alex, raising my voice to be heard above hers. "You need to push. You can't scream and push at the same time!"

She tried, putting her energy into pushing, but I could see she still wanted to cry out. And then the contraction passed, and she was left panting and crying.

"I can't," she kept repeating.

I bent down close to her. "You're exhausted. You're exhausted. It's okay. You're going to be okay. The baby, too. You just have to push a little more when the next one hits, okay?" She made no reply. "Okay?" I said more forcefully.

A feeble nod and then, "Okay."

I exhaled, feeling relieved, like I'd actually done something. "Okay," I echoed.

Alex pushed on the next contraction, straining the muscles in her neck and squeezing my hand, holding her breath and pushing as long as she could before gasping in more air to push again.

And then baby was out. All I saw was Dolores leaning in quickly and then backing away again, and she held the tiny pink baby in her hands, all covered in fluids that matted its hair and stuck to its skin. Already, Dolores was wiping at the baby's skin with one of the towels she'd kept nearby, and then it started to cry.

Alex was crying, too, and still breathing hard.

And I won't say I wasn't a teary mess myself. It was one of the most amazing things I'd ever seen, following a time when all I'd seen were horrible things, when I thought I'd never see anything amazing again.

"*Una niña,*" Dolores said. "Girl."

"It's a girl," I repeated through my tears.

"*Ayúdame,*" Dolores said, tipping her head to indicate I should come closer. She handed me a towel and then put the little baby in my arms. She wiggled a bit, and her arms and legs twitched.

Dolores grabbed scissors, poured alcohol over them, and cut the cord. She held it for a moment to stop the flow of blood and then turned back to Alex.

I moved closer to Alex, thinking I'd hand her the baby. But then there was one more contraction, and the placenta came out. And with it a lot of blood.

"*Dios mio,*" Dolores said, grabbing for cotton pads and pushing them up against Alex. I looked at her face, and saw fear there. She looked pale, like someone about to throw up from motion sickness.

"*Ayúdame! Ayúdame!*" Dolores shouted.

"What do I do?" I yelled back.

Alex moaned, and the baby cried.

I felt everything coming apart.

And I got a look at how much blood was pouring out of Alex. If she'd been in a hospital with doctors and nurses and all the right equipment...if she'd just had the baby a month before, she would have been fine. But with just me and Dolores there to help her on the floor of an abandoned drugstore, with no more doctors or nurses alive anywhere, and with all that blood...

Dolores tried. I can't imagine anything she could have done differently or better with the limited resources she had. But after an endless minute or two, Alex was gone. She never even got to hold her baby.

I couldn't believe it.

Dolores and I just sat there, both of us weeping along with the little orphan baby in my arms. I tried not to look at Alex's face, her eyes open and staring up into the dark ceiling of the store. I knew that image would haunt me, and it did. I'd seen so much death in the last month, had reached a point where it had stopped bothering me. But this was something new, and it took me a long time to shake it.

After a few minutes, Dolores covered Alex with a blanket and got up from the floor. Then she put out a hand to help me up and took the baby from my arms.

"Kayla," I said, glad Alex had thought to tell me, wondering if the poor woman had really known something was going to go wrong or if it had just been worry.

Dolores barely nodded. There was a package of diapers for newborns and she put one on the baby; then she used some medical tape on the end of the umbilical cord before beginning to wrap Kayla in a towel.

"*La leche*," she said.

Milk. Without her mother, the baby was going to need formula, bottles, all sorts of things. I nodded, took a lantern, and found a shopping cart, wiping at my tears with the back of my hand and moving into the dark of the store in total disbelief.

* * * * *

The rain had stopped by the time Dolores and I walked outside with the baby and our cart full of supplies. I don't think I considered running from Donovan for even a second the whole time we were in the store. Yes, I still wanted to get away from him, and I still wouldn't have minded seeing him dead or hurt in the process, but for now we needed him, needed his bus and his resources and whatever else he had in Riverside that had allowed him to beat the fungus for as long as he had.

When he saw just Dolores and me coming out of the store, he stood up inside the bus, opening the door and coming down the steps. He still held his gun and waved it at us now. I could hear him mumbling something inside his suit and guessed at what he was saying. But I didn't feel like putting forth the effort it would take to yell an answer across the parking lot.

THE GIRL AT THE END OF THE WORLD

"She's dead," I said simply and directly when we got closer. "No thanks to you."

Then I walked past him and let Dolores hand the baby to me once I was halfway up the steps into the bus. We ignored Donovan, loading the supplies from the shopping cart once I'd handed Chad the baby and told him unceremoniously to be careful. My tone must have told him everything he needed to know, because he didn't ask a single question, just took the little bundle from me and watched in silence as I helped Dolores.

Donovan waited outside, also watching, not doing anything to help. When we had everything inside, he followed us in and got Dolores and me locked in to our restraints again with Dolores holding the baby.

"What happened?" he finally said once the last lock had clicked into place.

"She bled to death," I answered.

He just stood there for a moment, thinking about it, probably trying to ferret out any trickery that Dolores and I or maybe even Alex had cooked up. He must not have thought of any, just nodded. Then he went to check for himself, or at least that was what I assumed. He left the bus and walked away only to come back a few minutes later and climb the steps to the driver's seat without saying a word.

And then we were off again, continuing east, with one more survivor as part of Donovan's herd.

CHAPTER TEN

Donovan drove the bus straight through the night, but with stops along the way. He let us out of the bus to relieve ourselves behind cars, always with the threat that he'd start shooting the others if one of us didn't come back.

I could only guess that he was taking care of his own business inside that suit he wore, probably wearing an adult diaper. During the breaks in driving, I watched him, seeing that his protective suit fit loosely enough to enable him to pull an arm out of his sleeve and move it around inside the suit. He must have had inner pockets with supplies of some kind inside, as I saw him drinking something from a straw, maybe a protein drink or something else to keep him hydrated and energized. If he'd been on just liquids since he'd started his trip from Riverside, there might have been some way he'd been urinating into a bag or something. Even so, he was probably ready to get out of that suit, as his impatience with our stops suggested.

The first time the baby needed feeding, it was quite a production with all the packaging that needed to be opened and instructions that needed to be read. And then the baby needed changing and cleaning and swaddling, and Dolores couldn't do it all with her hands chained. Finally Donovan gave up in disgust and let her ride unbound, probably reasoning that she wouldn't do anything to jeopardize the baby while we were driving. That meant she handed Kayla to me several times while she got up and rummaged through the supplies we'd brought onboard. I remember holding her that night, worried that the swaddling cloth was too tight, amazed at this warm little package on my lap, and haunted by the image of her dead mother and the fear that the baby wouldn't have inherited Alex's immunity. I kept looking at her nose for signs of bleeding; finding none, I'd relax for a minute and then be forced to look again.

We reached Donovan's compound just after sunrise. A large, open piece of land off the beaten track, it didn't look like much. I could see only a bit of it through the bus's windshield: dry grass and old cars and an older house on the other side of a chain link fence.

Donovan opened the gate with a remote control, and the bus rolled into the compound, driving past the house to stop in front of a small outbuilding made entirely of gray cinder blocks. It had a single door and no windows that I could see; from its roof a huge antenna sprouted, the kind I'd seen before on the homes of ham radio operators. When I saw it, I immediately thought of the Australian TV station I'd been so desperate to reach when I'd gone to the solar house.

Donovan killed the engine and turned in his seat. "You're going in one at a time. I'm telling you right now, this was a good trip for me. I got more of you than I needed, so if I need to hurt one of you, or worse, it's still good for me. I don't want to have to, but don't push me."

I tried to figure out what he meant, but there wasn't much point. What he claimed to have needed was beyond me, and how he could now have more than he needed was also confusing. I was convinced that he was his own kind of crazy, had been before the fungus hit and now had found a way to bend what was left of the world to fit his twisted vision.

He said nothing more, just exited the bus, closing the door behind him. I moved as far forward in my seat as I could so I could watch him go.

He disappeared from my line of sight for several minutes. If I'd been fully able to trust Chad, I would have used this time to talk about escape or working together to trap or trick Donovan, maybe even hurt or kill him, so we could escape with Dolores and the baby. But I couldn't be sure of him. Not after what he'd done to me at the observatory. So I just sat still and waited.

Craning my neck, I felt relieved to see Donovan finally returning. He approached the metal door of the block building. With his back between the bus and the door, I couldn't see how he opened it, but seconds later the door swung inward, and he disappeared inside.

This time, he wasn't gone long. He came back and pulled us out of the bus one at a time, Dolores and the baby first, me last. Getting out of the bus, the first thing I noticed was the rumble of a motor, a generator I realized, guessing that Donovan had fired it up when he'd first gotten out of the bus. When he shoved me through the doorway into the little building, I saw it was lit with fluorescent bulbs hanging from the ceiling. Chad and Dolores sat against the wall—Chad with his arms bound behind him, Dolores connected to Chad with leg shackles but with her hands still free so she could hold Kayla.

"Sit," Donovan said, pointing to a spot on the other side of Chad. As always, he had a gun in his hand, so there wasn't much point in arguing with him. A minute later, my ankles were bound to Chad's just like Dolores' were. We couldn't walk, not without cutting off Chad's feet first, but we were free to pass the baby back and forth by reaching across Chad's chest.

There was another door at the back of the building; this one looked bigger, more heavy duty, almost like the kind of thing you'd expect to see in a bank vault. It had an electronic lock that must have only just recently come back to life with the generator firing up. Now Donovan went to it and punched numbers on the keypad with his back to us. Seconds later, I heard a hiss and the door popped open.

I watched as Donovan pulled it open and then glanced back at us. He pointed up, to where the corners of the building met the roof; cameras were mounted in each corner.

"I'll be watching," he said. Then he stepped through the door and pulled it shut behind him with a loud click. A hiss followed and the sound of motors and other machinery. I could only guess that Donovan had built a chamber that would keep him safe from all sorts of contaminants. Other people had worried about energy pulses and weather catastrophes, earthquake clusters and even zombies. Donovan had worried about disease, and it looked as though he'd won the paranoia lottery, building a sealed chamber with enough filters and air purifiers to keep even the microscopic fungus spores from reaching in and claiming his miserable life.

I'd wondered on the bus how long Donovan could get by in his sealed suit. He'd have to run out of food or water sometime, would have to empty his bowels or—I hated the thought—change the diaper he must have been wearing. Now I saw he had his chance; he'd made it back to his lair and was now going to enact the next phase of his plan, whatever that might be. Collecting his little group of survivors had been the first step. I still couldn't guess what was next, but was determined not to find out if I could possibly help it.

It was hard to argue with the chains, though. And now the idea that I might somehow get away without Chad's help was entirely unimaginable. I'd have to take him into my confidence even if I didn't trust him entirely and doubted I ever would.

"We need to get out of here," I said, my voice just above a whisper.

"How?" He didn't hesitate in his response, didn't have to process what I'd said. That was good.

"I don't know. But we have to be on the lookout for anything."

Then he said something that made me wonder if I'd been reading him wrong, if it had been unfair not to trust him, to think such bad thoughts about him and his role in getting me captured. "If one goes, we all go. Agreed?"

Now it was me that hesitated. What he said made sense. It was what I would have wanted him to say. But could I really agree? If there was some total fluke, some once-in-a-lifetime breach in Donovan's plan, a person would be a fool not to take advantage of it even though the others might not be able to. I couldn't imagine what the chance might be, but I wondered if I'd be able to let it slip past if it turned out to be a chance for me alone.

"Agreed," I said regardless of my qualms.

The airlock on the vault door began hissing again, and then it clicked open. Donovan came into the room wearing a different suit than the one he'd had on our trip from Los Angeles, this one not quite as bulky. He wouldn't need to have all his food and water contained in the suit now that he was home; the new suit let him move around more freely.

"We may be here a while," he said, his voice muffled behind his mask. "And we may not. Here's the rules. There's an outhouse. You go when I say you go. We all go out there together, and then you're inside one at a time. There's food to last, and water. But you eat what I say, when I say. No arguments."

I hadn't eaten since being captured, so I was glad when he stopped talking and broke out a box of energy bars, giving two to each of us along with a small bottle of water.

He went out after that without another word.

* * * * *

All that really happened over the next few days was that Chad and I got the chance to talk. And I got the chance to trust him a little more. Donovan spent a lot of time down in his chamber, and after a while we couldn't help starting conversations even if we did worry that Donovan had the room bugged and was listening to our every word.

On the first afternoon, I was holding Kayla after she'd been fed and changed, and she was upset, just crying and crying. I rocked her a bit in my arms and tried humming a little tune, but it did no good. I didn't want to say anything, but I wondered if this was the first sign that she was sick, that her mother's fears had been well founded and that the baby hadn't inherited Alex's immunity to the fungus.

Chad may have been worrying about the same thing, but if he was it didn't show. "Try sticking your pinky in her mouth," he said.

I thought he was joking, like he was saying we should shove something in her mouth to force her to be quiet. I just gave him a weird look.

"Seriously. Try it," he said.

I shrugged, considered my finger for a moment, and hoping it wasn't too dirty, popped it in between Kayla's lips. She latched on instantly, and the feeling of those little lips and gums and her tongue on the tip of my finger made me want to laugh. But she'd stopped crying.

Giving Chad a look of amazement, I said, "How'd you know?"

He shrugged. "My girlfriend used to babysit a lot. She would do that when there wasn't a pacifier around. They just want something to suck on even if they're not hungry. Must make them feel secure or something."

I watched the baby going to work on my finger. "What was her name?" I asked.

He looked at the floor. "Becca."

I let the silence hang between us for a second or two, not sure if I should say more. "I'm sorry," I finally ventured. "Were you together a long time?"

"Six months. Before...you know."

"Yeah."

147

"What about you?" he asked. "Boyfriend?"

I shook my head. "No one serious."

There'd been little things, going to the movies, some kisses at parties, but no boy had really gotten to me. Jen and I used to talk endlessly about it, but it was really just something to giggle about. Not that my mother would have let me have a boyfriend at fourteen. Fifteen might have been a different thing. But my mom was gone, and the idea of boyfriends now…another silly thing from the gone world that we had spent so much time thinking about, using up our time on, when in the end it just didn't matter.

"It's hard to think about everyone who's gone," I said.

He just nodded and looked at the ground again. "I try not to. It was easier before, in the city."

I knew what he meant. "You had to keep busy," I said.

And then, at the same time, we both said, "No time to think."

Grim as the topic of our conversation was, we both smiled at that.

In another minute, the baby had fallen asleep, and I eased my finger from between her lips. "Thanks," I whispered, and he just nodded. I remember feeling glad that Kayla was out for a while, but also a little sad that Chad and I couldn't keep talking then, not wanting to wake her. It had been the first conversation where I'd really let my guard down, not worrying about whether I could trust him or not, and I wanted it to go on. Instead, I just leaned my head back against the wall and closed my eyes, wishing sleep would come as easily for me as it did for the newborn.

* * * * *

With Chad's and my bad Spanish and Dolores' bad English, we were able to figure out that she was from Oaxaca in Mexico. She and her husband had made several trips across the border over the years, sometimes going back to Mexico on their own when the work here dried up, and sometimes getting caught and sent back. She had lived in a tiny town in Mexico and had had three children, all boys. They'd all been delivered at home, from what I could tell, by a midwife, which probably accounted for Dolores knowing what to do when Alex was giving birth. She and her husband had both been working in a Hollywood hotel when the fungus hit; she'd been expecting to die like her husband and everyone else and still didn't know what was keeping her alive.

Arranged side by side the way we were, it soon became impossible not to begin feeling close to Chad and Dolores. Donovan had brought in thin mats before the end of the first day, and the three of us had eventually gone to sleep chained together. More than once, I woke up with my head half on Chad's arm, like it was a pillow, and I remember lying awake at night, my face inches from his as he slept, his steady breaths blowing on my cheek.

After the first day, Donovan let Chad have his hands loose like Dolores and I did, but he never tried anything, never let his hands slip or wander, never even suggested that there should be something between us. I think about that now, but at the time I wasn't even worried about it. Romance was off the radar; the idea of getting free again crowded everything else out of my mind.

Actually, the possibility of escaping was just about all we talked about, and when we weren't whispering our way through some ridiculous and unworkable plan, I worked at the puzzle of our freedom on my own, hoping for an opportunity but not seeing any, not anywhere. I kept thinking about the generator and how Donovan must have been stockpiling gasoline to keep it running. If we could find where he stored it, we might be able to start a fire. Or if we could come up with another way to destroy the generator, then Donovan would only be able to last so long. We would just need to convince him we didn't deserve to die in the mean time. And then there was the question of how we could get to the gas or the generator in the first place, chained together and watched the way we were.

Chad and I also spent time talking about Donovan's plans for us, whether or not he was really crazy, and what he'd do once he realized his plans weren't going to come to anything. On the one hand, it seemed possible that he'd get tired of keeping us and just let us go, but then again it wasn't hard to imagine him making good on his threats and just shooting us all out of frustration before killing himself. His filters wouldn't last forever; the time would come when he'd be exposed to whatever spores were still around, and that would be it. Would he be content to just let us outlive him? I doubted it. He still seemed too angry for that.

On the third day, he came out of his chamber with an iPhone in his hand, and for a second I had the absurd thought that he'd gotten a call. He walked up to me and leaned over.

"I want to record your voice. Say your name and a few details about yourself. Say you're a survivor of the plague, that you're immune, and that I've got you, that I'll kill you if someone doesn't come and make a deal with me. Got it?"

I didn't get it, but I nodded anyway.

He pushed a button on the app he had open and held the phone out to me. I could see it was recording. I swallowed and said, "My name is Scarlett Fisher. I'm fifteen. I lived in Pasadena before...before the plague, the fungus, whatever it was. I'm immune. Everyone I know died. Now I'm here, with Donovan. He's got me and three other people, including a newborn baby." I hesitated, looked at the cold eyes behind the clear plastic shield of Donovan's suit, and said, "He's going to kill us if someone doesn't make a deal with him."

He clicked off the recording, held the phone close to his head, and played it back. Then he went to Chad and had him do the same thing. He didn't bother with Dolores, had really made no effort to communicate with her the whole time we'd been held here. He just played Chad's recording back and then turned back to the door into his chamber. I heard him say something that sounded like, "Now they'll believe me." And then he was gone again.

"He's crazy," I said to Chad when the airlock had shut again with its ominous hiss.

"I know. But what do we do about it? He's always got his gun. And we're always chained up."

The rest of that day, I forced myself to think about escape and nothing else. When my mind wandered, taking me into memories or thoughts of other places, I forced it back to the problem at hand. By nighttime, I had gotten nowhere. Every possibility seemed like a dead end. Convinced that Donovan was bound to lose what was left of his mind, though, I didn't let myself give up, not wanting to be around when the shooting started.

Our nightly trip to the outhouse came around. Donovan let us go maybe four times a day, with the last trip being sometime after the sun had gone down. As always, he got us on our feet, fastened manacles on our wrists, and then linked the chains to others that went between our legs to connect to the wrists of the person behind us. The chains were slack, so whoever held Kayla wouldn't have a problem and also so we'd be able to take care of our business in the blue plastic outhouse. Out we marched in a little line with Donovan at our backs, a black handgun pointed at us as we crossed the tall dry grass. I remember how we'd hear crickets chirping and toads distantly croaking when we'd come out of the bunker and how they'd all stop when we started tromping through the grass, one or two starting up again by the time we had all finished.

I held Kayla as we walked this time. Fixated as I was on escape, I kept looking this way and that as we made our way to the outhouse. It was dark, but the moon was up, and Donovan's property at night seemed bigger than in the light of day, the fence more distant, the ground we'd need to cover more imposing. And yet, I told myself, if we were going to get away, it was most likely going to be at night. And that meant escaping during one of these evening outhouse runs. So I tried keeping an eye out for any details, anything Donovan might have missed in setting up his little prison for us, any weakness in his plan. None came to me.

When it was my turn in the outhouse, I passed Kayla to Dolores and let Donovan take my chain out of the loop that held us together. Then I went in and sat down, locking the door out of habit. No one was going to walk in on me, so there wasn't much point in twisting the little lock that made the sign on the outside switch from "Vacant" to "Occupied." Still, I did it anyway and then thought about that as I'd thought about everything else related to our captivity that day. The locking mechanism on the door was just about the only metal part of the outhouse, and it was secure in its fashion, having been meant to provide a little bit of privacy at carnivals and construction sites, but not high security at any rate. Still, it got me thinking.

When we were finished and back in the bunker, Donovan turned the lights out, and we lay down on our mats, still chained together at the ankles as we'd been since the first day.

"I think I have an idea," I whispered to Chad once the door had sealed on Donovan's airlock.

"What is it?"

"Do you think he'll really shoot one of us if there's trouble?"

"That's your idea?"

"No! Just…do you think he means it?"

"He went to a lot of trouble to catch us. I don't think he'd kill one of us if another one got away. But that doesn't mean he wouldn't hurt us."

"Yeah." The more unstable Donovan really was, the more bent he was on controlling and using us, the riskier my plan seemed. Still, it was all I had come up with. "I think we can use the outhouse," I said after a moment's thought.

"How?"

"I'll say I'm sick, can't come out when he says it's time. He'll probably threaten to shoot somebody like he did when we were on the bus."

"What then?"

"*Que pasa?*" Dolores whispered.

I didn't know how to explain to her what we were talking about. "*Nada*," I lied. "*Hablar mañana.*" I was pretty sure that wasn't correct, but I wanted her to understand I'd tell her about it tomorrow. She must have gotten the message, as she didn't press the issue.

"You watch Donovan," I continued to Chad. "He'll get up close to the door, maybe even try pulling at the handle. When he gets close, you signal me, and I'll push the door open hard. With luck, I can knock him off balance, maybe even get him in the face with it. You have to be ready to jump on him. We get the gun away, knock him out, get the keys, and we're gone."

Silence lay between us for several seconds. "You're counting on luck an awful lot," Chad finally whispered.

"It can work."

"And if it doesn't?"

"Then he probably smacks me in the face and maybe leaves me tied up alone somewhere, but that's it."

"And we're screwed," he said.

"And we're screwed if we don't try something. You got a better idea?"

"Wait for him to make a mistake."

"Does he seem like the kind of guy who's going to make a mistake?" I asked.

"Everybody makes mistakes."

He was right about that; I knew that too well.

"Even so," I said, "I don't think we can afford to wait. Whatever his scheme is, it's not going to work out. I don't think we should still be here when he figures that out."

Another long silence followed. Finally, he said, "So how do I signal you to hit him with the door?"

I wanted to sit up and say, "You'll do it?" but I restrained myself, just pausing for a breath before whispering, "What if you just shout my name? Like you're trying to get me to cooperate with him?"

He thought about it. "Could work," he said after a few seconds. "Tell me if you think of something better."

* * * * *

I found it difficult the next day not to keep checking in with Chad to go over the plan a few more times before nightfall. But I didn't want Donovan to get suspicious; even if he was just watching us on the monitors inside his sealed chamber, there was a good chance he'd know we weren't just making small talk. Even Dolores had known something was up just from the tone of our whispers. I imagined Donovan getting suspicious from our body language or facial expressions. I also wanted to keep Dolores in the dark as I knew I couldn't adequately explain the plan in my lousy Spanish, nor could I persuade her to go along with it if she did understand and tried to talk me out of it. Her agitation would be another red flag for Donovan.

So I kept quiet about it, trying to give Chad meaningful looks throughout the day just to confirm our solidarity. If I was going to fake being sick tonight and risk Donovan's wrath, I wanted to be sure it was a risk worth taking, one that Chad was going to back me up on. But when I did catch his eye, he didn't say or do anything to show that he knew what I was getting at, let alone that he was still onboard with the plan. He seemed distant throughout the whole day, and I wondered more than once if I'd made a mistake taking him into my confidence.

When I couldn't take the worry any longer, I whispered, "Are you having second thoughts?"

"Sort of," he admitted. "But only with part of it."

We were sitting side by side on our mats. Dolores dozed on Chad's other side, the baby asleep beside her in an empty dresser drawer that Donovan had brought in for us to use as a bassinet.

When I raised an eyebrow, Chad said, "I should be the one inside the outhouse. I can hit him harder with the door."

I thought about it for a few seconds, weighing the differences in the plan.

154

"I don't know," I said. "I think I could hit him pretty hard from inside. But if it was you inside, and he didn't go down…I might have a tough time getting him off balance outside."

"I don't think you'd need to," he said.

He sounded so sure of himself, almost cocky, not the way he usually sounded.

"That's not what you're worried about," I said after a few more seconds.

Chad looked at me quickly, and then looked away.

"If it goes wrong," I said, "and it's you in the outhouse, then it's you who's going to get punished. Right? Even if it just looks like I'm following your lead outside? That's what you're worried about?"

His silence was answer enough.

I shook my head. "Don't worry about me, Chad. If it goes wrong, it's bound to get ugly for both of us. But chances are it won't go wrong if it's me inside and you out. Odds are way better that way than the other."

"You think?"

"Don't you? Who's got a better shot at tackling Donovan once he's off balance?"

He nodded. "I guess I do."

I let that sink in for a few seconds. "We're in this together. Right?"

He nodded again.

"If we're worried about anything, then let's worry about protecting Dolores and the baby, okay?"

"Okay."

I wished we could shake on it to seal the deal, but it would have been completely stupid to do something like that with Donovan's cameras trained on us. It would have been like shouting, "Hey! We're conspiring here!" So instead, we traded nods, and that was that.

The rest of the afternoon and evening just crawled by. We didn't talk any more about our plans, and we hadn't talked at all about what we were going to do if we succeeded, so I filled the time by imagining the kinds of things we'd need to gather once we made it to Riverside and what we'd do after that. It was hard not to let my nerves get the better of me, hard not to feel jumpy and tense. I forced myself to eat the canned beans and fruit Donovan handed out, but my stomach felt like a tight little ball, so when I was done eating I just leaned my head back against the wall and closed my eyes, just willing the time to pass and steeling myself for the moment when I'd shut the outhouse door.

Finally, it was time. Donovan's airlock hissed open, and he came out in his hazard suit with the gun that may as well have been joined surgically to his hand. Out we went, as always with the length of chain joining each of our manacles, passing between our legs to the person behind us. It was me in front, then Chad, then Dolores, who held Kayla. Donovan followed, always watching.

I let out a little cough as we crossed the tall, dry grass between the bunker and the outhouse, raising my hand to my mouth as I did. This pulled taut the chain between Chad and me, rubbing uncomfortably between my legs. I held it there for a second, and then gave it two quick tugs.

I waited for Chad to tug back, waited for anything, any signal from him that he was still with me and ready to go.

Nothing.

My heart sank, and I began lowering my hands, taking some of the tension out of the chain. And then it jerked, just the littlest bit. And again.

Two tugs back.

It was hard not to smile as I lowered my hands all the way and let the chain go slack.

I stopped in front of the outhouse door and waited for Donovan to unlock the chain connecting me to Chad. He kept the keys in a Velcro pocket, and as he pulled the pocket open, I said, "Please hurry. I don't feel so good."

He just looked at me, no sympathy in his eyes, no concern— only a you've-got-to-be-kidding stare, as if my problems couldn't compare to his in the tiniest way and my asking him to hurry was the height of arrogance. I found myself hoping his plastic facemask would crack when I hit him with the door; then he'd know what real problems were.

Once he had me unchained, but still with my hands loosely manacled in front of me, I bolted into the outhouse and slammed the door shut, making sure to lock it. I crouched beside the door and gave a few grunts and moans, hoping they sounded like I was in some distress. Then I stayed quiet, just listening.

Come on, I thought. *Get impatient with me.*

It didn't take long. I'd been inside only a little longer than normal when there came a tap on the side of the outhouse. "Come on," came the muffled command.

Not that side, I thought. *By the door! Stand by the door!*

"Sick," I said, trying to sound like I had terrible cramps and could barely get the word out.

"I'm not gonna stand out here all night. You can get sick in the grass while the others go in. Come on out."

I let out a little moan. "I can't," I gasped.

He pounded harder on the plastic wall, and a second later I felt the door move just a little as he pulled at the handle, probably frustrated that he hadn't thought to remove the lock. If my plan didn't work, this would be the last time any of us would be locking the door.

Now? I thought, waiting for the signal from Chad. Was Donovan standing close enough to the door for me to have any hope of doing some damage with it? Or had he reached for the handle from his position beside the outhouse? *Come on, Chad*, I thought. *Come on.*

"I'm gonna hurt somebody out here if you're not out in ten seconds," Donovan said, his voice louder but still coming from the side, not in front of the door.

"I think I need help," I moaned.

I could imagine the look of disgust on his face as he wondered what kind of help I could possibly need.

"Then unlock the damn door," he shouted.

Okay, I thought. *Unlock it now and wait for Chad.*

I reached my hand to the plastic knob that would unlock the door, but before I reached it, I heard Donovan say, "What the hell?" He no longer sounded angry, more surprised, almost awed.

Then his voice was farther way. "We'll get her in a minute. Come on."

And then Chad's voice. "Scarlett?" he called. He sounded farther away than he should have been, and a little scared. Then again, "Scarlett!" but from a greater distance still.

What the heck? I wondered, filled with frustration. It had almost worked. Why had Donovan taken the others away from the outhouse? And just when I'd been about to whack him with the door? Now there'd be no way to try this again. He'd break the lock off the door the next chance he got; he might even take the whole door off its hinges.

I crouched there, waiting, wondering, my heart pounding. I wanted a sign, anything. *What do I do?*

I pressed my ear to the door. Nothing.

Slowly, I twisted the lock so the sign outside now read "Vacant." Then I just waited a few seconds. Maybe Donovan had backed away and was waiting for this. Maybe now he'd pounce.

But I caught no signs of life through the door, no signal from Chad.

Carefully, slowly, I pushed the door open, just a crack. Again, there was no sign from outside that anyone was around to notice. So I pushed it farther and poked my head out.

I was alone. The door faced away from the bunker, so I couldn't see what was going on. All I knew for certain was that I'd been left alone. I could run for it and try to hop the fence with my manacled hands. I remembered the promise Chad had extracted from me: If one of us goes, we all go. But should I keep the promise? If I didn't take this chance, another would never come. Chad would hate me for it, but if I got away, maybe I could find a way to come back for the others.

It's funny how you don't notice some things when your mind is occupied with something else. I think that's especially true if you're excited about whatever is running through your head. That was me as I pushed the door open the rest of the way and carefully stepped out, my mind racing with the possibilities beyond Donovan's fence. I'd need to find a car with the keys in it, probably a dead person behind the wheel. And then I'd need to drive away from here before Donovan had a chance to catch my trail in his bus. A hardware store in Riverside should have something for me to cut the chain between my wrists, and then I'd look for military surplus and find a way to rescue Chad and Dolores and Kayla.

So I was completely taken aback when I peeked around the side of the outhouse, wondering what had drawn Donovan back to the bunker and hoping that, whatever it was, it would still be a strong enough distraction to keep him from noticing my flight to the fence. All I saw was Donovan standing in the circle of light that surrounded the bunker, a silhouette against the night beyond. He must have forced Chad and Dolores back into the bunker while I'd been pressed against the outhouse door trying to figure out what was going on.

Then I saw what he was looking at—and instantly realized I'd been hearing it for several seconds without even realizing it, its distant rhythm almost indistinguishable from the hum of the generator but getting louder now.

There was a light in the sky, and it was moving.

It was coming in low from the north and getting lower still. The closer it got, the more its sound broke from the hum of the generator, and I could hear it for what it was. Seconds later I had dropped to the ground, wanting to hide in the grass that did almost nothing to conceal me from the sweeping light of the helicopter as it got closer and closer.

Had it not been for the dirt digging into my chin as I pressed myself onto the ground, or the dust in my eyes from the artificial wind the rotors created, I might have thought it was all a dream. There were no more helicopters flying in this world, no more pilots to fly them. There were no more people besides me and Chad, Dolores and Kayla and Donovan. They were all dead. This couldn't be happening.

But it was.

The helicopter set down in the wide expanse of grass and gravel that separated the bunker from the fence and the road beyond. Even in the dark, I could see that it was a military helicopter, big and green with white numbers stenciled on the side.

The army! I thought. How perfect that they'd come to rescue us, how perfect that they'd found a way to survive. Somehow, the military's scientists had worked it all out, and we were saved. They were probably going around plucking up little pockets of survivors all over the country. How they'd found us, I couldn't guess at first, but then I remembered Donovan going on about his plans. They'd actually worked. The ham radio antenna had done its job.

I watched as a big door on the helicopter's side slid open. I saw some movement and then three soldiers hopped out onto the ground. They wore the same kind of suits as Donovan, but looking even more heavy duty than his, if that was possible.

Contrary to what I'd been hoping, the soldiers weren't immune to the disease. They weren't cured. They hadn't been inoculated or otherwise protected. They'd survived the same way as Donovan, by shutting themselves off from the contaminant.

I watched as they approached Donovan, guns pointed at him. They stopped about ten feet from him. Probably following shouted orders that I couldn't hear, Donovan dropped to his knees.

One soldier approached him while the other stayed back, his gun still trained on Donovan. The first soldier patted Donovan down, eventually making him lie face down in the dirt; then he waved toward the helicopter, and four other soldiers came out, all wearing the same type of suit.

They may as well have pointed their guns at me. I didn't move. I couldn't. I wanted to jump and shout my thanks to them for rescuing us, but at the same time I was too scared. What if this was a case of "out of the frying pan and into the fire"? I'd made mistake after mistake since the plague had struck. The last big one had been to put those lanterns out on the wall of the observation deck in the Hollywood Hills, so sure had I been that any other survivor who saw them would be thrilled to find another person alive, imagining us teaming up and going on together, maybe all the way to Australia. I'd been wrong that time, and wrong and wrong and wrong before with countless things I'd only lucked my way through. This time, I was going to wait and see.

Seconds later, two of the soldiers came out of the bunker with Chad and Dolores between them. They were still chained together, and now the soldier guarding Donovan found the key ring fastened to his suit, unclipped it, and tossed it to one of the others. Dolores held the baby, and after she and Chad had been released from their chains, another soldier came out of the bunker carrying bags of the baby supplies we'd brought on the bus. Then the fourth came out carrying more. Along with my former fellow captives, the four soldiers moved toward the helicopter, seeming to shepherd Chad and Dolores along, gently guiding them with pointed hands, not pointed guns.

Chad got inside the helicopter first, turning to take Kayla from Dolores, who followed quickly. Then the two soldiers with the baby supplies climbed inside. The first soldier, who hadn't moved since Donovan dropped to the ground, came forward now and seemed to be consulting with the two who had just come out of the bunker. They appeared to talk for a moment, and then all three turned and looked around the compound, each clicking on a bright flashlight mounted to his helmet.

They're looking for me, I thought. They'd heard the recording Donovan had made of my voice. Chad had probably confirmed to them that there was one more survivor, had probably told the soldiers I was out here somewhere.

After a few seconds of scanning the compound, two of the soldiers turned toward the helicopter.

They're leaving without me, I thought, and a stream of images flooded my brain: me alone in this compound, me alone trying to get back to the observatory, me alone foraging for food in lonesome houses filled with desiccated corpses, me alone remembering conversations with Chad and wishing I could see him again and knowing I never could. Me alone, just alone.

And I sprang from my hiding place in the grass, feebly shouting, "I'm here!" as though my little voice could penetrate the hazard suits and equipment and the spinning rotors.

And in the same instant there was a flash and a boom as the soldier who'd been guarding Donovan put a bullet in his head.

I just stood there in disbelief. One of the soldiers must have seen a flash of movement, as he quickly focused his light on me, and there I was—revealed like a flushed rabbit and staring just as defenselessly into the light, watching as the soldier who'd killed Donovan stepped away from the body and wishing that I'd stayed down for just a second longer, knowing now that these weren't saviors, that these weren't good men. Yes, we were saved from Donovan, but what worse treatment did we have to look forward to now?

There was nothing for it. I could have run, but they'd have caught me, or shot me. I knew they wouldn't ask me politely to stop. The soldiers were all business.

Now the one who'd shone his light on me began walking slowly away from the helicopter and Donovan's body. With one hand he waved me toward him encouragingly, but with the other he still held his rifle; though it pointed at the ground, I knew it would be whipped up and aimed at me in half a second if I made any kind of unwanted movement.

What could I do? I started walking toward him, shaking as I went. There was some comfort in knowing they already had Chad in the helicopter. Whatever awaited me now that the soldiers had me, I wouldn't have to endure it alone.

When the soldier and I got within six feet of each other, he held up a hand for me to stop. I did. Then he motioned for me to turn around. Again, I complied. Then I felt his gloved hand patting me down. He did it quickly but thoroughly, running his hand down my sides, my legs; I didn't like it and was glad when he stopped. Next, I felt his hand on my shoulder, gently turning me.

He was close enough for me to see his face through the plastic mask and breathing apparatus of his suit. He was young, maybe twenty. But he looked hard, too, and kind of edgy—not like he was scared right now, not scared of me, but more like he'd been scared for a long time, like it had become his normal mode of operating, and he wasn't handling it well. I was glad I hadn't opted to run when he started toward me.

"Are you Scarlett?" he asked, his voice as muffled as Donovan's had been.

I nodded.

"Come on. You're safe now."

I hesitated a second, looking at those wide eyes beyond the plastic, and then started walking toward the helicopter. I wanted to ask him what "safe" even meant anymore, where they were taking us, why they'd killed Donovan, but I didn't ask anything. I couldn't, really. It would have meant turning back and looking into his eyes. It wasn't just that I was scared of him. I *was*, of course, but it was more than that. I was scared that maybe I looked the same way after all I'd been through; if I didn't look at him, the fear of what all this had done to me wouldn't be so strong. So I kept walking, aware of him and his gun and his eyes every step along the way, and wanting nothing more than to see a different set of eyes when I got inside the helicopter to find Chad waiting for me.

CHAPTER ELEVEN

I don't know exactly how long we were in the air—probably more than hour, but less than two. The soldiers had put me into a hard seat next to Chad and told me to buckle in with a heavy harness, and then we'd lifted off. I was next to a window, but could see only dark sky when I looked out. If I wanted to look toward the ground, I had to stretch against the harness and lean closer to the window, but it was just slightly less darkness, the land lit up just a bit by the half moon. I couldn't really make anything out until we crossed the mountains that separate the Los Angeles area from the high desert that stretches to Las Vegas and beyond. I'd made that trip a couple times before with my mom and sister on getaway weekends that seemed a thousand years ago.

When not trying to look outside, I tried shutting my eyes, just wanting the flight to be over. None of the soldiers had said a word to us since we'd gotten onto the helicopter. When I'd asked where they were taking us, having to raise my voice above the engine and the rotors, they'd just ignored me. For all I knew, we were going as far as Colorado or Washington, D.C.—as far as a helicopter could go on whatever fuel it had. And while I kept telling myself this could all turn out just fine, that survivors like Chad and Dolores and Kayla and me would be treated well, I still felt scared. I couldn't forget how they'd killed Donovan. And I still remembered the angry look on that woman's face when I'd fled my burning neighborhood; I'd been getting out, and she hadn't. Her jealousy hadn't made any sense, but then again emotions aren't logical. While these soldiers were maybe supposed to be taking care of us, I wouldn't have been surprised to find them angry and frustrated at having to deal with us, all the while questioning why we didn't need filters and masks to survive while they did. *Why me? Why not me?* How much suffering had grown out of people asking those two questions when things had gone wrong for them and right for someone else?

Kayla cried on and off throughout the trip; she was maybe hungry or maybe wet. There was no way to know and no opportunity to mix formula or dig through her supplies to find diapers. Dolores just held her, rocking and cooing and singing Mexican lullabies that I wished I understood. It seemed to help only a little.

Between the noise of the helicopter and the baby crying, it was just about impossible to say anything to Chad without raising my voice, even though he sat right next to me. I didn't have anything super important to say to him, just wished I could make small talk to help the time go by, and since I didn't want that kind of thing broadcast to the whole cabin, I kept quiet. At one point, though, as I sat there with my eyes closed, I felt his arm brush against mine— our seats were right up against each other, and they weren't that roomy. He probably hadn't meant to nudge me, was just moving his arm to stay comfortable. My reaction was automatic; I moved my arm, too. Not away, but toward. And a second later, we were holding hands.

I felt a little tingle as he squeezed my hand and I squeezed back. *We're going to get through this*, I thought. *We're going to get through it together.* I still had my worries about our destination and the soldiers' intentions, but they eased under the pressure of Chad's fingers intertwined with mine.

Sometime after that, I remembered my backpack with the photo of my family inside. It was still in Donovan's bunker, sitting in a corner. Now it would sit there forever, just gathering dust. I pictured spiders crawling on it and mice tearing at the fabric for nesting material and my photo inside, zipped up in darkness. I felt terrible about having lost it, and I squeezed Chad's hand a bit harder without thinking about it. He squeezed back, but it didn't really help. I let out a couple of big sighs and tried to think of something else.

When I felt the helicopter begin its descent, I opened my eyes, looking first at Chad and then toward the window. Chad gave me half a smile, both reassuring and worried, and I knew he was having the same thoughts as me: we didn't know what the soldiers had planned for us, but it looked like we were going to find out pretty quickly, and neither one of us was feeling optimistic. Out the window, all was darkness, and when I looked down, the view revealed nothing more than endless desert, barely lit by the moon. I couldn't see lights or a building or even a road; what we descended toward was a mystery.

We were almost on the ground before I could really see anything—some lights not far in front of us. I couldn't actually see the lights through my limited view out the window, could just tell we were heading toward something brighter. And a few seconds later the lights revealed a fence that we passed over. Contained within were several military vehicles and then small buildings clustered around a much bigger building. It was low to the ground but vast, spreading out past my line of sight. In a few seconds, I saw we were above a large helipad on top of the building where other soldiers stood waiting to receive us.

"Here we go," I said, mostly to myself. I squeezed Chad's hand again and then let go, flexing my fingers and pushing myself up in the seat, ready to unstrap myself once we were down.

The soldiers led us out one at a time—Dolores and the baby first, me last. They didn't point their guns, waving us along with one hand while holding their weapons at their sides. It wasn't threatening, but it also wasn't reassuring. I'd feel better when I could deal with someone not armed; I doubted I'd have that chance any time soon, however.

Three other helicopters rested on the helipad, and I could see a few other soldiers all watching intently as we filed across the open space toward a doorway. All the soldiers wore the same full-body suits as the ones who'd taken us from Donovan's compound—no immunity here—and though I couldn't see their faces through the light reflected off their face masks, I could tell that each had his head turned to watch Chad and Dolores and me walk toward the door.

A soldier led us, and the rest flanked us. When we reached the doorway, the leader punched a code into a keypad and the lock clicked. He twisted at the big metal handle, and we went inside. It was all very industrial: gray walls and gray tile floor, fluorescent bulbs in the ceiling. We were in a small room with nothing much there except a set of elevator doors. The soldier punched the call button, and a few seconds later the doors slid open.

We crowded in. I was right next to Chad, pressed close, and I took his hand again. It made me feel better, but only a little bit. The soldier hit a button and the elevator dropped; there was no digital display to show how many stories we went down, but it couldn't have been too far. Several seconds later, we slowed to a stop.

When the doors opened, it was to more gray walls and floor. The only thing before us was another set of doors. These were big and metal, painted black and yellow, and in their center were the words "Warning: Biohazard" and under that "Authorized Personnel Only." The soldier who'd called the elevator punched a code into another keypad, and the doors slid open with a hiss much louder than the door into Donovan's chamber. Inside was a small room with another set of doors on the other side. The soldier motioned us but didn't follow.

As soon as the four of us were inside, the doors closed with a loud click and then another hiss. Immediately, the doors behind us opened, and we turned to find a brightly lit corridor with ceiling, floor, and walls all painted the same dull gray. Two people stood before us: another soldier with a pistol in his hand, and a woman who I didn't think was a soldier. Both wore the same white biohazard suits as the soldiers we'd already seen, but rather than carry a gun, the woman held a clipboard. She wasn't very tall, and I could see she wore glasses under her facemask. Her skin was dark, and I would have guessed she was Indian or Pakistani. When she smiled at us, I told myself it looked like she'd been practicing.

"Good evening," she said. Her voice was muffled but not as much as Donovan's had been—better technology, I guessed. "I am Dr. Sharma. I trust the rescue went well?"

Chad and I exchanged glances, not sure how to respond. Sure, the rescue had gone well, if you didn't count the murder outside the bunker and the lack of all explanation on the part of the soldiers. I opted to nod meekly, and I think Chad did the same.

"Good," she said. Glancing at her clipboard, she said, "So we have Scarlett and Chad and Dolores. The baby?"

"Kayla," I said.

She nodded and made a note.

"The mother?"

I guess it was obvious that neither Dolores nor I had given birth recently.

"She died," I said. And when Dr. Sharma looked up from her clipboard and gave me a questioning look, I added, "In childbirth."

Another nod and another note. Then she said, "You're in a military facility that was designed in part to study infectious disease, germ warfare, chemical warfare and other biohazards. We're going to do our best to make you comfortable here, but our primary mission is to find a cure for the F2 infection that's just about wiped us out. Can I count on your cooperation?"

"Sure," Chad said, a little hesitantly.

"Yes," I added, not sure I meant it. I was all for helping find a cure, but my cooperation was going to depend on just what they wanted of me. Medical experiments weren't high on my list of favorite activities.

"Wonderful." Then she took a couple of steps and put herself in front of Dolores, immediately switching to what sounded like flawless Spanish. I heard her say her name, and was able to pick out a couple of other words, but the doctor rattled off her Spanish so quickly that I got lost almost right away. Dolores nodded as Dr. Sharma spoke, and then she said, "*Sí.*"

And that was that.

With the soldier following us, the doctor led the way along the corridor, past a door marked "1", stopping in front of another marked "2". She turned to the door. "Chad?" she said. "If you would…"

He stood there for a second, glancing first at me and then back to the doctor. "What about them?" he asked, not giving any hint that he was ready to move, not doing anything to show that he was ready to make good on his promise of cooperation.

The doctor smiled behind her mask. I think it was supposed to be reassuring, but it just looked condescending instead, as though she really didn't have time for the little teenager and his chivalry. "Your companions will be fine, all in safe accommodations identical to yours." She waved a hand toward the door, the smile on the verge of burning out like an old light bulb ready to pop.

I thought about the soldier behind us, not sure of where Chad's mind was going but ready to follow his lead if he decided against cooperating. Holding my whole body tense in anticipation, I almost jumped when Chad's hand found mine again. He squeezed my fingers—not hard and determined and readying me to fight, but tenderly, a quick goodbye. A second later, he let go, and we looked at each other, just a quick glance. Then he was gone, passing through the door after Dr. Sharma had punched a code into its keypad.

As soon as the door had shut, we moved on, turning a corner at the end of the hallway. Now the doctor led the way down a long, doorless corridor, our footsteps echoing as we walked. I told myself to pay attention to the route we took in case I needed to find my way out again, but there were no landmarks, and I feared this might be a challenging maze to run if it came to that.

We had reached the end of the corridor and now turned right. Immediately, I saw a door marked "3" and we stopped in front of it. The doctor began speaking Spanish to Dolores, who nodded and said "*Sí.*" I tried to watch the doctor as she input the code for the door, but all I saw were the numbers 5 and 3. She punched others, but the angle of her hand kept me from being sure of what they were. The door popped open and then Dolores was passing through just like Chad had done. She gave me a quick, uncertain smile before going.

"She'll have things for the baby in there?" I asked.

The doctor flashed her condescending smile again. "We'll take care of everything," she said and began walking again.

I knew there would be a door marked "4" coming up and that I'd have to go through it. Unsure of who or what I'd be dealing with on the other side made me nervous, and I wondered how long it would be before I saw Dr. Sharma again. With a million questions in my head but no real certainty about whether I should ask any of them, I managed to blurt out, "Why did they kill Donovan?"

"You would have preferred your kidnapper be shown mercy?"

"I just...there's so few people now."

"And killing one seems a waste of precious resources?"

"I suppose," I said.

"What you say makes sense from a scientific standpoint. If our species is to survive and prosper again, we need to consider maintaining genetic diversity. Every set of genes is thus of value. However, from a tactical standpoint, we also need to consider the type of person who has survived—someone who will help us make the most of our limited resources, or someone who will place a drain on them. Your Mr. Donovan already placed a considerable drain on our resources by insisting we come to him, by insisting that we *rescue* him rather than volunteering to bring the survivors he'd found to *us*. The helicopter, the fuel, the manpower...all were wasted meeting his demands. Not to mention the future drain on resources needed to guard the man if we had let him live, considering his propensity for following his own rules rather than those of society."

As I'd thought, the door marked "4" was on our left now, and the doctor stopped in front of it, turning to face me. "You could have just left him there," I said.

"He thought of you as his possessions. We had to weigh the risk that he would try following you to our facility," she said. "We haven't the time or the resources for dealing with such people now. And, frankly, we don't have the patience. Mr. Donovan took a risk, an exploitative and self-serving one." She punched her code into the keypad on the door. This time I couldn't see the numbers at all because of the way we were standing. I heard the same click I'd heard before. "It didn't pay off for him. For you, though, and your friends...for us here trying to understand what happened with F2, it may well have turned out to be something of a gift Mr. Donovan gave us. Will you step through, please?"

I didn't say anything, didn't even nod, just stepped through like she'd asked, wondering if this was the beginning of blind obedience. It wouldn't do to be a loose cannon, not when they had all the guns and all the codes for the locks.

The room was dark, but fluorescent lights clicked on the moment I passed the threshold. *Motion detector*, I thought as the door shut behind me. I turned at the sound, but it was too late.

Sharma hadn't said another word, just locked the door once she'd gotten me inside.

I let out a big breath, telling myself to relax.

"Please enter," said a computerized voice. It sounded slightly female.

I ignored the invitation, my feet planted right beside the door as I took everything in. The room was maybe twenty feet long by ten wide, all painted and tiled the same gray as the corridor outside. Directly across from me was a row of vertical window shades, all closed, that started about four feet up from the floor. A small table and a single chair were in the middle of the room, and there was a small bed along one wall. Toward the back of the room, not far from the entrance I was peeking out of, there was a partition about six feet high, and behind it a toilet, sink and shower stall.

"Home sweet home," I said.

"Please enter," the computer repeated in the same almost friendly tone. I wondered if it would change if I made it repeat a third time, but didn't wonder that much. I entered.

"Please shower and deposit your soiled clothes in the bin marked *Waste*," the computer immediately said. "You will find fresh clothes in the supply closet."

Again I looked around the room, trying to see a motion detector or camera. There was nothing, at least not anything obvious to me. Still, the computer had needed some confirmation that I was now in the room, or else it wouldn't have given the new command. That was what it was doing, I told myself, *commanding* even if the commands came in the politest tones.

Not ready to rock the boat yet, I followed orders—if a bit tentatively. The supply closet was at the far left end of the back wall, and inside were plastic cups and plates, toilet paper and several other things for hygiene, and a change of clothes sealed in a plastic bag. These I examined quickly—stiff camouflage pants, a khaki t-shirt, socks, underwear, and a sports bra. Everything looked a little big for me, but probably close enough to fit reasonably well.

I felt uncomfortable taking my clothes off, even behind the shower partition, and kept looking at the corners where the walls met the ceiling to try and spot a hidden camera. I couldn't shake the thought that someone was watching me undress—maybe Dr. Sharma, maybe someone else. I finally decided the best thing would be to get it over with as fast as possible, and so finished getting out of my clothes. I found two towels on a shelf and wrapped one around myself as I gathered my clothes.

A drawer built into the wall had a handle with the word "Waste" on it. It hinged open to reveal a trash chute. I checked the pockets of the jeans I'd worn since being taken from the observatory and then dumped them into the chute, not exactly sorry to see them go. Then I showered as quickly as I could—the first time since the solar house in Hollywood—before drying off and getting dressed.

Patting my hair dry with one of the towels, I thought about cutting it short. That would have been the practical thing days ago, but I hadn't thought about it—just kept tying it into a bun or fixing a ponytail. It would be good to be done with it. Curious, I went to the supply cabinet again to see if they'd given my scissors or even a sharp knife, but there was nothing. I thought of prison movies I'd seen; just like in those scenarios, my keepers didn't want any suicides, so they'd left me nothing sharp. Not only were there no shoelaces for me to strangle myself with, but there weren't even shoes. It was a good thing I didn't want to kill myself, just my hair.

On the opposite wall was the row of windows, still hidden behind vertical blinds. A control panel was to my left, and at intervals along the windowed wall I saw three boxes built into the wall. Investigating, I saw they were metal and had hinged tops, but they were tightly sealed and didn't even have an edge I could grip to try and pull one open.

The wall panel controlled the blinds and lights, and these I could manipulate, dimming the lights for sleeping, opening and closing the blinds. When I punched the "Open" button, the slats shifted sideways, giving me a look out the windows.

I looked out into another corridor, this one painted and tiled in bright white, almost blinding. Across from me was another set of windows and closed blinds, and above them was a red number 1. *Who's in there?* I wondered. *Someone else they caught?*

Diagonally across from my chamber, the blinds slid open below a red number 2, and Chad looked out at me. We smiled at each other and waved feebly. I felt so glad to see him there. It would have been awful to be completely alone. This wasn't much better, but seeing him was a huge help. He touched a button on his panel, and I was afraid he was closing his blinds again, but his command sent the slats sliding down their rails to reveal a full view of his quarters, not one divided by all the slats. I looked again at my control panel and decided hitting "Open" a second time was my best option. It worked, the slats sliding away from me with a *whish*.

The way the cells were arranged, I couldn't see Dolores' cell but when Chad shifted his gaze to look straight across the hall, I assumed the blinds in the third chamber had opened as well. Catching what must have been a questioning look from me, he mimicked rocking a baby and then gave the thumbs up sign.

Now what? I wondered.

Chad and Dolores may have been thinking the same thing, but none of us had an answer. Chad and I just stood at our windows, waiting, and I assumed Dolores was doing the same. It was late, sometime after midnight I was sure, but I had no thought of sleep. Too much had gone on, was still going on in my mind.

It was maybe five minutes later that I caught sight of movement to my left, and then Dr. Sharma came into view. She didn't wear her hazard suit anymore but was in clothes similar to what had been left for me—camo pants and a khaki shirt. She got to wear shoes, though, with laces. No worries about the doctor killing herself, I thought. She looked to be about 35 and had her black hair tied in a tight bun, probably all very regulation. Like before, she held a clipboard.

Behind her came a thin man, mid-twenties, pushing a cart. He was dressed the same way as the doctor but had a gun holstered around his waist. Another soldier, not medical staff, but here to help the doctor, or at least be her back up if we gave her trouble. It was hard to imagine the kind of trouble we could give on the other side of this glass, though; it looked pretty thick.

From the top of the cart, the doctor picked up what looked like a remote control. After pressing a button, she began to speak, and her voice came to me through the speakers hidden inside my cell the same way I'd heard the computerized voice giving me instructions earlier.

"I see you've all had a chance to freshen up," she began. "Thank you for cooperating so nicely. You'll find we just want what's best for you and are going to do our best to keep you comfortable." She repeated this in Spanish, turning toward Dolores' cell as she spoke. Then she continued in English, stopping every few sentences to repeat for Dolores. "Of course, you are still in a hospital and military environment in the middle of the greatest threat human beings have ever faced, so your comfort will likely be minimal. I'm sorry for that, but I'm sure you understand. We have to have some higher priorities.

"My job is to determine what genetic or environmental factors have allowed you to be immune to the F2 outbreak. To do that, we will need blood and tissue samples and will also need to do some extensive interviews regarding your background, medical history, and your family's medical history. I trust you will be cooperative?"

She looked from Chad to me, and we both nodded. "Good." Then she repeated the last bit for Dolores and probably got another nod. "Without your cooperation, those of us not lucky enough to be immune would be doomed. This facility can house us only for so long, and resources are finite, so the day will come when we have to go out into the contaminated zone and face it so we may begin rebuilding our society."

"Are there many other survivors?" I asked automatically, forgetting she wouldn't be able to hear me through the glass. Those closed blinds across the corridor still had me curious.

The doctor cocked her head and then said, "Use the intercom button."

I went to the panel, saw the button, and pressed it before repeating my question.

She hesitated a second before answering. "We know of some, but all quite far from here, too far for us to have access. No doubt there are others nearby, but without the resources to contact us. We are searching, but resources are limited, as I said."

"What about Australia?"

She raised an eyebrow. "There may be survivors in other parts of the world, yes. Isolated pockets spared by wind patterns from being exposed to F2. I don't know anything specific about Australia." She paused, giving me a sterner look than she had before. "Don't plan on booking any flights, though."

I didn't need that, but let it go.

"If you will each pull a chair up to the metal box in the center of your chamber, we will begin."

She began with Chad, then moved on to Dolores and Kayla. Room 2, then 3. *Going by the numbers*, I thought. *How military*. I sat before the box and watched as Dr. Sharma pulled a wheeled stool up to each of the cells, opening a door in the wall below the windows and doing things I couldn't see with her back to me. When she had finished with Chad, I made eye contact with him. He smiled and gave me another thumbs up; I nodded, not knowing what else to do.

Finally, Dr. Sharma came to me.

I watched as the metal box on my side of the windows popped open with a hiss and a click. Two red rubber gloves, long enough to reach past someone's elbows, lay inert at the bottom of the box, their ends connected to the wall. The doctor leaned forward, and the gloves came to life as she snaked her hands into them. At the bottom of the box was a chrome handle; Sharma pulled it up to reveal a drawer full of medical supplies.

She used the gloves deftly, opening the supply drawer and taking out packages that contained a syringe, alcohol swabs, a rubber tube, and bandages.

"Make a fist," she said.

I complied, and in seconds she had the tube tied around my arm and the swab spreading alcohol over my skin. She tapped the veins in the bend of my elbow and then popped the needle into my arm. There was another drawer in the side of the box; this one had its own keypad, and the doctor entered her code to pop the door open with another hiss. The full syringe went inside before she was back in the lower drawer for more supplies. She bandaged my arm and then swabbed inside my cheek, popped the sample into a test tube, and placed it in the same drawer as the syringe full of blood.

"Any health problems before the outbreak?" she asked.

"No."

"Are you on any medications?"

"No."

"Pregnant?"

"No!"

"All right. Keep the bandage on until morning. There's food in the cabinet beside your bed. Try to get some sleep. We're going to do our best to keep you comfortable here, but there are going to be some unavoidable inconveniences. I'm sure you'll understand."

I nodded. "I'll do my best."

She didn't like that response, just gave me a cold smile. Then she closed the drawer where she'd put the samples, hit more buttons on the key pad, and pulled her hands back out of the gloves.

"Close the lid, please."

I did, and then she was doing something else with the keypad on her side. I heard a *whirring* sound and felt the wall vibrate. When it stopped, Dr. Sharma hit more keys, and then I saw that she had a small, sealed box in her hand. It was the same gray as the walls inside my cell and had a bright yellow hexagon on each side with the word "Biohazard" printed in black in the center.

It had my blood and saliva inside. The air in the chamber it had come out of must have been removed before the box could be taken out on the doctor's side of the glass; otherwise she wouldn't have exposed herself to it without a hazard suit, contaminated as it must be by everything on my side of the wall.

I realized as she walked away that the colors meant something. Gray meant contaminated; white meant safe. Each of our chambers and the corridors where Sharma had first met us were all gray, all connected to the outside world through the elevator shaft, all dangerous places for anyone not immune or without a biohazard suit. On the other side of the glass, all was white and pure, clean and safe; the doctor and the soldiers and whoever else still lived in this installation could move around in the white zone without protection in what I now knew was a larger, far more sophisticated version of the underground chamber in Donovan's bunker.

When the doctor was gone, I glanced across the corridor to see Chad looking back. He gave a little wave, and I could see his arm had a bandage like mine. Using my index finger, I made a big U on the glass, then O and K and a question mark. *Primitive texting,* I told myself.

Chad nodded, pointed at me, and drew a question mark on his window.

I nodded my response before trying something more complicated, slowly making letters and checking in to be sure he was following along. It was hard remembering to make the letters backwards so they would make sense on Chad's side of the glass, but I managed, writing, "THINK WE'RE SAFE?"

He shrugged and wrote back, "DOES IT MATTER WHAT WE THINK?"

He had a point. We were here, locked in, and no longer by just one crazy guy with guns. Now it was lots of people with guns and locks far tougher than the ones Donovan had held us with. If we were safe, if Dr. Sharma could be trusted, then we were probably in a good situation. And if the doctor had lied, if we were in danger, knowing about it wouldn't do anything to make the guns and locks less of a problem. Still, there was something to be said for keeping one's head in the game. I wanted to stay alert for any sign of trouble, and also for any opportunity to get out of what might be nothing more than a giant hamster cage.

"MAYBE," I wrote back. "KEEP YOUR EYES OPEN."

He nodded and then just looked at me, a little sadly I thought. He put his hand up onto the glass, his palm against it and his fingers spread out. I did the same and felt a little tingle as I did. After a few seconds, he smiled and nodded and then turned to his control panel, shutting his blinds a few seconds later.

"Goodnight, Chad," I said before closing my blinds as well.

I didn't turn the lights off but explored the rest of my supplies first. The food Dr. Sharma had mentioned consisted entirely of military rations, sealed packets of ready-to-eat meals. They didn't look or sound appetizing, and I wasn't hungry anyway. I was glad to see several bottles of water, and I drank half of one before telling myself I should conserve. After all, the doctor had said the resources in this place were finite.

Then I had a terribly unpleasant thought: what would happen to us if the white zone outside the windows got contaminated? What if the equipment or one of the soldiers made a mistake and the F2 spores breached the barrier? Everyone not immune would die. And where would that leave the rest of us? Locked in, separated from each other, waiting to starve or suffocate or die of thirst.

I wanted out. I wanted out badly. Panic began rising in me as I thought of how far down we'd come in the elevator. I paced my cell, looking again for a camera, for anything that connected me to the doctor and the soldiers, for any way to let them know I didn't want to be here anymore and was done cooperating.

But there was nothing, and I thought about the possibility that maybe they weren't watching me after all. *Impossible*, I thought. We were too valuable to go unobserved.

After a while, I calmed down, telling myself that even though things *might* go bad, they hadn't gone bad yet. We were safe for now, probably safer than we'd been with Donovan. Yes, men with guns still had us locked up, but I didn't think they were crazy or angry or bitter because we were immune while they weren't. Isolation and shock might start chipping away at the soldiers' discipline, but it would probably take a while, and until then I'd do what I could to figure out a way to protect myself should the time come and the neat barrier between gray and white, between health and illness, become blurred or break down altogether.

Eventually, I turned out the lights, slipped off the stiff pants, and got into bed—nothing more than a cot with a pillow and a single blanket. The lights in the corridor stayed on, and enough came through the edges of the window shades to keep my cell from being pitch dark.

I lay there, looking at the slivers of light, and waited for sleep to come. At least this was more comfortable than the floor of Donovan's bunker, which already seemed a long time ago and very far away. In comparison, it felt like an eternity since I'd lived in the observatory. And my old life, my old home, my neighborhood and family...all of that felt somehow unreal now, like it had been a dream or a long and wonderful movie about some other girl name Scarlett that I'd been caught up in. Somewhere along the way, the credits had rolled, and the lights had come up, leaving me to find my way in this other world. And now I was alone in the dark again, but with no movie running and nothing to distract me but the hope of better dreams.

CHAPTER TWELVE

In the end, the worst part of my time at the base was the bore-dom. There was nothing to read, nothing to do. Chad and I tried writing messages back and forth, but that got old, and it was hard to sustain a conversation of any substance writing backwards letters with our fingers on the windows.

Dr. Sharma came frequently the first couple of days, taking more samples and interviewing us as she'd promised. I decided to be truthful with her, reasoning that if I actually did help her learn about our immunity, it might mean freedom from the cell.

If she decides there's no way we can help them, I wondered, *will they just let us go?*

The thought kept me on edge, looking for any sign of the doctor's intentions, but I couldn't tell what was going on behind those glasses she wore.

Sometime during our first full day there, the blinds across the corridor opened, and I saw the occupant of room 1. It was an old man, probably in his seventies. He had gray hair and a scraggly beard, and he looked awfully skinny. When he saw there were other people in the chambers across from him, he just stood at the window and stared, looking from my windows to Dolores' and back. He had piercing little eyes and a wild look about him. The man made me nervous.

I tried writing a message on the window as I had done with Chad, asking if he was all right. The man gave no sign of comprehension; he didn't even seem to notice I was writing anything. After I tried a second time, he moved his fingers on the glass, too, but didn't make any letters, and I realized he was mimicking me.

Like an ape in the zoo, I thought.

I wanted to know who he was and how long he'd been here, how the military had found him and what they'd done to him since. It would have been such a help to know even a little something. But his mind seemed gone, which made me feel incredibly frustrated. Had the doctor done something to make him like this? Or had he been this way before coming here? I guessed that the latter was more likely. Anybody could be immune to the fungus, even crazy people. I didn't see how there could be any real purpose to Dr. Sharma doing something to this man that would result in him being this way. What would be the advantage? No, I decided, he was probably someone who'd already been on the fringes before the disease struck, maybe even a hermit or something, someone who wandered the desert, someone easy to spot from a helicopter when the soldiers had been out searching for survivors.

I did my best to explain to Chad who his neighbor was and what I thought of him, but it wasn't easy to get big ideas spelled out across the glass. Still, I was pretty sure he understood. For his part, he did his best to keep me updated on what he could observe of Dolores and the baby. It seemed like they were doing okay.

A guard patrolled the corridor between the cells once every fifteen minutes or so. Every eight hours, the guards changed, but I noticed there were only three all together. The first was stocky with a thick neck and thick fingers. He walked up and down the corridor without really looking at any of us, and he struck me as nervous and scared. The second was older, taller, and more professional in his demeanor, probably a career soldier as opposed to the first guard, who I guessed was in his early twenties. The older guard smiled and nodded when he first came on shift but had no other real interactions with us.

The third guard, though, was different. She didn't look old enough to be a soldier, but I suppose she had to have been at least eighteen. It wouldn't have surprised me to learn that she'd been in high school just six months before, had probably graduated in June and gone straight to boot camp. The military recruiters who came to all the high schools had sold her on this as her future, her career, her ticket to the world and a college education after a few years of service. And here she was with the world all fallen apart around her, no such thing as college anymore, and maybe no such thing as a future. She was Latina, and I could see the name "Muñoz" on her uniform.

The first few times Muñoz patrolled the corridor, she looked pretty neutral, giving us little nods as she went, but not smiling. She didn't seem angry or scared or pleased or hopeful or much of anything, really—just did her job and moved on. With her being so close to me in age, I felt like she might be able to relate a little, might be willing to make things a little easier on us.

My feelings were affirmed a couple of days later when I noticed she had stopped in front of Dolores' cell, and when I pressed my face to the glass and turned my head the right way, I saw that she was speaking, her hand on the keypad below Dolores' windows. Muñoz nodded and even smiled. Then she made a little waving motion with her fingers, and I could tell she was trying to get Kayla's attention.

Great, I thought. *She's human.*

After a few seconds, she seemed to remember herself and continued with her patrol. When she got to my cell, I expected a friendly greeting as well, but her eyes barely shifted from dead center as she walked. The little wave I wanted to give died on my fingertips. Muñoz walked past and didn't come back, disappearing through the door that the doctor and the guards always passed through just out of my line of sight.

* * * * *

Dr. Sharma took more blood after two days had passed. I tried engaging her, too, to see if there was any progress with her research. She was uncommunicative, though, barely answering my questions with nods or not at all.

"You know," I said when she'd finished and I was pressing the bandage against my flesh to stanch the bleeding, "I am cooperating voluntarily. You could at least be friendly in return."

It was a stupid thing to say, childish really, but I was angry and annoyed, and the confines of my cell were beginning to get to me. All I wanted was a little glimpse of what my future looked like—how long she thought we'd be here, what was going to happen next. It didn't seem like so much to ask for.

But Dr. Sharma didn't see it the same way. Maybe she'd been having a bad day, or was frustrated by her research, or was going a little stir crazy herself even though she could move around in all the white spaces of the base. At any rate, she answered my insolence with a cold stare and said, "Your cooperation doesn't have to be voluntary."

That stopped me cold. My mind took me to a dark place, and I imagined myself on a surgical table, my arms and legs restrained and an IV drip hanging above me, feeding drugs into my veins to keep me sedated and compliant. They'd get their cooperation any way they could, and a few soldiers coming into my chamber with their guns drawn would be enough to get the job done. I pictured Muñoz behind a hazard mask, a little grin on her face as the doctor popped a needle into my arm and made the world melt away.

I said nothing. Sharma said nothing either. She just nailed me with her stare and then pulled her samples from the chamber once it was safe for her to open the little door.

* * * * *

"WE NEED TO ESCAPE," I wrote on the glass the first chance I got, my fingers making the letters as carefully as possible with Chad watching across the corridor.

Directly across from me, the old man had his blinds open and was simply staring at me. He did that a lot. At first, it gave me the creeps and I tried to avoid his gaze, but after a while I got used to it; his eyes didn't seem to register, didn't seem to be focusing on me or anything at all. So I told myself he wasn't really *looking* at me, just pointing his eyes in my direction without really seeing anything.

"BRILLIANT," Chad wrote back. "WHEN DO WE LEAVE?"

It might have been meant as a joke, a way to take the edge off the tension I might have been revealing with my expression. But I didn't think so. He didn't look amused. In fact, he looked almost disgusted.

"WHAT'S UR PROBLEM?" I wrote.

"WON'T WORK. Y TRY?"

"HAS 2 B A WAY."

"LIKE BEFORE?"

He shook his head then and stepped away from the window. Conversation over.

I was angry and crestfallen at the same time. I wanted to keep sending messages, was mad at myself for having started this line of talk and getting him mad in the first place. And I was also frustrated that it looked like I was the only one who wanted to get away or felt like it was worth looking for an opportunity to escape.

I knew why he was upset. I had been all about escape at Donovan's, too, even roping him into my plan to find a way out. I'd gotten him to feel some hope. And it hadn't gotten us anywhere. The helicopter and soldiers had seen to that; Donovan's plan had overshadowed mine, even if it didn't work out for Donovan.

It wasn't my fault things had worked out this way, but maybe it was my fault that Chad had gotten back whatever sense of independence Donovan had scared out of him, only to have it squashed again when we got locked inside these cells. He didn't want to hope anymore, and I suppose that made me sadder than anything else.

I was as likely to get cooperation from the old man who still stared at me. Absurdly, I waved at him and he, predictably, waved back—the only sign I ever got from him that he was actually aware that there was a person across the corridor.

Then I turned from the window and went to my normal spot— my cot, where I lay on my back and looked at the ceiling and replayed the night we'd arrived at the base, convincing myself that there must be some flaw in the compound's security, some little thing they'd missed, something I could exploit to get myself out of here. They were the same questions I'd asked at Donovan's, and escape had seemed just as impossible then; the outhouse plan would have worked, I was certain. Now I just needed to come up with something similar...and win Chad over to my way of thinking once more.

Of course, I'd take the others with me; more than ever, escaping alone wasn't an option now. The thought of going on alone out there in the gone world was too much to consider. Even if Chad was being kind of a jerk right now, one of the things that helped me get through the long days and nights in my cell was the thought not just of being out of here, but being out of here with him, of running through the desert sand and toward the city and the ocean beyond, his hand in mine the way it had been on the helicopter.

* * * * *

A week must have passed before Dr. Sharma came back.

Since I could shut off the lights in my cell whenever I wanted, I'd been sleeping a little more than normal. Sleeping and dreaming helped keep the boredom and despair at bay, but also caused me to lose track of the days. The lights in the corridor were always on, so the only way of really telling the passage of time was with the changing of the guards, but every now and then they switched the order of their shifts, so I could never really be sure when I woke up and waited for the next patrol whether I had been out for one hour or ten.

When I could, I sent messages to Chad. The subject of escape hadn't come up again, which was just as well since I didn't have any new ideas. We tried playing 20 Questions on the glass and other things to pass the time. At times, I felt like we were actually having a conversation, but the feeling would never last; the glass and space between us was too complete, too unbreakable for the fantasy to really get a strong enough hold to make me forget my reality.

Around three days into Sharma's absence, I noticed someone else conversing with Chad. Apparently, Private Muñoz had decided not to limit her friendliness to Dolores. Though she kept refraining from making eye contact with me, she did stop every now and then to look in on Chad. The first time I saw her stop and hit the intercom on Cell 2's control panel, I thought there might be something wrong with Chad.

He wasn't in my line of sight when Muñoz stopped in front of his windows, and I imagined him lying on his cot, maybe sick. But then he came to the window and pushed the button to respond to her. They talked for less than a minute before she moved on.

"WHAT WAS THAT ABOUT?" I wrote once she was gone.

"JUST BEING FRIENDLY," he replied.

"HOW NICE 4 U," I wrote back, crossing my eyes to show him I wasn't mad or anything. And I wasn't. Chad couldn't help it if the guard wanted to talk to him and not me.

On her next shift, Muñoz stayed longer. I could see Chad smiling as they talked, and when Muñoz turned away from the control panel to finish her rounds, she looked amused as well.

I just put up a big question mark on the glass once she had left.

Chad shrugged. "SMALL TALK," he wrote.

"ABOUT?"

"LIFE BEFORE F2."

I nodded. "TELL HER I DON'T HAVE COOTIES IF SHE
WANTS SOMEONE ELSE 2 TALK 2."

He laughed. "K."

After that, it was every shift. She'd ignore the old man, linger at
Chad's cell for a few minutes, chat with Dolores, and then pass by
my cell on her way out of the chamber. I'll admit to some feelings
of jealousy. I mean, who wouldn't feel kind of weird in that situation? Muñoz's attentions also made me realize how much I'd come
to think of Chad. Had we not been thrown together into this
situation, had we met each other in the times before the F2, those
feelings might never have developed, but we weren't in those old
times, and my mind kept turning to thoughts of Chad now, probably as often as it lingered on thoughts of escape and memories of
my old life.

Absurd as it was, I wished we were back at Donovan's, able to
talk to each other and sleep side by side. I remembered the feeling
of his breath on my cheek when I'd lay awake next to him in the
night and longed to be that close to him again. In truth, I longed to
be that close to *anyone* again, but Chad became the focus of my
longing during all those days in the gray cell. Strangely enough, I
felt lonelier there than I had at the observatory when I'd been
convinced I was the last person left in all of California.

When Dr. Sharma did return, it was with a small plastic case
and her omnipresent clipboard. This time, she started with the old
man, who seemed to cooperate readily, as though he'd been conditioned like an animal in an experiment. With her back blocking
much of my view, I couldn't tell what the doctor did, but it looked
like she put something *inside* the drawer before leaning forward to
put her hands in the gloves. After a few seconds, she withdrew her
hands, punched buttons, and then took something back out of the
drawer. She made notes on her clipboard and then moved on to
Chad.

With him, she stayed a bit longer, but not much. I could see
them talking. Then she repeated the same process. This time, from

the different angle, I could definitely tell she took something out of her little case and dropped it inside the airlock chamber. She made a note on her clipboard, leaned forward to put her arms in the gloves, and then pulled her arms out to wait for the decontamination process to finish inside the drawer before she took the same thing out. A few more words exchanged with Chad, and she crossed the hall to Dolores.

There, the angle was all wrong; I couldn't see much of anything, but assumed the doctor was going through the same routine. All I could do was wait for my turn.

It came soon enough.

"Good morning, Scarlett," Dr. Sharma said when she pulled her stool up to my window.

That was odd. First, because she was never so friendly, and second because my internal clock had me convinced it was late afternoon. *Morning*, I thought, trying to reorient myself.

"Good morning," I replied automatically.

"We've made some advancements and are ready for the next phase of our experiments."

"Okay. What's that going to involve?"

She didn't answer directly, just opened her little case to reveal four syringes. Three looked empty; the fourth had about half an inch of yellow liquid in the tube. Taking the fourth syringe from her case, she looked at the label for a moment and then wrote something on her clipboard before setting it aside. Then she punched her code and placed the syringe in the decontamination drawer.

"What's in that?" I asked.

"Just some neutral agents that we plan on suspending the vaccine in once it's ready. We need to make sure the delivery system has no adverse effects."

"Wait," I said, drawing back from the glass. "What kind of adverse effects?"

She raised an eyebrow and said, "Nothing to worry about. If the vaccine is going to cause nausea or insomnia or euphoria, we'd like to know about it before we begin subjecting men with guns to it."

I thought about it for a second before scooting back to the glass. Her reference to men with guns hadn't been random. She wanted me remembering who had the power here. If I refused to participate in this portion of her experiment, she had ways of changing my mind. Now I imagined Muñoz as the one forcing me onto a table while the doctor strapped me down. I still didn't like the idea of her shooting something experimental into my body, but I also knew I didn't have much choice. My desire to escape this place increased by about a thousand-fold, however, as I sat there and let her swab the spot on my upper arm where she'd chosen to inject me. I glanced in Chad's direction, hoping to find him watching so I could give him a meaningful stare, but he wasn't anywhere in sight.

A few seconds later, the needle was in, and I felt a burning sensation spreading out from it as well as a quick feeling of intense pressure. Then the needle was out, and the gloved fingers were applying a little bandage, and that was it. The pain decreased but didn't go away entirely.

"Are you all right?" the doctor asked.

I nodded. "Hurts, but it's going away."

"Good." She pulled her hands out of the gloves and readied herself to go. "Thank you for cooperating," she added.

"You're welcome." I felt like I had to say it, like I'd been bullied into it by her imitation of politeness.

Then she was gone, and I was left to rub my arm and fantasize about breaking through the glass and running away.

* * * * *

I must have slept. Or maybe I just lay on the cot and stared at the ceiling, but I doubt I could have done that for long without dozing off. At any rate, I definitely had the feeling that some time had passed when I sat up and looked around. I felt a bit dizzy, and the room seemed elongated, distorted.

The shot, I thought. *She lied.*

My adrenaline started flowing then, the idea that Dr. Sharma had given me something more potent than "neutral agents" made me angry and scared at the same time—but mostly angry. I wanted to shout and hit things. I wanted her sitting across from me with her neat little clipboard and her stupid glasses and her smug look so I could tell her what I really thought of her and how I wished she'd just get it over with and die.

But then I realized that the dizziness was gone. Maybe my anger had counteracted it, made it go away. Even so, I still felt angry, but also a bit less scared.

A bit tentatively, I got off the cot. Still feeling fine, I went to the window. And there I saw Chad at his window, waiting for me.

I had never seen him look like this, and I was alarmed immediately, more adrenaline coursing into my system. He looked scared and agitated and was rocking back and forth behind the glass. When he saw me, his expression changed a bit, adding relief to the mix. How someone could look relieved and scared at the same time, I don't know, but Chad pulled it off that day.

"KAYLA," he wrote on the window, his fingers flying so I could barely get the letters.

"?"

"THEY TOOK HER."

Now my heart started beating even more rapidly. At first, I'd guessed he was feeling side effects from the injection, too. Probably worse side effects than I was having. But now I knew otherwise.

"Y?" I wrote.

He shrugged and held his arms up in a sign of bewilderment.

"DID SHE GET A SHOT 2?"

"COULDN'T SEE. CAN'T ASK DOLORES."

Chad's Spanish was far worse than mine, and I didn't have the slightest idea of how to ask, "Did the baby get an injection?" in anything but English.

"IS SHE UPSET?" I asked.

Chad nodded vehemently. Dolores was probably freaking out in the cell next to mine, and there was nothing I could do to help her.

"WHEN DID THEY TAKE HER?"

"A WHILE. NOT LONG AFTER SHARMA CAME."

"U SAW?"

He nodded.

"WAS IT SHARMA?"

"THINK SO."

"AND SOLDIERS?"

He nodded again.

I could picture it—the doctor and the soldiers all in hazard suits, the soldiers with their guns drawn in case Dolores put up a fight, and Dolores probably crying and begging them not to take the baby.

If I'd hated Sharma before, it was nothing compared to what I felt now.

"WHAT DO WE DO?" Chad wrote.

I thought about it for a few seconds, wanting to write *ESCAPE* on the glass, but now wasn't the time for I-told-you-so. Even if he had been willing to conspire with me, I didn't think we'd have found an opportunity before this new kink in our situation.

"TALK 2 MUÑOZ," I finally wrote. Maybe there was something there. Maybe the young guard had a little crush on Chad or was just sympathetic to our plight. That she didn't seem to care for me wouldn't matter: it was Chad and Dolores she seemed to like, and if those two were upset over what had happened to Kayla, they might find a sympathetic listener in Private Muñoz. And maybe some information that we could work with to get ourselves out of this bind.

Chad didn't even need to think about it, just nodded right away. He must have seen the possibilities of talking to the guard even as I was thinking them.

But Muñoz didn't come. It was the middle of the mean-looking young guard's shift when Chad and I messaged each other. Then the thin, older guard had his turn. Muñoz should have been next, but no. The third guard was one we'd never seen before, an African-American soldier in his thirties who made no eye contact with us as he patrolled, just got out of the corridor as quickly as he could.

Chad and I gave each other quizzical looks and shrugged. "SHOULD GET SOME SLEEP," Chad wrote.

He was right. I'd been fighting sleep for a while now, waiting for Muñoz. Now that she hadn't shown, the idea of staying awake until this guard's shift was over seemed an impossibility.

"WHAT ABOUT MUÑOZ?" I wrote.

"WE'LL CATCH HER AS SOON AS WE CAN."

I nodded, not wanting him to be right but seeing no way around the situation. We needed sleep; Muñoz wasn't here; if we slept through her shift, one of us was bound to be awake during another shift. I was determined that I'd get her to talk to me if Chad was asleep and I wasn't.

I closed my blinds, dimmed my lights, and lay down. Telling myself this was just a catnap, I didn't take off my clothes and didn't cover myself with the blanket. I didn't want to get too comfortable, didn't want to fall too deeply asleep. It wouldn't do to crash out for six or seven hours, not when so many odd things were going on.

The deterrent didn't work. I don't know how many hours passed, but I know that I was deep in sleep when the booming woke me. I sat up and put my feet on the floor, completely disoriented for a few seconds, not knowing where I was or how I'd gotten there. For some reason, I was trying to figure out what day it was, even though days had stopped mattering on my birthday…how long ago now?

But then the boom hit again, and I sat up straight, adrenaline kicking in and bringing me back to my weird, confined reality. It was loud but not incredibly so—more of a reverberating, distant boom rather than a sound that spelled immediate danger. Still, during all the time I'd spent at the base, it was the first sound that had penetrated my cell without passing through the intercom.

Darting to the control panel, I opened my shades before turning on my lights. And when I saw what was happening, I dropped my hand from the panel, leaving the lights off, no longer caring about them.

Across the hall, the old man had gone crazy. His beard was streaked with the blood that poured from his nose, and he had torn off most of his clothes. I could see that he was shouting, and every few seconds he picked up the metal chair he'd used in his interactions with Dr. Sharma and heaved it at the windows. They shook with each concussion, looking like they must burst outward with the next strike. But the windows held, and still the old man tried breaking them with all his might. The crashing booms must have been deafening on his side of the glass, but reached me only as the low reverberations that had awoken me.

It didn't seem possible. The blood, the aggression…I hadn't seen anything like this since the first days of the outbreak. And now this? I knew the old man was going to die, that he'd pass out in a few minutes and sprout stalks and that would be it. But how? And why?

Maybe he hadn't been immune in the first place, I told myself. Or maybe something had gone wrong with…

The thought just hung there at the forefront of my mind, like a hammer poised to strike a nail. At the same time, I watched the old man lift the chair again to run, seemingly in slow motion, at the window again, raising the chair as he went and swinging it with all his might as his mouth contorted in a scream I couldn't hear. The chair hit the window in the same instant that the hammer fell in my mind.

The injection! I thought.

"The injection!" I shouted.

And then I looked to Chad to see him standing at his window in a panic. He couldn't see what was happening in the cell next to his, but he definitely understood that something had gone wrong. His face conveyed more fear than I'd ever seen him express, and I had to wonder if he was so upset because he couldn't fathom the situation, or if it was something else.

We had the injection, too! I realized. Was Chad next to go mad? Dr. Sharma had administered the shots in one-through-four order, with the old man first and me last. Was I going to have to watch Chad go crazy and then wait, knowing Dolores would follow before I lost my mind and died?

I barely had time to process any of this before something else happened across the hallway. A soldier entered the old man's cell from the back, from the gray corridor where Chad and Dolores and I had first met Dr. Sharma. He burst into the cell and stood there for a second, pointing his gun at the old man and probably shouting. In his hazard suit, I couldn't tell for sure who he was, but I thought I could see dark skin behind the face mask and assumed it was the new guard. He'd only just been assigned this duty, and now he faced a trial by fire.

Everything happened so fast then.

Out of the corner of my eye, I saw more movement in the hall-way. Dr. Sharma running in—no clipboard, no escort.

In the cell across the hall, the old man dropped the chair, turned and lunged at the guard.

I expect all the guards had been instructed not to use deadly force on their immune "guests" in the cells. It wouldn't have done to reduce the number of immune human beings even by one, especially in a setting where doctors and scientists were studying the genetically lucky to find a cure for the rest of humanity. But training and instruction can only go so far; instinct kicks in at some point. The guard did what just about anyone else would have done with a crazy man coming at him like that, a crazy man who looked to be infected with the most deadly disease human beings had ever encountered.

He fired his gun three times just as Dr. Sharma reached the edge of the cell. The first bullet caught the old man in the neck, jerking his head back and spraying blood across the window as the bullet passed clean through him. The second bullet missed, hitting the glass and sending a hundred cracks out in every direction. The third bullet hit the glass as well, just as the old man fell to the ground, shattering the window into thousands of little pieces. And it kept going, heading straight for the window of my cell, straight for me where I stood in the line of fire.

The bullet hit the window with another boom, and I just stood there watching as it struck the thick glass, peppering my shirt with a fine spray of glass dust. I looked down to see the light from the corridor reflecting off the miniscule shards, expecting blood to start darkening the fabric.

But I wasn't hurt. The bullet didn't pass through, but was right there in front of me, lodged in the glass, a smashed little cylinder at the center of a spider web of cracks that spread out to the window's metal frame.

In the hallway, my view of her distorted by all the cracks in the glass, Dr. Sharma had turned from the wreckage of the old man's cell to look at me inside mine. She looked panicked, and held her ground for only a second before turning away to start running from the chaos around her.

If I hadn't just been watching the old man, it might have taken me a few seconds to think of what to do, but as it was, I acted immediately, grabbing the chair where I'd sat with the doctor and swinging it at the glass with all my strength. The window exploded outward with a crash and a thunderous pop and a rush of air. Instantly, I could hear alarms sounding; they'd probably been triggered with the first broken window across the hall, but I hadn't been able to hear them with my glass intact.

I raked the chair along the lower window frame, brushing the last bits of glass aside. Then I set the chair on the floor, stepped onto it, and hopped into the hallway. For the first time now, I saw double doors at the end of the hallway, and Dr. Sharma desperately punching her code into the keypad. She glanced over her shoulder toward me as I ran in her direction, paying no attention to the glass on the tile floor even though I almost slipped on it twice. I ignored Chad, ignored Dolores, ignored the blaring alarm, ignored the soldier still in the old man's cell; nothing mattered any more, nothing but getting to the double doors before they closed after the fleeing doctor.

At the last second, I leapt at the doorway, my arms wrapping around Sharma's ankles as she cleared the threshold. She went down in front of me, and I struggled to hold onto her as I hit the ground hard. The doctor turned under me and struggled to kick free, but I wasn't about to let go. All the anger I'd felt in the weeks since the world had ended—anger at the people I'd lost, anger at Chad and anger at Donovan, anger at Dr. Sharma and Private Muñoz and everyone else in this compound who had conspired to hold me here against my will—all of it came out now in a rage directed at the doctor, the full extent of which she did not deserve.

But it served me well. In seconds, I was straddling her chest and hitting her in the face. Her glasses flew off, cutting the bridge of her nose.

"What did you do? What did you do?!" I shouted. "What did you give us?"

She didn't answer, just struggled to fend off my blows. Finally, she shouted, "Just let me go!"

"Why the hell should I let you go? Why?" I yelled, holding her down by the shoulders.

A look of absolute defeat came over her then. "Because I'm already dead," she said, her voice just louder than a whisper. "I'm already dead."

I couldn't hurt her any more than I already had. From the moment the old man's window had shattered with Dr. Sharma right there, her life had been over. Running away from me had just been automatic, if entirely futile.

"What did you give us?" I said, more calmly.

"Different solutions. We developed several possibilities. You didn't all get the same ones."

"And one of them made him sick? You gave him the disease?" I shook my head in disbelief. "How could you?"

"We didn't intend it to go that way."

"But you knew it might."

She didn't respond, just shifted her eyes away.

I was filled with disgust.

But I couldn't do anything about it.

A door opened to my right, and the soldier who'd shot the old man stepped into the corridor. He still wore his hazard suit and still held his gun. Now he pointed it at me.

"Let her go," came the muffled command.

I hesitated for a second and then lifted myself off of Dr. Sharma. Maybe it was just training from my past life, but I immediately felt sorry for having attacked her, felt like I was in trouble now and had to atone. Even though she didn't deserve an apology, I wanted to give one.

But the "Sorry I hit you" that was rising to my lips never got there. The second I was off the doctor, she was scrambling to her feet, groping for her glasses, and then running as fast as she could. She never looked back. I was death to her, I realized. I was pestilence and plague and every horrible thing from every nightmare she'd ever had. And she wanted away from me. A few seconds later, she rounded a corner, dashing away like a scared rabbit, and was gone.

I turned to the soldier. He looked unsure of himself, but also agitated and maybe even angry.

He waved his gun toward the double doors, which had closed after the doctor and I had tumbled through them. "Back in there," he said.

"It won't do any good," I began. "The whole area's contaminated now."

It was true. The white zone had become the gray zone, and his expression told me he knew it as well as I did. His frustration and fear rose to the surface now, and he shoved me against the door, slamming my shoulder and elbow into it. I think I cried out in shock and fear more than pain.

"Get back in there!" he shouted now. Looking into his face, seeing the fear and anger barely controlled, I felt lucky he hadn't already opted for his weapon. That would be next.

"You have to open it," I said meekly, hoping to calm him. I stepped away and watched him punch the code. 53137. The door clicked open.

"In," he said.

I stepped through and half turned, expecting him to follow, expecting him to do something to subdue or punish me, to lock me up or restrain me—to contain me and the threat I represented outside my cell. But he didn't do anything. He just stood there for a second; fear and anger and frustration had overridden his training, and he looked at me in complete disbelief, like he'd just watched the world end all over again. Then he let the door shut between us, content, I suppose, to have the little barrier between us before he ran to find the doctor, maybe hoping to save her or at least to save himself.

CHAPTER THIRTEEN

Back in the corridor between the glassed-in cells, the alarm still sounded, a short, sharp tone that grated with each repetition. I tried to ignore it, tried to think about what was next, but the alarm wasn't any help in getting my racing, colliding thoughts to line up. It also didn't help that my most persistent thought was of the injections we'd received and the possibility that Chad and Dolores and I were about to go as crazy as the old man had.

So as the door clicked shut and I stood in the bright white corridor with the litter of broken glass upon the floor, I didn't really stop to think—just ran to Chad's window and his intercom button.

He was right there, his hands pressed against the glass as though he were trying to part it like water and reach me on the other side. I didn't bother putting my hands on the glass opposite his. There wasn't time for little gestures like that. Instead, I hit the intercom button on the panel beside the window.

"Are you okay?" I asked, trying not to sound scared.

"Yeah," he said. He sounded surprised that I had asked, confused. "What's happening?"

I shook my head. "The shots they gave us…they might have taken away our immunity."

"What?" he shouted.

I repeated what Dr. Sharma had told me about the experiment they'd been running on us, and ended by saying, "You're not feeling any symptoms?"

He hesitated a second. His silence made me nervous. "No," he said. "Nothing. What happened in the other cell?"

"The old man went nuts. They shot him."

"He's dead?"

I nodded. "The bullet cracked my window. That's how I got out."

"I thought you just used your chair. Thought you got super strength or something."

I smiled briefly.

"What now?" Chad asked.

"I get you out. And Dolores. Then we find Kayla and get out of here."

His face fell.

"What's wrong?"

"You can't get me out of here."

"I can," I said. "I saw the guard put the code in. I can go through the old man's cell and open your door from the back corridor. We'll—"

"No!"

I raised an eyebrow.

"You can't," he said. "I might be sick. You said it yourself."

"Well I might be sick, too!" I countered. "But at least we'll be out of here."

"Scarlett, listen! If I'm sick and you're not…who knows what this new strain is? Sharma said they gave us different formulas?"

I nodded.

202

"Scarlett, I could get you sick. If they gave you something that had no effect and me something…that did. I don't want to do anything to hurt you." He looked down at the floor; it seemed like he couldn't face me as he said it.

It was almost the exact same argument I'd used on my mom the night of the Dodger game when I'd insisted she and Anna leave before I made them sick. Coming out of Chad's mouth, now that everything had changed so much, it sounded absurd, and yet I understood exactly how he felt and why he was saying it. My mom had resisted the argument, but eventually I'd gotten her to see the wisdom of it. That wasn't going to happen now, though. Chad wasn't going to talk me into leaving.

"I'm not leaving without you," I said, trying to sound as adult and determined as I possibly could.

He looked up then, his eyes taking me in. He smiled for a second and then looked past me. His face changed, the smile fading into a dead stare.

"You get out," he said. "Get out while you can."

I turned to look over my shoulder. In her cell, Dolores stood before the glass, her hands in the air and her eyes aimed at the ceiling. I could see her mouth moving. She looked like she was praying. But that wasn't what I focused on, wasn't what had brought the change in Chad's expression. No, it was the blood streaming from her nose and running down the front of her khaki t-shirt.

"Oh my God," I said.

"Get out of here, Scarlett." He said it calmly, but I knew he was scared, as scared as me.

I didn't want to go; I didn't think he was right. He wasn't having any symptoms, and neither was I.

Standing there, looking from Chad to Dolores and back again, I hadn't really been paying attention to the airflow in the corridor. But that was before it stopped. There were vents high in the ceiling, one just behind me, and cool air had been blowing down on me. Then the whole place seemed to shudder for a second and I heard a distant popping sound.

My first thought was that we were having an earthquake, just a little one. But I also felt the airflow cease, the cool air no longer hitting the backs of my arms.

I must have looked alarmed, as Chad said, "What happened?"

"They shut off the air conditioning."

He raised an eyebrow. "Is that a problem?"

I looked up at the vent. Being a few floors underground like this, in a building designed for the study and control of disease, air conditioning might very well be a problem, perhaps not right away and with only a small group of people breathing the limited air supply. Still, it was another reason to think about getting out of here as quickly as possible.

But then there was another shudder, and the airflow started again, this time in the wrong direction. I could hear the ventilation system working now, and if I stood still and concentrated, I definitely felt air passing by me, but flowing upward now toward the vent.

"They're sucking the air out," I said at the moment of understanding. "They're trying to control the contamination."

"What contamination?" Chad asked.

"When the windows broke. The gray zone crossed into the white zone. They're trying to keep it from spreading to the rest of the base."

Chad looked up and put a hand in the air. There would have been a vent in his ceiling, too. "Nothing's happening in here. Still cool air coming out."

"Then it's just the white zone."

I couldn't feel any difference in the air yet, had no difficulty breathing. But I guessed that wouldn't be the case for long.

"I gotta go," I said. This time I did put my hand on the glass, and he put his up to match it. "I'll come back for you."

"Don't."

He meant it, but so did I.

Then I was gone. Taking only a moment to glance at Dolores and wish I could do something for her suffering, I ran to the broken window of the old man's cell, hoping the soldier had left the door open after he'd shot the old man and seen what was happening in the corridor. Shards of glass stuck up from the window frame, so I darted across the corridor, reached into my cell, and pulled my chair into the white zone. Placing it on the floor next to the old man's cell, I stepped up and then found a spot on the window frame where I could put my foot without getting cut. Then I was up and in.

The old man lay dead at my feet, a hole in his throat and blood everywhere. There was no avoiding it. If I tried hopping over the pool of blood, I might slip when I landed, and I didn't want to fall in it. So I stepped gingerly in the puddle, my military-issued socks soaking it up right away, and got past the old man's body as quickly as I could. I couldn't stand the feeling of his blood on my feet, so I peeled off the socks as soon as I had crossed the cell and went barefoot to the door at the back.

It was still open. That was one lucky thing. Our captors had installed keypads only on the outside of the cell doors, so knowing the code wouldn't have done me any good on the inside, which was why I hadn't opted to get back into the gray zone through my own cell.

Now I was in the gray zone again, in the same spot where we'd first met Dr. Sharma. To my right was the long corridor she'd escorted us along before depositing us in our cells. The door into Chad's cell was maybe thirty feet away. I hesitated a second, thinking of how vehement he'd been about my staying away from him, and then I ran to his door anyway. I punched the code, and the door clicked open.

"Chad?"

"I told you to stay away!" He sounded scared, as scared as I had the night of my birthday.

"I'm not coming in. I just wanted to unlock your door." I paused, swallowing back a little sob. "In case I can't come back. I don't want you…trapped in there. The code for the doors is 53137. In case," I repeated.

He didn't reply. I waited a second, and then turned to run back the way I'd just come.

Past the door into the old man's cell, I saw the doors that would lead to the elevator the soldiers had brought us down on our first night at the base, and one more door that I hadn't noticed at the time. It was to the left of the elevator, and I'd had my back to it that night. It had a keypad mounted beside it and a sign prominently displayed in its center that read "Entering Sterile Zone."

Not so sterile anymore, I thought.

For a moment or two, I considered hitting the elevator's call button and getting away on my own. Dolores was as good as dead. I probably wouldn't be able to keep Kayla alive even if I could cross the desert with her and get her back to the city. And Chad…he didn't want me rescuing him, didn't want me risking my life in case he was the next to fall ill with a new strain that might infect me, too. I imagined crossing the desert on my own, making my way back to the observatory…alone. And I left the elevator for later.

53137 worked on the door into the sterile zone. The door was extremely heavy, and when it closed with a click and a hiss, I found myself in a small room, maybe six feet square. On one wall hung four hazard suits, looking almost like limp bodies hanging from their hooks. Along the opposite wall was a black metal box about two feet high and five feet long; mounted to the wall above that was a blank screen that looked like a computer monitor or a small television. Directly across from me was another door with the same sign about the sterile zone and another keypad like the ones I was used to seeing.

I tried the same code on the second door, but it didn't open. I tried it again with the same results.

"It's like Donovan's airlock," I said aloud, reasoning that if the base's personnel could just pass from the gray zone to the white zone, it wouldn't be very sterile. Looking up, I saw that the ceiling was almost completely made of metal vents.

"Okay, then," I said and turned to the control panel above the metal box. For the first time since I'd been at the base, I had real appreciation for military efficiency. It wasn't enough to assume that all the personnel had been trained on using the airlock. No, the administration had seen it necessary to put redundant precautions in place to protect its people—and its investment as well.

Seeing no controls, I touched the screen. It blinked to life with the words "Prepare to Enter Sterile Zone" printed in bright red across its center and two squares at the bottom marked "Cancel" and "Continue." I continued, and the computer walked me through the whole process, directing me to the oxygen tanks stored in the metal box at me feet. These were precautions only in case of emergency or malfunction, the screen assured me, but I was strongly advised to utilize the equipment before proceeding.

Knowing that the air on the other side of the door might be as compromised as it had been in the hallway with Chad, I opened the lid and saw four tanks in black harnesses with breathing masks attached. I pulled a tank out and closed the lid. The computer screen showed me how to check for airflow and supply, which I did, and then I slipped my arms into the harness, wearing the tank like a backpack.

The program walked me through a few more screens, and then it was time to hit the "Initiate Sterilization" button. Immediately, machinery whirred in the ceiling, and the whole room seemed to vibrate. I felt the air rush upward as though a wind were blowing from below my feet. Then it stopped. All was still for a second. This was the point where a staff member who'd opted to ignore the warnings about oxygen may have second-guessed that decision. A loud click followed and then a hum; at the same time, I felt the air pressure in the room change. My ears began to hurt the same way they always had at the bottom of the deep end in Jen's pool. I tried to get my ears to pop, but it was no good, and I began to feel panic rising up inside me.

And then it was over. I felt air whoosh back into the chamber, and the air pressure returned to normal. I swallowed and felt my ears pop. A second or two later, I felt normal again. The computer screen now read "Sterilization Complete." And it directed me back to the keypad I'd tried using before.

Now the code worked, and with another loud click the door popped open. I was in the white zone, still wearing the oxygen mask. I took it off just to see if anything was different on this side of the chamber and then put it right back on. The air was so thin here I felt like I was drowning as I tried to breathe. Panic rose in me before I got the mask back on.

After that, I just stood still for a few seconds, taking in big gulps of air and looking around to get my bearings. I was in a long white hallway. Like the space between the cells we'd been in, the walls and floor and ceiling were white and almost blindingly bright. *Sterile*, I thought. I could see several doors in either direction and prepared myself to start opening them one at a time.

But not everything was white. The door I'd just come out of, for one thing. It was gray and had a big sign on it that read "Entering Contaminant Zone." And it didn't just have a keypad mounted next to its metal handle. There was also a card reader, a little machine with a slot running down the side. *Extra security*, I thought. Dr. Sharma and her team didn't want just anyone entering the gray zone; you had to have clearance, probably a special card with a coded strip that needed to be run through the reader before the entry code would work.

I looked at it, dumbfounded, telling myself I'd just locked myself out of the gray zone, out of the one part of this floor that still had air being pumped into it, out of the only access to the ground level that I knew of.

Panic kicked in again, but only for a few seconds. I looked left and right, hoping I was wrong, and in looking saw the next door down, marked only with numbers above it, a sign reading "1-4." It was the door I'd just tackled Dr. Sharma outside of, the door the soldier had forced me back through. I went to it. The same keypad I was used to seeing, no card reader. The same keypad I'd watched him enter 53137 into and it had opened. Nothing stopped me from doing it again, climbing through the old man's window again, getting into the gray zone again. I walked to the door; Chad and Dolores were on the other side, and it would be nothing to open it again now and talk to Chad some more about what I'd found so far and what I should do next.

But after a few seconds of standing there, I left the door and the keypad alone, opting to move along the hallway instead. I told myself it was because my air supply was limited and there wasn't time to waste getting all tingly in my throat from talking to Chad. The real reason was that I was scared the key code wouldn't work any more, that they'd done something to heighten security with the breach in the white zone's sterilization. If that were true, then I was in trouble. I didn't want to know that just yet.

I saw doors marked "Medical Supplies" and "Janitorial Supplies" and some with the names of people whose offices were inside. None of these interested me. But then I came to another gray door with a card reader and the same sign about the contaminant zone. The door next to it had "5-8" above it.

Four more, I thought. Four more survivors, four more guinea pigs being experimented on. Maybe four more dead people, victims of Dr. Sharma's failings. Maybe Kayla.

I passed the door with the card reader and, hesitating a second, entered 53137 into the keypad on the next door. It opened with a click. Relieved, I stepped through, a bit hesitantly, and looked around before letting the door close.

I had tried to tell myself to be ready for anything—more mayhem like there'd been in our cells, more bloody victims, maybe even another broken window. I might not actually have been ready for those things, but I had steeled myself. Of course, there was nothing like that on this side of the door. What I *did* see, however, was about the last thing I would have expected.

The chamber was the same horseshoe configuration as the one we'd been kept in—two windowed cells on either side and a white space in between where the doctor and staff could interact with patients. One of the chambers farthest from the door was dark, the other three lit. In the cell to my left was a crib, but the relief I felt upon seeing it was short circuited by the blood spattered across the windows of the cell to my right.

I approached the window slowly, my oxygen mask still pressed to my face. On the other side of the glass, a soldier lay dead on the floor, face down in a pool of blood. Two stalks poked out from under him.

Which one? I thought. He might have been one of our guards, or one of the soldiers who'd rescued us from Donovan's. Or he might have been someone I hadn't seen before.

I'd been looking at him for only a second when a pounding noise from behind made me jump. Immediately, I turned, ready to run or fight if I needed to.

In the last lit cell, Private Muñoz stood banging on the window with the palm of her hand. She looked angry and confused and scared all at the same time.

But she was alive.

Inside the gray zone.

I approached her cell with caution, and she went straight to the intercom.

"What the hell is going on?" she said.

I just stared at her for a second, wondering what to make of her presence there—my former guard in a cell and me out here looking in. My feelings of animosity towards her hadn't gone away, and they weren't eased by the fact that I was in her position now: free to ignore her or not, free to leave when I wanted. Still, walking away wouldn't do me any good. So I took a deep breath, pulled the oxygen mask from my face, and answered. "There's been a breach in the sterile zone."

Her expression said *Yeah, and I'm looking at it.* But she didn't say anything.

I took another breath and continued, giving her the fewest details possible. "The old man went crazy and they shot him. Window broke. That's how I got out."

"Where's Sharma?"

I shrugged. "Infected maybe. She was right there when the soldier blew the windows out."

"Which one?"

I described him as best I could.

"Anderson," she said, looking thoughtful.

"Is that bad?"

She shook her head but didn't answer me directly. "If Sharma's got it, then we're all screwed."

"Why?"

She looked at me for a second, dumbfounded, as though she couldn't see how I could be so stupid. Then it clicked for her that I wasn't one of them, that I didn't know everything she did, and she answered, "'Cause she's the only doctor left."

I raised my eyebrows. All this time, I'd imagined a team of scientists, all wearing hazard suits and bent over microscopes as they studied the samples they'd taken from us survivors. I had a hard time believing it had only been Dr. Sharma the whole time.

"Serves us right, I guess," Muñoz said.

"What do you mean?"

She shook her head, didn't answer at all this time.

I needed to move on, needed to figure out how I was going to get Kayla out of her cell and then get back to Chad. But seeing Muñoz inside the cell was just too strange, and had filled my head with too many questions. It got the better of me, so I took another breath and asked, "So what are you doing in there?"

She hesitated before answering, sizing me up, I realized, seeing if I was worthy of being told anything more.

"I volunteered," she finally said. When I raised an eyebrow and cocked my head to show I didn't understand, she went on. "The doctor needed control subjects—someone without immunity to see how the formulas would work on the rest of us."

I nodded my head to indicate the soldier behind me.

"He volunteer, too?"

She gave me a mean little smile. "He was voluntold."

I grimaced at that and then said, "So he's dead and you're alive. Does that mean you're cured?"

"Maybe. There were two serums. I might've got lucky."

"Unless you were immune the whole time," I said.

She gave me a look then—anger and amazement and incredulity. I could see her working through the possibilities, how she thought she'd been lucky to be in the white zone when the plague had struck, but maybe she'd just been lucky the whole time and would have survived anyway, anywhere. Finally, the thought made her smile ironically. "Guess we'll never know."

"Why would..." I began, looking for the words that seemed so impossible to put together. "Why would Sharma make another version that *caused* it though?"

Anger in her voice, she blurted out, "'Cause that's what she—" And then she stopped herself, looking at me to see how much I understood. Then she swallowed and said, "What do you mean, 'caused it'?"

"The old man," I said, my mind racing. "He went crazy before the soldier shot him. He was immune and then he got sick after the serum." I hesitated and then added, "Dolores, too."

Her face turned stony.

"She dead?"

I shrugged.

"The other serum must have neutralized their immunity," she said. "Any spores they had on them from outside or had already breathed in before the serum…they took off after the injections."

I thought about it, remembering when Dr. Sharma had given the injections—the case that held the four syringes, the notes she'd taken while administering the shots. It had been random. Dolores and the old man had lost out. I hadn't. And Chad…as long as there really were only two versions of the serum, then he was safe, too. If there had been three or four variants…then he might already be dead.

I couldn't let myself think that. Something else nagged at me. When I'd asked about Sharma's formula causing the disease, Muñoz had misunderstood me, letting something slip before catching herself and answering the question the way I'd meant it.

"Before the outbreak," I began, not wanting to say the words but making myself anyway, "they didn't just study diseases here, did they?"

She gave me a hard stare through the glass. It may as well have been a loud, bold, "No."

"So this is where it started?" I asked.

She shrugged. "Could've been. If not here, then somewhere like it. There were a lot of facilities working on biological weapons. Something got out, somewhere. It was just a matter of time before someone screwed up. Even soldiers and doctors are human, yeah?"

"Yeah," I said quietly, my heart pounding. "That's what you meant before…when you said we got what we deserved."

Again she shrugged.

"So you got a plan?" she asked.

"Get the baby and go."

She raised an eyebrow. "You can take care of her?"

"Enough."

I don't know what she'd been thinking in regard to Kayla, maybe that it would have been more merciful to let her die now, when she was too little to understand what had happened to the world and hadn't yet had much chance to suffer in it.

"Did they give the baby any of the injections?" I asked.

She shrugged. "Beats me. I doubt it, though. Even Sharma has her limits. I don't think she'd be so messed up to give a little baby any of that stuff." She gave me a long look then before she said, "And Chad? He going, too?"

I hesitated. "I don't know. He doesn't want to. Says he's scared of making me and the baby sick. You know…if he got a different serum?"

She looked thoughtful.

"Too bad," she said. "You could make a little family."

I couldn't tell if that was supposed to be sympathetic or sarcastic.

Without thinking, I said, "You in love with him or something?"

She gave me another angry look before saying, "No. All of you…survivors. Just made me feel good to talk, like you were people from my old world."

I told myself that might have been true, maybe especially about Dolores. But I also knew she was lying. There'd been something about the way she'd talked to Chad, something more to it than a connection to life before the F2 plague.

Breathing in first, I said, "I thought you hated me."

Again came the angry expression. Then she shook her head. "Just jealous."

Of me and Chad, I thought.

But then she went on. "Why you? You know? You and me, we're practically the same age. You look like girls I knew in high school. It just…made me angry you were gonna make it, and me…I was gonna die in here with Sharma and all these soldiers."

I nodded. "Is that why you volunteered for the serum?"

"I guess."

"Looks like it paid off," I said.

She smiled. "I guess it did. Wasn't sure till you showed up."

"You coming with us?" I asked.

Honestly, I didn't want her along, not really. I didn't want Chad to get to choose between us. I liked the idea of me and Chad and Kayla being a little family like Muñoz had said. Having her with us just wouldn't fit. But then again, I didn't know that Chad would be coming, didn't even know that he was still waiting back in his cell, alive. On top of that, it would just be stupid to leave Muñoz behind; her training, her know-how, her experience...she could probably save us in ways I couldn't even imagine. If that meant losing Chad to her, so be it, I thought.

Maybe she sensed my ambivalence.

"I don't know," she said. "Need to see what's left for me to do here first. I mean...if I really am cured, if that serum really worked, whoever's left should know about it. Here, or in D.C. or Atlanta."

"There are still people there?"

"Supposedly."

I let that sink in for a moment. "Well," I finally said, "either way, we need to get you out of there."

"You already have the code, right?" she said.

"I do," I said, a little pride at my cleverness creeping into my voice.

She just raised an eyebrow. "No other way you could've gotten this far." She turned around and went to her cot. From under it, she pulled a little leather case, unsnapped the cover and took something out. Then she came back to the window and talked me through the menus on the control panel that would open the sealed box on her side of the glass. She held her military identification card up to the window and then placed it inside the box that the doctor would have used to access a patient's samples.

"Take it," Muñoz said.

I hesitated a second and then entered the code. The wall between us vibrated and hummed before the little drawer on my side of the window popped open and I had her identification card in my hand. "Patricia Muñoz," it read next to a very serious looking, grainy picture of her.

"Okay," I said. "I'll be back."

"You better be. Leave me in here and I'm gonna haunt you."

We nodded to each other like we would have in a high school hallway, and then I turned away. I checked on Kayla through the window and then passed through the door again.

Getting back into the gray zone now was a snap. The card reader took her ID, and then I was inside a chamber identical to the one I'd found the oxygen in. Passing through was no big deal either; it didn't matter that much if you went from sterile to contaminated as long as the doors were shut behind you. Going the other way was the more crucial operation. I left the oxygen behind and entered the gray zone on the other side of the airlock.

I wanted to check on Kayla first, but went past her door to the entrance to Muñoz's cell instead. Seconds later, the door popped open and we were face to face. For just a moment, I worried that I might have made a mistake in trusting her. Here she was in front of me, with no glass between us. If she'd been faking when I talked to her, if she was still loyal to the military and the ideas they'd drilled into her about germ warfare and national defense, then I was in trouble and could expect to be subdued and dragged inside the cell to wait for the rest of the soldiers and Sharma's team.

But she just smiled at me. "Thanks," she said.

I held out the ID card. "Do you need it back?"

She thought about it for a second. "You might need it still. I can get another one."

I raised an eyebrow.

"A lot of us died. There's a lot of dead soldiers' stuff in the barracks. Bound to be an ID or two in there."

"Okay. Thanks."

"Good luck."

"You, too."

And then she was gone, bolting down the hallway for the airlock and the white zone. I didn't know what her plan was, or even what mine should be. It was only after the door had closed behind her that I thought to ask about the best way to get out of the compound. But the door had already closed, and I knew that once she'd started the decontamination process, it wouldn't open again from this side until she had gone.

I had figured this much out on my own, I told myself. I'd figure out the rest, too.

Only one more door to open, and then I was in the baby's cell. She lay there awake, just looking up at the ceiling. They had her dressed in one of the same little one-piece outfits that Dolores and I had gathered from the store the night she was born. It seemed like an awfully long time ago.

"Hi baby," I said.

She blinked and made a little noise at me. I was surprised at how much bigger she seemed; we'd been held at the base for something like three weeks, and I felt like she had turned into a different baby somehow. She looked more alert, and her nose wasn't so squished. During our time in Donovan's bunker, all three of us had taken turns holding and feeding and changing, but here it had all been Dolores, and I felt like I was coming back to Kayla as a stranger. All the confidence I'd had in my ability to step into Dolores' shoes just evaporated as I looked into the little face.

"You remember me?" I asked and gave her my finger to play with. She grabbed it and squeezed, and that made me feel better right away. "Gonna go bye-bye," I said and took my finger back to see what supplies I could take with me.

The soldiers had transferred everything they'd brought from Donovan's bunker to Dolores' cell, and then they'd moved it here when they'd taken Kayla away. The supplies had run low, though. On the floor behind the crib were a single unopened pack of diapers, two canisters of formula, and a bag of baby clothes. The bottles and nipples were probably in the bathroom area, but I suddenly didn't care about that or the question of where I was going to get more supplies when these ran out. My eyes had darted over the little pile of baby things, and sticking out from under them was what looked like my black backpack.

I went to the pile, and moved aside the bag of clothes. I hadn't seen the soldiers with my backpack the night of our "rescue," but they must have gathered it up with all the baby things; it had been with Dolores the whole time. Goosebumps ran up my arms as I pulled the zipper tab and found my things inside, including the photo of my family. I just looked at it for a moment, not tearing up the way you'd think I would. It felt strange looking at it. When I'd been twelve or thirteen, I'd gone through a box of books that had been stored in my closet, and at the bottom had discovered a Barbie doll that I'd lost when I was around eight. I remember wailing about that doll when it had first gone missing. Coming across it years later, there wasn't any feeling of elation or relief; it was just a curiosity, like I'd found something in an antique shop that had belonged to me in another lifetime. It wasn't mine any-more. I wasn't the same person who had lost it, and I no longer felt connected to it. Looking at the photo didn't feel quite that strange, but almost. Not only had I gotten used to the idea that I'd never see it again, but I had come so far now from the girl I'd been in that picture, and the faces in the frame seemed like people I'd only heard about or dreamed about and never really known. I still missed them all terribly, but my day-to-day life had become about so much more than missing them. I was glad to have it back, of course, and I touched a finger to each of the faces, even my own dimpled smile, before slipping the photo back inside. Then I zipped the backpack closed, knowing that if I lost it again, I'd be fine.

I gathered bottles and nipples, formula and clothes, and about ten disposable diapers. Most of these I shoved into the backpack, discarding a couple of my own belongings from my days at the observatory to make room for Kayla's things. I slipped my arms through the straps, turned and scooped the baby up, holding her against my shoulder. "Here we go," I cooed, and then we were on our way.

Back in the gray hallway, I went right for the airlock again, following the steps Muñoz had taken just minutes before. It was awkward to get a new oxygen canister out of the storage locker while holding the baby, but I managed. Testing the tank and checking that it was mostly full, I started the airflow and then tried holding the mask to Kayla's mouth. It covered just about her whole face and made her start crying. There wasn't anything else I could do, though, so I started the process on the touchscreen to get the chamber decontaminated.

The noises and all the strange sensations must have been scary. Kayla cried a lot, especially when the air pressure changed, and I tried to comfort her, but short of holding her close and making happy sounds, there wasn't much I could do. In the back of my mind had begun to grow the possibility that the soldiers might be back on this level any second, that the decontamination process in the white zone might have been completed and they'd be on their way to reclaim it from me—maybe led by Muñoz, maybe stepping over her body. Their guns weren't something I could argue with, and I felt a chill at the thought of being put back into one of the cells.

"Not gonna happen," I said, more to myself than to Kayla. But she made a little gurgling sound back at me, and I gave her a nervous smile.

When the lock clicked open, I stood there for just a second, steeling myself for what I might see on the other side. And then I pulled the door open.

I was still alone in the long white corridor. Why the soldiers hadn't put on their hazard suits and come to get Chad and me under control again was beyond me. My only thought was that they were in a panic, maybe trying to save Dr. Sharma and probably assuming that I was still locked safely away. The soldier who'd killed the old man had shut me inside our cellblock, and they probably had no reason to assume I wasn't still in there, just waiting. Maybe they thought Chad and I would die like the old man, and probably Dolores, and so we were the least of their worries. I assumed there were cameras that had caught my actions, but maybe the base was so short-staffed that no one was monitoring them, especially with the breach in their precious white zone. At any rate, I was still on my own.

Taking a deep breath from the mask, I held it as tightly to Kayla's mouth as I could, one of the tank's straps over my shoulder so the canister dangled off of me. I should have thought to strap the tank on completely and let the backpack hang instead, but it was too late now to rearrange. I moved as quickly as I could back to the door I'd first come out of, leading to the gray zone behind the old man's cell.

It seemed to take forever—between the awkwardness of the tank bouncing against my side, the baby crying and trying to squirm away from the oxygen mask, me holding my breath, and my need to look and listen for any sign of returning soldiers.

But we made it, and once the door had closed and sealed behind me, I leaned against the wall and let the tank slide down my arm to rest on the floor. Kayla still cried, but now I didn't care.

"We're gonna be okay," I said, more to myself than her.

I just breathed in the air, ignoring the crying and the grating sound of the alarm that still echoed through the hallways. Then I straightened up and moved into the gray zone.

When I got to the door of Chad's cell, I froze. I had left it open for him; now it was closed. Was he still inside? Had he shut the door himself to keep his illness contained? Or had someone else shut the door...Sharma, one of the soldiers, maybe even Muñoz? I hesitated only a moment, picturing myself setting the baby down in the old man's cell and creeping through the broken window to check out the rest of the cells. But then I thought of seeing Chad through the glass, thought of having to watch him suffer or finding him dead already. It was more than I could take.

53137. The door clicked, and I opened it, the baby held close to my chest.

"Chad?" I called out tentatively.

He didn't answer, and I held my breath without meaning to as I entered the chamber.

He sat on his cot, his back to me, his neck bent forward. He had his elbows on his knees and his forehead rested on his hands, like he was deep in thought. Or grieving.

"I told you not to come in here," he said.

"I know."

"You're so stubborn."

"It's one of my better traits," I said, hoping he'd laugh.

I approached carefully, still not sure that he was all right.

"Dolores is dead."

I looked at the windows. There was no blood on the glass, but that didn't mean anything. Dolores could have died on the other side of her partition, banging on the door to get out. I had to look down again, couldn't say anything for a few seconds.

"You watched her suffer," I finally managed.

"She saved me," he said. "When I was sick…before Donovan."

"You couldn't have done anything for her," I said, hoping it sounded helpful. "No one could have."

"I tried."

He stood up then and turned toward me. I gasped at the sight of all the blood on his shirt. *No!* I wanted to scream, thinking it was his. But his face was clean, his nose too.

Then I understood. "You went to her," I said, my voice quavering as I pictured him running along the same corridor where Sharma had led me and Dolores on our first night here.

"All I could do was hold her while she died. I couldn't even understand what she was saying."

He had tears in his eyes, and I wanted to hug him, would have even with the baby in my arms and the blood on his shirt, but as I stepped toward him, he took a step back.

"I don't want to watch you go through the same thing," he said. "Especially not because of me."

The cot was between us. When I took another step toward it, he didn't retreat any farther, so I kept going, clearing the corner of the cot to stand right in front of him. If he really was infected, this put me in a vulnerable position, but if he was losing his mind, I still believed there was enough of Chad in there to keep him from attacking me with the baby in my arms.

"I don't think anything like that's going to happen," I said, my voice soft, reassuring. "I don't think you're sick. I think you and me got the same dose. I think we're going to be okay."

He looked up, his eyes just passing by Kayla, barely seeming to recognize her.

"You don't know that," he said.

"You don't know either. You don't know when you're sick." I shifted Kayla to the crook of my left arm and lifted my right hand to touch his cheek just above the downy growth of beard.

"You should go."

He sounded so sad. I leaned forward.

"I can't," I said, my voice just above a whisper. "I'm here now. If you're sick, then I'm sick, too, now. And you know what?"

"What?"

"I wouldn't want it any other way."

I leaned forward, my hand slipping down to his neck. Then I leaned in and kissed him, just lightly.

"I can't go on alone," I said, tears in my eyes. "I can't go back to living like I was before you came. If it means we die, then we die."

And I kissed him again, longer this time, deeper. And he was kissing me back, his arms around me. It almost made me forget where we were, what we still had to do. All my worries about his loyalty, about how he might have felt about Muñoz…all of it just dropped away, and it was just he and I together, connected.

I don't know how long it lasted, but it couldn't have been more than a few seconds, not with Kayla starting to squirm in my arms as I held her between us. I broke away and smiled at him as I wiped away my tears.

"You okay?" he asked.

I nodded. "Yeah." Then a nervous little laugh escaped me. To say that I was "okay" was a ridiculous understatement. I still didn't know what was going to happen, didn't know if one of us might still get sick, didn't know how we'd get out of here alive. But now I knew we'd be going together, and that was really all that mattered. It was the only thing that had mattered for a long time now; I just hadn't been ready to admit it to myself.

He shook his head, kind of in disbelief. "I've wanted to do that for a long time."

"Well why didn't you?"

"I could never get you alone."

I almost laughed again at that, at the absurdity of it. In a world with almost no one left alive, he'd still had a tough time finding some privacy with me.

"Come on," I said. "Enough worrying about who's got what disease. I think we can get out of here now."

He stood up with me. "You don't think they'll try and stop us?"

"They might. They haven't yet, though. I don't think there's many soldiers left here. Muñoz said that Sharma was the only doctor."

"Muñoz? You talked to her?"

I gave him a quick rundown of what had happened since I'd left him before.

"You really think she's got immunity now?"

"That, or she always had it to begin with."

We had shoved the remaining food rations into the backpack while I talked, and now we each took a bottle of water as we prepared to leave his cell. I looked away for a second when he peeled off his bloody shirt and took another one from the supply closet along the back wall.

"You want me to take her?" he asked once he popped his head through the clean shirt, and I handed Kayla over before slipping on the backpack. She only weighed maybe ten pounds, but I was glad to pass her off to Chad. Then we went into the hallway, only getting a few steps from the doorway before we stopped and exchanged a worried glance, each of us practically frozen mid-step.

"You smell it, too?" I asked. He nodded, and we both looked up.

I couldn't see it at first against the gray paint, but when I'd looked at the ceiling long enough, I began to make out thin tendrils of smoke coming through the vents.

"They trying to gas us?" Chad asked.

I thought about it for a second and then shook my head. "The place is on fire," I said.

"How?"

"Who knows? The fungus maybe…people going nuts already. Maybe something else. We better go."

We moved faster then and made it to the elevator doors. I punched the call button.

"You sure it's safe?" Chad asked.

"No."

I thought about all the times I'd ever been in elevators and how every single one of them had a sign outside warning you not to use it during a fire. There was always a little stick figure drawing of a person taking the stairs instead.

The elevator doors slid open a few seconds later.

"What if it gets stuck?" Chad said.

I hadn't explored the whole floor out in the white zone, but I had been around the hallways of the gray zones enough to remember not having seen any doors marked "Stairs." With very little breathable air out in the white zone, and a fire burning somewhere in the complex, I didn't like the idea of rushing around this whole floor looking for another way out. I didn't like the idea of being trapped in an elevator while the whole underground complex burned around us either, but I figured we had better odds if we got out now, when things were still just beginning to fall apart, rather than wait and search and hope for a way out of the maze as it collapsed around us.

A second later, the sprinkler system kicked in, water spraying down from the ceiling. That decided it for me. The chaos of locked doors and sprinklers raining down on us, of airlocks and fire in a building I didn't know my way around—and where armed men might be showing up at any moment—was all too much.

"We take our chances," I said and stepped inside.

Chad didn't even hesitate. He and Kayla were there beside me, and the doors closed.

CHAPTER FOURTEEN

There were no choices for floors on the elevator panel. Just up and down. I reasoned this was because the floor we'd been on was the only floor that was part of the gray zone, the only floor with a direct connection to the outside world. There must have been other elevators in the compound, but they all would have needed to be part of the white zone, all with sterilization chambers and layers of security to keep the scientists safe.

No, I told myself. *Not to keep* them *safe. To keep the rest of us safe from them and what they were making down here.*

Nervous about it, I punched the Up button. With my right hand holding Chad's, I kept my left on the elevator doors as we zipped up to ground level, hoping not to feel the metal grow hot. A few times on the ride up, I thought maybe it was heating up, but when I moved my hand the door felt cool again, and I decided it was just my imagination and paranoia.

The ride didn't last long. The elevator slowed and stopped, and then the doors slid open. Chad held up a hand, cautioning me to wait. We both listened for any sign of trouble, any challenge to our presence here. Hearing nothing, we exchanged nods and then stepped out onto the roof.

I hadn't really known what to expect from the top level, probably hadn't consciously been expecting anything. But I remember feeling surprised to find it was light outside. The last time I'd been here, out in the fresh air on the roof of the building, it had been the middle of the night, and it had been cool out here in the desert. So it was kind of incongruous to find that the sun was out, dipping to the west and the distant mountains that separated the desert from the sprawling city on the other side.

The helipad was in front of us, two helicopters sitting there and reminding me of giant grasshoppers just waiting to spring away into the air. To our left and right stretched row upon row of solar panels; when we'd arrived in the dark, I hadn't been able to make out the black panels, or if I had, my feelings of overload and confusion had kept me from comprehending the panels' purpose. Now I knew how the whole complex had continued to have power even though all the power stations in the region had shut down. And now that I knew, I didn't really care.

"Which way?" I asked.

Both of us looked around for a moment. We were atop a large low building, no hint that it spread deep into the ground. Across from us, on the other side of the helipad, was one edge of the building, and I scanned along it for a second.

"There," I said, pointing at what looked like a metal handrail curving up from the building's side. "Stairs, or a ladder. Something."

"Okay."

Chad led the way, walking past the first row of solar panels. I followed, wondering what we'd find when we got to the ground and where we'd go from there. We were maybe a dozen steps from the elevator when I heard something on our left—maybe a footstep, maybe the brushing of a hazard suit against the side of a solar panel.

I didn't have time to process what I'd heard or to say anything to warn Chad that something was wrong. A soldier stepped out from the shadows between the panels, a hazard suit protecting him from the atmosphere. He held a rifle, and had it trained on Chad, who looked frozen to the spot. The littlest movement of the rifle's barrel, and it would be pointed right at my chest.

"Stop right there," he said, his voice muffled but clear enough to understand.

We had already stopped.

"Hands up."

Chad raised one hand, holding Kayla to his chest with the other. I raised both of mine, my mind racing to find a way to get us out of this. The handrail and freedom were just so close. Our bid for escape couldn't end this way, I told myself. At the same time, I couldn't think of a way around the gun.

"Down," the soldier said. "On your knees."

Chad complied, going down carefully and slowly with the baby held to him. I hesitated only a second and then followed suit.

The soldier approached. I couldn't remember having seen him before. He might have been part of the crew that rescued us from Donovan, and he might not have been. At any rate, he didn't look happy, and I felt sure that if Chad hadn't been holding Kayla, he'd already have had the soldier's rifle butt across his forehead.

"The building's on fire," I said. "We had to get out. We weren't trying to escape, I promise."

He seemed to consider this for a moment.

There's no way to know what he would have done next. My hope was to play on his sympathies, to get him to let us stay here until he had more information on the fire. Maybe he'd relax his grip on the gun and one of us could make a move then. There had to be something.

But it didn't go that way.

The soldier seemed to react to something behind me, and when I turned my head, there was Muñoz stepping out of the elevator doors. She had armed herself with a handgun, and now she pointed it at the soldier.

"Let 'em go," she said.

"You crazy?" he replied. "You're gonna die out here Muñoz. Where's your suit?"

She ignored the question. "The only one that's gonna die out here is you, Darren. Let 'em go. This place is gonna go up any minute. There's no more military for us. You better make your peace with it."

He seemed to consider this for a moment. Then he shook his head. "Drop your weapon, Muñoz. And get me some handcuffs for these two."

She didn't hesitate, just pulled the trigger without another word.

I think I screamed, and Chad and I both ducked. Kayla started wailing. The soldier with the gun went over backwards, his body when it hit the rooftop seeming heavier than it should have been. Dead weight.

My ears rang from the gunfire, and I turned to see Muñoz approaching us, a stupid smile on her face.

"Changed my mind," she said. "Better odds with you guys."

I began to get up off my knees. And then there was another gunshot. A little hole appeared in Muñoz's forehead, and her body crumpled.

I couldn't speak, couldn't really even think for a few seconds. This couldn't have just happened. I couldn't have seen it. It was like everything got slowed down—the desert breeze on the rooftop, Kayla crying, Chad shouting, and Muñoz's body bouncing just a little as it came to rest.

And then I was kneeling at her side. Her eyes were blank, no longer taking in the sky. Tears streaming down my face and rage ripping through me, I turned to see the soldier who'd killed her approaching across the helipad, his rifle pointed down, his gait relaxed—as though killing a fellow soldier was nothing to him, and as though the teenagers and baby with the body were no threat at all.

I didn't even think, didn't consider what awaited us back down in the gray zone where we were sure to end up, prodded along by the rifle's tip. I picked up Muñoz's handgun, swung it around, and emptied it into the soldier's chest. He didn't even have the chance to raise his weapon.

Kayla was screaming now. Chad looked at me in complete disbelief.

"You killed him!" he said, his voice coming to me from far away, somewhere past the ringing in my ears.

I didn't say anything, just lowered the smoking gun. I gave myself a silent little pat on the back, remembering all the target practice I'd done in the observatory parking lot. *You finally got something right,* I told myself.

"We'd better go," I said after a few more seconds. "More might be coming."

Turning back to Muñoz's body, I closed her eyes and whispered, "Thanks."

I stood up, bent over the body, and then stooped to remove her belt, along with the gun's holster and a little leather case with a box of ammunition inside. Then I untied her shoes.

"What are you doing?" Chad asked. He sounded scared, impatient.

"Set the baby down and open that guy's suit," I said.

"What?"

"Get his shoes. We need shoes."

Neither pair of shoes fit us well, but we couldn't cross the desert with Chad in socks and my feet still bare. In a few minutes, we had gathered our things along with the weapons and ammunition from the dead soldiers. Then it was across the helipad and down the metal stairs to the ground.

There was an open space maybe thirty feet across and then a high fence with razor wire along the top. The fence looked like it stretched all around the perimeter. There had to be a gate some-where, but it might be guarded. The thing that really caught my attention, though, and Chad's too, were a couple of Jeeps parked maybe fifty yards away.

We hurried, walking as quickly as the ill fitting shoes would allow, each of us glancing up at the roof of the building occasion-ally, worried that another soldier might be up there ready to pick us off. Then we heard a booming sound and felt the ground shake; something down in the complex had just exploded. Without saying a word, we started running toward the Jeeps, my backpack bounc-ing uncomfortably against my lower back, and Kayla crying in Chad's arms.

Please let there be keys, please let there be keys, I thought as we ran.

Luck was with us. The first Jeep had a silver key resting in the ignition.

"You know how to drive, I hope," I said as I piled my backpack and the rifles in the space behind the seats.

"Yeah," he said. "How about you?"

"Motorcycle." I took Kayla from him and tried to make a silly face to calm her down, but she wasn't having it. "No baby seat, kiddo. We're gonna get a ticket if we get pulled over."

Chad smiled at that, and then he started the engine. The three of us pulling away from the little parking lot made me think of what Muñoz had said about us being like a little family once we escaped, and the weight of her death hit me harder than when I'd watched her fall. I knew I'd been wrong about her, wrong about how it would have been if she'd come with us: we could have made it work with her along.

I wiped a tear from my eye and held Kayla tight as Chad took us along the gravel road beside the massive building. The gate was ahead of us, a guard station next to it. Chad slowed the Jeep to a stop and reached behind us for one of the guns. We exchanged glances, and when I nodded at him, he put the Jeep back into gear and went forward slowly.

RICHARD LEVESQUE

I was ready to duck and protect the baby if I heard gunfire, but there was nothing. The little kiosk was abandoned, its door hanging open in the breeze. Chad stopped the Jeep in front of it, and I passed Kayla over to him before getting out.

Inside the kiosk were a radio unit and three monitors showing the building from its other sides, a bodybuilding magazine, and a half empty bottle of water. All that interested me, though, was a small console with a big red button on it, the word "GATE" in white above it. I punched the button, and the gate began to slide open on its rollers.

Once we were outside, I wondered about closing the gate behind us, but I realized there wasn't much point. If the soldiers inside the compound survived the outbreak and the fire, they'd know we had gone soon enough, and closing the gate to cover our tracks wouldn't do any good. They might follow us, and they might not. The odds were that they wouldn't, though. Sharma had been exposed and would be dead soon, if she wasn't already. Without their chief scientist, the soldiers wouldn't know what to do with survivors. I expected that any soldier who made it through the next few hours would spend the rest of his life in the white zone, radioing for help the way Donovan had before they starved to death or killed themselves.

Beyond the gate, a gravel road snaked across the desert, and we followed it for miles. I couldn't help looking back at the compound as we drove. Smoke trailed into the sky from three different spots. *No*, I told myself, *they're not going to follow.*

Kayla calmed down before too long, and Chad took us west toward the mountains and the setting sun. In spite of all the horrible things that had happened in the last several hours—to the old man, to Dolores, to Muñoz, and even to the soldier I'd killed and all the others who'd be dead soon, too—I felt really good with the sun on my skin and my hair whipping in the wind. I couldn't help laughing. It had been the longest time since I'd laughed, and now there was nothing to stop me.

232

* * * * *

Eventually, we found a paved road, followed it to a bigger one, and followed that to yet another. By dusk, we'd made it onto Highway 395, which Chad said was good; it would lead us to the Interstate, he said, and he was right. The closer we got to the main road, the more clogged it became with wrecked or abandoned vehicles, and when it seemed too dark to keep going safely, we just stopped in the middle of the road.

Chad found blankets in an SUV; then he cleared the corpses from a Cadillac and gave Kayla and me the back seat to sleep in while he reclined in the driver's seat. It was a short night with not much sleep, and before dawn we were on the road again, opting for a big pick-up truck that Chad had outfitted with a baby seat. I didn't ask where he'd found it.

Outside Victorville, we broke into a convenience store, loaded up on salt and sugar, and gathered up one of each map they'd had for sale in a rack by the register. Then we got back on the road again after talking about our options.

We had to stay off the Interstate because it was completely jammed with cars and dried out bodies, but the maps we'd found showed the back roads that got us into the mountains and eventually onto the highway that led to Big Bear Lake, the mountain resort where my family had a cabin, where my mom and Anna had headed when they left me the night I turned fifteen.

For a variety of reasons, Big Bear seemed like a better choice than going back down into the city: there would be abundant water from the lake and the sources that fed it; there were plenty of stores and homes and resorts that we could scavenge enough supplies from to last us for years; there was less likely to be another Donovan in the mountains, or any other survivors who might mean us harm. The winters would be hard, but we'd have plenty of firewood.

I didn't say it out loud, but it was hard not to fantasize that my mom and Anna had made it, that they shared my immunity and had fought their way through all the madness of those first days of the disease to reach the cabin and set themselves up nicely. I imagined a perfect homecoming with my mom and Anna opening the door of the cabin to welcome Chad and me and Kayla, the scent of a turkey dinner wafting through the air as they took us in with hugs and tears.

But of course that didn't happen. Big Bear was a ghost town. Deer had gotten used to wandering the streets, and they looked at us with insulted surprise when the pickup truck rolled through town, raccoons and squirrels scattering, too.

When we got to the cabin, I walked up first, knowing I'd find no one there but needing to see for myself. It felt silly knocking on the door, but I did it anyway. When there was no answer, I tried not to sigh. Giving Chad a brave smile, I walked past him to the lone black rock among all the white and gray ones that lined the walkway. The spare key my mom had hidden a long time ago still sat there in the wet earth, undisturbed for ages. I picked it up and squeezed it, knowing my mom had been the last one to touch it, telling myself it was our last little connection and making myself believe the key gave me a little of her spirit.

Chad followed me in, Kayla sleeping in his arms. The cabin smelled musty; it had been closed up for a long time and would take some airing out. It felt strange for it to be so silent and dark, so empty and cold. Summer was long gone, and autumn had already begun to grow chilly in the mountains. I knew the lights wouldn't work, but the fireplace would. I crossed to the hearth and squatted before it while Chad laid Kayla on the couch and began unpacking a few things from our bags. Using the iron poker, I pushed aside the ashes and charred bits of wood around the grate.

"Welcome home," Chad said behind me.

I gave him a little smile and stood up to hug him. He kissed me and then said, "Here."

I stepped back, and he handed me the little framed photo from my old house.

"Thanks," I whispered and set it on the mantle, placing it between two empty candleholders. Then I took his hand and leaned into him before the hearth, letting him hold me there for a long time.

EPILOGUE

That was three years ago.

We spent the rest of that fall getting ready for winter, realizing pretty quickly that there were better, nicer, less drafty places for us to live. After a few days in my family's cabin, we moved into a place with solar panels on the roof, finding a crib and baby furniture in a store in downtown Big Bear.

There were bodies to dispose of—mostly the suicides and accident victims. The people who'd died from the fungus had all been consumed, their bodies transformed by the F2 into barely recognizable lumps, but we gathered as many of those as we could and burned them in a vacant lot. They were just too unpleasant to leave lying around.

When we weren't working at storing food and supplies and planning for our survival and taking care of Kayla, we both read as much as we could—raiding the library for books on agriculture and medicine and childcare.

The little town was really perfect for us. There were plenty of stores and houses from which we could gather clothes and tools. The lake had plenty of fish in it, and the water was fresh.

We spent the first couple of months nervously watching for signs that someone from the base had survived and wanted us back; several times, I had nightmares about helicopters coming over the mountains or crossing low over the lake. But we never saw or heard anything. And no one else has crossed the mountains to find us, drawn by the smoke from our fires or stumbling into the valley through dumb luck. There have been times when we saw smoke in the distance, but we never went to explore and so never knew if it was someone traveling through the mountains or a small, distant forest fire that the wind never pushed our way.

Kayla has grown into a sweet little girl, and I think we've done a good job of taking care of her—even though Chad and I spent a lot of time worrying about little illnesses that always turned out to be nothing. I think our biggest fear was that something catastrophic would happen to her and we'd be helpless to save her. Now that she's not a baby any more, we worry less, and I'm planning on teaching her as much as I can about the world that used to be and the one she's inheriting.

Chad and I talk about having kids of our own, but the thought makes me nervous. I can't get out of my head the picture of Kayla's mother bleeding to death after she'd given birth. I'm terrified of something like that happening to me, but probably more terrified of leaving Chad and another baby all alone in this very lonely world. Soon, though, it's going to be time. The world needs repopulating, after all.

I wonder about who else is still out there, about other groups of survivors in what's left of the cities or in small towns like we've settled into. They must be out there. Counting myself, there were four people with immunity in the area around Hollywood, and there had to have been more that I never knew about, and more than that in other parts of the country, other parts of the world. I wonder about Australia and the people I contacted there. And I wonder about the little islands that the breezes spared, where maybe ships' crews settled when they knew no ports were safe. There's not much point in wondering, though. Maybe my grandkids or great-grandkids will be able to explore the world again and find other human beings to try and put the world back together. For me, though, just getting through the day-to-day things is enough.

A few months ago, I decided to start writing my story. There are plenty of books about the old world, the world that used to be. But someday, someone's going to want to know what happened to it and how the few of us who survived managed to get through the crisis. So here I am, writing late into the night with pens and paper while Chad and Kayla sleep upstairs. I don't know who'll ever read it, probably Kayla one day, but maybe someone else long from now when the world feels new again. I hope they're happy, whoever they are, and that they're not making the same mistakes as we did.

But mistakes are bound to happen, accidents and disasters. We keep going, though, pushing on through the night the same as this pen scratching across the paper, never quite knowing where we're going, just always forward, forward, forward into the unknown—a little bravely, a little scared, but at least not alone.

ABOUT THE AUTHOR

Richard Levesque was born in Canada and grew up in Southern California. By day, he teaches composition and literature—including Science Fiction—at Fullerton College, and by night he works on his novels and short stories. He joined the ranks of independent novelists in 2012 with the release of *Take Back Tomorrow* and followed that with *Strictly Analog* and the first Ace Stubble novella, *Dead Man's Hand*. In 2013, he published a second Ace Stubble novella, *Unfinished Business* as well as *The Girl at the End of the World*. When not writing or grading papers, he spends time with his wife and daughter, works on his collection of old pulp magazines, and tries to be better than a mediocre guitar player.

You can learn more about Richard at
www.richardlevesqueauthor.wordpress.com.

Made in the USA
Las Vegas, NV
22 September 2023